H🎈T AIR

DENISE KAHN

Praise for Denise Kahn

Peace of Music

What a thrill this novel is, especially for me, since I am Greek and a singer and have lived in many of the places in the book. It portrays beautifully the history of my country, some of which I lived through. Most of all, I truly love the way music is intertwined in the story.
Musicians will not be able to put this book down, nor anyone else who appreciates a good novel.

Nana Mouskouri
Opera and contemporary singer,
UNICEF Ambassador, Author

Music to Your Eyes.
This magnificent work of literary art spans four continents and the lives of the unforgettable and colorful characters.

Jada Ryker, Bestselling Author

This is an exquisite book. A beautifully woven tale covering several generations of one family whose paths are intertwined with an amazing Chinese vase. Although the story begins in China, the plot covers a range of countries and continents as well as several centuries as the magic of the vase touches the lives of the family to whom it belongs. The writing is beautiful, the characters are rich and varied and the pace changes from the smooth to the rough of World War. Be prepared to lose yourself in an amazing world of music, laughter and intrigue as you follow the vase from thirteenth century China to modern day Europe.
This novel will not fail to capture the imagination of the reader.

Sonya C. Dodd, Author

Obsession of the Heart

This tale is centred around a singing diva called Davina. From the first page the story whisks the reader along, from one crisis to another as we meet many other colourful characters along the way. This is very much an adventure story with love, deception and loyalty thrown into the mixture. The pace is quick as the action travels from country to country in a world of super stardom, yet very real human emotions. Hold onto your seats in this roller coaster of a journey!

Sonya C. Dodd, Author

Warrior Music

Denise Kahn wrote a masterpiece directly imagined from her heart as her own son, a U.S. Marine was in Iraq in harm's way… My hat is off to the author and most respectfully to her son and to all that serve in the United States Military. A must read for anyone looking for a love story with non-stop action.

Marc A. DiGiacomo,
Multi-award Bestselling Author/Law Enforcement Officer

Just an incredible read for me and brought back memories of my 20 + years in the military. Most highly recommended with additional Hoo-Rahs and a Bravo Zulu to this author.

A Navy Vet/Amazon Top 500 Reviewer

It will soon be categorized as a historical novel because it superbly chronicles the life of a soldier in the desert of Iraq, post 9/11… Ms. Kahn's son is a veteran of the Iraq War, and this novel is her love song to him. Her pride of him and all veterans shines through in this novel of love, war, and music.

P.A. McAlister, Author

Split-Second Lifetime

This book will become a classic! Isabel Allende, Paulo Coelho, Denise Kahn. What do they have in common? They are all amazing writers and storytellers with a touch of mysticism. Ms. Kahn's writing is fluid and elegant. The characters are original and compassionate, the story is intriguing and fascinating, and the settings are international and exotic. Unique scenes will stay in the back of your mind for a long time. Each one of these authors has a specialty or unique ingredient that puts them in a class of their own.
Denise Kahn's 'Split-Second Lifetime', like 'House of Spirits' and 'the Alchemist', is bound to become a classic.

Racquel, Amazon Reviewer

A Beautiful Quilting of Sounds and Images. The author took on a panoramic project with her book. She did a magnificent job. I learned more about other cultures and ways of thinking. At the same time, the writing style was lyrical, entertaining, and brought together images, sounds, flavors, and sensations. The book even encompasses humor., The entertaining and unexpected puns made me laugh out loud.
.

Jada Ryker, Bestselling Author

Denise Kahn's writing is highly sensual. "Dodi's words were music to my ears and a symphony in my heart." Her work is further enriched by her exposure to different nations, as she describes details from foreign settings and cultures.

Uvi Posnansky, Bestselling Author

Around the World in 80 Quotes on Photos

As I sit here in the frozen tundra of New England, I can say that I truly appreciated this photographic journey around the world, especially to warmer places! The quotes added a certain serenity to the experience, and I can honestly say the author has rekindled my desire to travel!

James Tredeau
Professor of French

Inspirational, beautiful and informative.
Take 80 inspirational quotes that will get you thinking about a variety of life's greatest truths, add in a wide array of stunning photos from every corner of the Globe and you have Denise Kahn's Around the World in 80 Quotes on Photos. The photos are as thought-provoking as the notable quotations - and add an element of beauty that only they can. If you wish to take an entertaining trip around the world without leaving your desk chair, this book will provide you with your round-trip ticket. I highly recommend this beautiful and stimulating book.

Dr. Joe Rubino,
www.CenterForPersonalReinvention.com

When looking at the beautiful pictures I dream away whilst the quotes give me food for thought. What a beautiful world we live in!

E. N. Heek, Author/Publisher
Amsterdam Publishers

Books by Denise Kahn

Novels
Hot Air
Split-Second Lifetime
Peace of Music
Obsession of the Heart
Warrior Music
Music trilogy

Photo Book
Around the World in 80 Quotes on Photos

Travel Tales
(Short travel stories)
We were 12 at 12:12 on 12/12/12 (Mexico)
Entertained by the Gods (Greece)
Sai Baba's Ashram Rendezvous (India)
Gstaad Grace (Switzerland)
Thanksgiving in 24 Hours (Mexico)

Short Stories
Miraculous Moments;
True Stories Affirming that Life goes on,
By Elissa Al-Chokhachy

ISBN 978-1506195674

Published by 4Agapi

www.DeniseKahnBooks.com
Denise@DeniseKahnBooks.com

DEDICATION

To the Gallant People of New Mexico,

And to First Responders

Once you visit New Mexico
You get the itch to return every year.

Georgia O'Keefe

I stopped scratching.

Denise Kahn

You haven't seen a tree until you've seen its shadow from the sky.

Amelia Earhart

Pilots are a rare kind of human. They leave the ordinary surface of the world, to purify their soul in the sky, and they come down to earth, only after receiving the communion of the infinite.

José Maria Velasco Ibarra
President of Ecuador

BALLOONIST'S PRAYER

The winds have welcomed you with softness,
The sun has blessed you with its warm hands,
You have flown so high and so well,
That God has joined you in laughter
And set you back gently into
The loving arms of Mother Earth.

PARARESCUE CREED

It is my duty as a Pararescueman to save lives and to aid the
injured. I will be prepared at all times to perform my assigned
duties quickly and efficiently, placing these duties before
personal desires and comforts.
These things I do, that others may live.

H🎈T AIR

_____

DENISE KAHN

PROLOGUE

The most photographed event in the world, the Albuquerque International Balloon Fiesta in New Mexico, was welcoming tens of thousands of people from around the globe as it hosted its annual world-class event. More than five hundred hot air balloons were scheduled to take off in a mass ascension in less than an hour, and Sean Sandoval, one of the pilots, meticulously checked the equipment—the basket, the uprights, the burners and the large envelope which waited to be inflated into a globe. It patiently lay on its side snuggled against the grass, among many more waiting in the same formation, all lined up as precise as a military operation. The Balloon Fiesta was over forty years old, and every year people would return for the unique event. Those who witnessed it for the first time usually found a way to return. New Mexico was famous for its multi-colored sky and landscape. The Balloon Fiesta gave it an additional dimension of color when hundreds of iridescent globes became living Christmas ornaments in the blue of the sky. It added even more fascination to the Land of Enchantment.

The Balloon Fiesta lasted a little over a week and Sean was as excited as a child. Everyone in New Mexico was, especially in the Albuquerque area. And they were extremely proud to be hosting the biggest ballooning event in the world. From the anticipation leading up to the celebration until the opening day, every person, no matter what age, was as enthusiastic as Sean.

It was barely four o'clock in the crisp October morning when the delightful sensations started travelling through Sean's body. This happened every time he communed with air, and anything that took him up into it. This was his natural high and he loved every one of the sensations, both physically and emotionally. Sean had been in awe of anything that had to do with flying ever since he was a child. He had followed this passion and made it his path in life. But at this particular moment something wasn't right. He could sense it. Was it his father's Native American heritage warning him? His Irish mother's Celtic roots? A combination of both? Or maybe the sharpened sixth sense from his military service. Whichever it was they were all screaming *danger!* and Sean knew better than to ignore warning signs. He looked over every inch of the hot air balloon, inside and out, although he knew the equipment was fine.

"Hey Sandoval, what's up?" Nico, Sean's best friend and fellow pilot, asked.

"Oh, you know me, always double checking everything." What could he say? *My gut is saying something might be wrong?* He didn't have any proof, and he didn't want to worry the man, although Nico would have understood when it came to gut feelings.

"So we're good to go?"

Sean pondered a few moments before answering. Would he be putting them in danger? He knew Nico would probably talk him out of it anyway. He was that kind of guy—a daredevil with a Spartan sense of loyalty and adventure. "Let's do it, time to get up in the air and fly!"

Nico grinned. "Sounds good to me."

As Sean and Nico were ready to take to the skies the man with half Navajo, half Irish blood still had the gnawing signals in the pit of his stomach. Something wasn't right. He sensed it, it was coming, and his instincts had never been wrong.

CHAPTER 1

A young nine year old Sean was awakened by the smell of warm cinnamon that wafted from the kitchen to his bedroom. His mouth immediately watered at the anticipation of his mother's delicious bread pudding, one of her specialties. He promptly jumped out of bed, and although he wanted to just run to the kitchen, he knew his mother would send him back as he had to go to school after breakfast. The boy quickly dressed. When he entered the kitchen a shadow from outside the window of the back door caught his eye. Curious about what it could be he looked out and saw a dark, ominous and immense round silhouette slowly hovering above their house. His heart skipped a beat, and although he was slightly scared, he looked up. The boy couldn't quite comprehend what he was seeing as the sun was only giving him a hazy outline. He put his face against the glass, slightly pushing his nose against the pane for a better view. And then he gasped as he saw the bright colors of a giant hot air balloon suspended over his parents' property. It was only a few feet above them! Talking distance! Sean's young heart changed from apprehension to delight.

"Someone is driving up," Tibah, his father, said. "I'm going to check it out."

"I'm coming with you, Daddy."

"Stay close to me."

"I will."

The Sandovals walked outside and looked up. Sean was mesmerized. This was the closest he had ever come to one of these hot air giants. He marveled at the puffy gores which to him looked like rows of turtle shells, but not with dull dark colors, rather it was sky blue with a magnificent iridescent rainbow swelling out from the globe. It hugged the entire balloon. Sean marveled at the cheerful design and desperately wanted to touch it. He loved rainbows and he thought how smart these two men in the basket were—they always carried their rainbow with them, even without rain. What he wanted even more was to stand in that basket below the balloon and fly. Oh, how wonderful it would be if they took him up for a ride! He squeezed his eyes as tight as possible and prayed. When he opened them his father was standing behind him, his hands on his son's little shoulders.

"Are they going to land here, Daddy?" He wondered and pleaded.

"It looks like it. They usually don't come over the Reservation. I hope everything is alright."

At that moment a van pulling a trailer with the balloon's logo *The Rainboyws* on its side drove up to them. The two men in the front waved. Tibah and Sean waved back.

"Hi," the driver said as he stopped next to Tibah.

"Good morning," Tibah answered back to the chase crew.

"We're really sorry to intrude, but the winds pushed the balloon over here."

It was an occurrence that happened often enough around the Albuquerque area, and most everyone was perfectly at ease with it, and knew that sometimes these multi-colored giants could even land in their back yards. The people loved their hot air balloons and their pilots, and actually looked forward to the impromptu visits.

"Yes, we can see that," Tibah said as he watched the hot air balloon make its descent close to where they were standing. The two men of the chase crew were ready as the aerostat landed gracefully. They quickly held the basket down. The pilots waved to the Sandovals.

"Good morning!"

"Good morning to you. Nice landing," Tibah said.

"Thank you. The winds decided to suddenly change and brought us to you. We're very sorry."

"That's quite alright, and my son seems very happy about it," he chuckled.

Sean watched, awestruck.

"Hey, little man," the pilot said, "what's your name?"

"Sean, Sir," the boy answered.

"Hi Sean."

The men introduced themselves as Jack and Ryan.

"Daddy, I want to ride in the big balloon," the boy said with the typical honesty of his age.

The men laughed at Sean's enthusiasm.

"I'm sorry, guys," Tibah said.

"No, don't be, we still feel that way, and probably always will," Jack said. The pilots reminisced back to their own ballooning beginnings, mirroring Sean's emotions. And they knew it would never change. There wasn't anything like piloting and flying through the sky. They were living their dream.

"Yeah, it just kind of stays in your blood," Ryan added.

"We have coffee, fresh squeezed orange juice and my wife Fiona's delicious bread pudding just came out of the oven. Would you all like to join us for breakfast? Tibah asked.

"That's sounds great, but we really have to get going."

"My mom makes the best breakfast in the world!" Sean exclaimed. "Could you please stay?"

The chase crew was holding down the basket, waiting until the pilots were ready to take off.

"If we stayed we would have to deflate and pack up here. We've already imposed enough," Jack said.

"Gentlemen, we have no problem if you want to do that, and the invitation still stands. I know Sean will be thrilled, and my wife loves company.

Jack and Ryan looked at each other and then at their chase crew. They also saw disappointment etched all over Sean's face.

"We're down now. We could call it a day," Jack said.

"I'm with you," Ryan answered. "And the guys would probably love a home-cooked meal." He turned to Tibah. "We gratefully accept your offer."

"YES!" Sean and the chase crew exclaimed at the same time. The boy jumped up and down, hardly able to contain his joy. They 'high-fived' each other, pleased with the outcome.

"It won't take us very long to pack up, and John and Adam are really quick," Jack said.

"That's fine. I'll tell my wife to set a few more plates," Tibah said as he headed toward the house.

"Can I stay out and watch them, Daddy?" Sean pleaded.

Tibah looked at the men already working on disassembling the equipment.

"That's fine with us," Ryan said.

"Alright then, just stay out of their way, Sean."

"I will."

"Uh, Sir, would it be alright if Sean helped us? Nothing dangerous, I assure you," Ryan said.

Sean's eyes grew as big and round as they had ever been. And, oh, how they pleaded with his father.

"I'm sure that will be fine. I'll come out and help right after I tell my wife that you'll be staying for breakfast. And please, the name is Tibah."

"Thank you, Daddy!"

"Yes, thank you, Tibah," Ryan said.

Tibah waved as he turned toward the house.

"Ready, Sean?"

"Ready!"

"You follow what I say so that you don't get hurt in any way."

"Okay."

"Stand right next to the basket until I call you."

Sean did and watched the four men with great enthusiasm. The basket lay on its side. Ryan was standing just in front of the gondola holding a rope.

"Sean, help me with this line." The boy was at the man's side in an instant. "Look up and you'll see a big circle at the top, that's the valve, also called the parachute, that releases the air from the envelope.

"The envelope?"

"Yes, that's what we call it, where the air is. Pull with me?" Sean nodded and put his hands on the rope. They pulled together and watched as the valve opened and the balloon quickly started to deflate. Sean was amazed how fast the air was going out. The emptying envelope gently cascaded to the ground. John was holding another rope on the other end, at the crown, guiding and pulling it down. Sean wondered if he would fall backwards. Adam, Jack and Tibah, who had come out to help, started rolling the sides.

"Sean," Ryan said, "help me with the sweeper." The boy went to him. The man produced a tube that looked very much like a big open 'O' with a handle on each side. Jack slipped it on the beginning of the envelope near the gondola. "Ready?"

"Ready," Sean answered.

Ryan and Sean each took one of the sweeper's handles and pulled the 'O' toward the crown. The balloon continued to deflate until all the air seemed to be out.

"Good job Sean."

John and Adam started folding the deflated envelope toward the basket. Jack and Ryan were ready with the carrier and placed it at the end where the folding would finish. The four men then put the envelope in its bag.

"Sean, put yourself across the bag and let the rest of the air out," Jack said.

Tibah lifted the boy and Sean lay on top. He could feel the material against his body. He thought the whole experience was better than any game he ever played.

"Okay, that's perfect. Now we tie the bag up and the basket goes into the back of the trailer along with the propane burners and uprights."

Sean watched them work. It was as if he knew every move they were going to make.

Adam backed up the vehicle toward the gondola. The other men lifted the front of the basket and when the trailer was almost touching the bottom of the gondola they quickly pushed it in. They put the rest of the equipment inside and closed the doors.

"Nice job everybody. Especially you, Sean, you're a natural."

Sean was proud of himself. "Thank you, Mr. Ryan."

Ryan had watched the boy touch and feel every part of the hot air balloon. No, it was more like a caress. The passion and the yearning had penetrated his blood, not the glee of a small boy or girl, rather an adoration, a passion.

"So, who's hungry?" Tibah asked. The group immediately cheered. "Follow me."

They all went into the house and sat down at the long table. Fiona had been thrilled at the unexpected company and welcomed each one into her home.

"Please have a seat, gentlemen."

They did as she asked.

"Thank you so much for your hospitality, Tibah and..." Jack said.

"Fiona, call me Fiona, and you are most welcome."

"Oh, you're Irish!" Ryan said, and wondered how this fair skinned and red haired beauty wound up in New Mexico and married to a Navajo.

"It's the accent, eh?" She chuckled. "If I'm not mistaken you sound American but... Canadian maybe?"

"Yes, indeed, from Toronto originally. Jack and I are brothers, twins actually."

"But you don't look the same," Sean said.

"Some of us do, others don't. We're fraternal twins, not identical," Ryan explained. "And this is John and Adam. They're college students at UNM, and the absolute best chase crew in New Mexico. They've been with us for a while now."

"Well, welcome lads. Now please, eat while it's still hot. You must be tired, that was quite a workout. I watched you from the window a bit."

"Thank you, Ma'am," they mumbled, their mouths already full of Fiona's delicious bread pudding.

"So, what made you fall in love with ballooning?" Tibah asked.

"That obvious?" Ryan asked.

Tibah raised his eyebrows and nodded.

"An avalanche," Jack said.

"As in snow?"

"That's right."

"Where? In Canada?"

"No, in France, in the Alps."

"You were watching an avalanche?" Fiona asked.

"No, we were caught in it."

"Oh my God, how did that happen?"

"Why were you in France?" Sean asked.

"Both Ryan and I were members of the Canadian national ski team. We were in Chamonix practicing on a run when a hot air balloon drifted above us. We both looked at each other and knew we had to get a ride in it."

"Did you?" The boy asked.

"We did. We booked a flight for the next day, took our skis with us and had our first ride in a hot air balloon. Oh, it was breathtaking! The view of the mountains and the dense trees covered with snow, the crispness of the air and the silence—that glorious silence that you can only have when you are away from the earth and in the middle of the sky, were incredible. If you listen carefully you will always hear something, the hum of a refrigerator, a mother's voice in the background, an animal howling in the distance, but never complete silence like when you are in the middle of the air."

Sean was following Jack's every word, practically sitting at attention as the man relayed their story.

"We were soaring like birds in the sky above the magnificent Alps," he continued, "breathing the same air that angels do, and probably the closest we had ever been to heaven. And that did it. We were both hooked."

Tibah watched his young son listening to Jack. There was something about the boy's eyes, a look of longing, of passion, of comprehension, perhaps even a soul connection with the pilots that had descended from the sky earlier that morning. Tibah understood this about his son, even though the youngster still didn't. But he knew he would, and soon. There was no question about it.

"Why did you take your skis?" Sean asked. He wanted to know everything concerning the trip, the skiing, and especially the balloon.

"Because after the ride we were going to ski down the mountain."

"Could they land?"

"No, there wasn't anyone there to help hold the basket so we just threw our skis out and jumped over the side."

"You could do that?" Tibah asked.

"Yes, they had explained it to us, just like helicopter skiing. They just hover over until you get out. The pilot dropped us off at the peak of the mountain. It was amazing! Beautiful untouched snow just waiting for us." Jack looked deeply into the emerald eyes the boy had inherited from his mother. "But they made a mistake."

"Who?"

"The pilot. He dropped us off on the wrong side of that mountain."

"How come?" Sean asked.

"His coordinates were wrong."

"So what happened?"

"Well, Ryan and I jumped out of the basket, waved goodbye as the balloon took off, and put our skis on. We stood there like gods above the grandeur of the Alps."

"It really was spectacular," Jack added. "I will never forget the beauty all around us. We couldn't get enough of the view and after a little while we were ready to go down the face of that mountain."

"And what a run that was," Ryan said. "It was our slope, our moment. We were one with nature, with the incredible Alps surrounding us and doing what we loved most—skiing. As we slalomed through the powder we made infinity signs in the snow... until we heard a roar, and we instantly knew it wasn't going to be good—it was an avalanche, and right behind us."

"Were you scared?" Sean asked.

"Terrified!" The twins answered at the same time.

"We skied as fast as humanly possible, and that was pretty fast since we were downhill racing champions," Jack said.

"But even though we were two of the fastest skiers in the world we were no match for that mass of snow chasing us."

"I think the scariest part was the noise," Ryan continued, "we went from heavenly quiet to the booming roar of a side of a mountain hunting us down."

"In less than a minute the avalanche caught up with us," Jack said.

"And played with us as if we were toothpicks in a storm," Ryan added.

"Oh, no!" Fiona gasped.

"Did you get hurt?" Sean asked.

"I'm not much of a gambling man," Tibah said, "but I would bet they did."

"Well, that sea of snow picked us up like ping pong balls and batted us back and forth between a few trees," Ryan said, as his eyes grew darker from the memory. "We were pretty badly hurt—broken bones, unconscious and buried about two feet below the surface."

"When the rescuers finally found us we were shattered marionettes, yet remarkably alive," Jack added.

Ryan laughed. "The hospital kept losing count. We broke almost all our bones including our backs."

"Oh, my God!" Fiona exclaimed.

"I'm sure He had a hand in us being with you at this moment, because the doctors weren't very optimistic. At some point they realized we really would survive, but they didn't think we would ever walk again."

"But we proved them wrong," Ryan said.

"Yes, but we had operation after operation, were laid up for months, and went through some horrific times with pain and therapy."

"And of course we would never be the athletes we once were. Our dreams of competing for our country, and being the best in the world were over."

"But at least we survived," Jack said.

Sean watched the brothers and was amused at how they continued each other's story.

"We did. Luckily we weren't paralyzed."

"But we're still a little limited physically. We can only do so much, but we're grateful to be alive and able to function on our own."

"We also became rich," Ryan said.

"How? Because of the avalanche?" Sean asked.

"That's right, little man. Because they dropped us off in the wrong spot," Jack said.

"Totally wrong spot—it was an avalanche zone! Their insurance paid us handsomely."

"With a little careful planning we can both live very comfortably to the end of our days," Jack continued.

"But because of the accident our bodies can only do so much, and we can't really work."

"But we remembered that amazing balloon ride and decided to look into it further," Jack said.

"It was as if we were obsessed. Something happened to us on that first flight, and now here we are."

"Yes, pilots of our very own balloon," Jack said.

"We left Canada and moved to New Mexico."

"The weather a wee better?" Fiona asked, chuckling. She was from a colder, wet country herself.

"Oh, yes, our bones are very grateful," Ryan answered.

"And we're in the land of hot air balloons," Jack added.

"Basically, we're in heaven on earth," Ryan concluded.

Fiona clapped. "Bravo, gentlemen, you followed your heart. You seem to be very passionate and happy."

"We are." Jack and Ryan said at the same time.

They continued eating their breakfast. When they finished Jack turned to Sean. "Hey, little man, do you think you can remember what our balloon looks like?" The boy nodded. *How could he ever forget?* "Tell you what. The Fiesta is starting soon. You come see us there, and if you like we'll give you a ride… if that's okay with your Dad," Jack quickly added.

Sean was sure his young heart was bursting out of his chest. "Can I Daddy? Can I, please?" He begged.

Tibah looked at the youngster. If he was any happier he was sure the boy would levitate. He also knew that Sean was already starting to follow the ambition he had seen earlier in the boy's eyes. He would help his son in every way he could. "I think it's a plan."

"Thank you, Daddy, you're the best!" He whirled around to the brothers. "And you too! Thank you so much! And I can help you again," Sean said, wanting to be useful.

"You're very welcome, Sean. And that's very kind of you to offer. I'm sure we could use all the help you can give us."

"Just make sure you get there early before we take off," Ryan said.

"We'll be there, thank you." Tibah said.

"Thank you, Tibah, and Fiona. Breakfast was delicious," Jack said.

"Yes, thank you very much," the college students said.

"You're very welcome," Fiona said, "come back and see us any time."

"Yes, please do," Tibah added. "If you need a landing spot you can always come here. Sean will surely be thrilled."

"Thank you again," Ryan said.

Sean thought this was the best day of his life. He wanted to become a pilot just like Mr. Jack and Mr. Ryan, and even though he had never been in a hot air balloon he knew he would be just as passionate as the brothers were. He watched them get into the van with the *Rainboyws* logo on the side. He really liked the design of the giant rainbow protruding out and around the entire sky blue globe. He stayed there and waved until they were completely out of sight.

"Sean!" Tibah shouted, breaking the boy's reverie. "Time to go to school!"

Oh, no, he had completely forgotten. Sean cringed and ran to his father. "Do I have to, Daddy?"

"No."

Sean's eyes shot up to his father's face. "Really?" He couldn't be serious.

"Really. But just this once. You're already very late since we had our guests this morning, and I thought maybe the three of us could spend a little time together. What do you think?"

"I think you're the best Daddy in the whole world!"

"Remember, just this once."

"Can we go riding?"

Tibah giggled. "I think that's a great idea. Let's go get your mother. Maybe she can make us some sandwiches. And go change, you're school clothes got a workout too and are now of course dirty."

Sean took off running to tell his mother the good news. When he arrived in the kitchen she was already preparing for their picnic. He loved how smart she always was.

That night when Fiona had tucked him in and turned off the light he kept reliving the sight of the balloon descending from the sky. How he wished he could fly. How wonderful would it be to become a bird, to soar above the mesas and mountains, to traverse across the blue horizon of New Mexico, to float through the oranges and crimsons of enchanting sunrises. He had heard stories from his Navajo people about shape-shifters, of men becoming deer or other animals and communing with nature. Sean and his two best friends would play at 'shape-shifting', pretend they had transformed themselves into mountain lions, deer, horses and many different animals. They would chase each other in a kind of 'animal hide and seek'. It was great fun, but Sean wondered if one day he would be able to do the same in real life. He, of course, wanted to be an eagle, the most majestic and powerful of all flyers.

Sean fell asleep with a smile on his face, and in moments he was in that sky, dreaming he was flying effortlessly like his noble raptor. The boy traveled to eastern France, to the Rhône-Alps region. The year was 1777 and a man, sitting on the ground and leaning against a house, watched laundry drying over a fire. Sean walked up to him with his hands in his pockets, dressed in the clothes of the era.

"What are you doing, *Monsieur?*" Sean asked, amazed and thrilled as he realized he was communicating to the man, but wasn't sure what language they were speaking. In dreams you could always communicate.

The man, in his twenties, seemed financially comfortable

as his clothes were not cheap, but was dreadfully unkempt. His knee-length breeches were wrinkled, as was his waistcoat. The ruffles of his silk shirt weren't standing at attention any more, rather they looked as if they had fainted. His shoes were scuffed and needed a good shine, and the large buckles in the front needed to be polished.

"I am looking at the laundry floating upward. Come, sit next to me," he said patting the ground, "but only if you are interested in something magical."

Sean immediately sat down. "Oh, yes, Sir, I am very interested!"

"I can tell," the man retorted. "What is your name, *mon petit*?"

"My name is Sean, Sir."

"So your name is Jean," he said, mispronouncing it.

"Uh, Sean."

"Yes, Jean, I know."

Sean chuckled inwardly as he accepted that his name would never sound correctly.

"And my name is Joseph."

"Pleased to meet you, Monsieur Joseph," Sean said extending his hand.

Joseph shook it. "Now let me show you something incredibly exciting. Watch how the laundry floats up." The man was so animated his eyes kept twitching. He put his elbows on his bent knees and held his face as he focused intently on the shirt making waves.

Sean looked at the wash hanging on a line, his eyes following the undulating see-through material of the shirt. There wasn't a spot of wind, but the clothes took on a life of their own. The trousers swayed up and down, the sleeves rippled, the dance was magical.

"That is so cool!"

"Cool?"

"I mean it's very interesting." Sean realized that the people back then didn't use 'cool' in the same way. "Why is it doing that? There's no wind."

"Hah ha! Exactly. Exactly!" Joseph said with delight as his limbs shook with excitement.

The man reminded Sean of a rabbit. At any moment he was sure he would start jumping around. "So why is the wash moving?"

"Because of the heat!" Joseph exclaimed excitedly. "It makes it go up!" He crumbled some paper and threw it on the fire. More flames jumped up. The clothes danced even faster. "The heat! The heat!" The man hopped up and did a few crazy steps from his own creative dance. He grabbed Sean's arms, pulled him up and swung him around lifting him right off his feet. "We're going to fly! Just like you're doing now, Jean! Man will fly! Yes! Man will fly!" He shouted with joy as he spinned Sean higher and higher.

Sean nodded to himself. He was right. The man really was a rabbit. Maybe Joseph would make furry creatures fly too. And he wanted to be right there with him when humans starting their flying, although he was already doing some of it now with the help of the man who was turning and turning and making him soar through the air.

CHAPTER 2

Sean woke from his dream with a smile on his face, and with one arm and leg off the mattress. He almost fell out of bed. Was he still spinning? Still flying in a circle powered by Joseph's arms? Had he really been to that far off land, with the people wearing funny clothes? It was in the past, a long time ago, yet he was sure he had been there. How had he traveled there? Had he shape-shifted? It was even better than being an eagle, he could go back in time as well! Right?

Little Sean wanted to see for himself, so he ran to the kitchen. He took his box of sweet cereal and removed the waxy paper containing the grains. He tore off the top and bottom of the carton and put the open-ended box over the sides of the toaster. He did this so that the light plastic supermarket bag he wanted to inflate wouldn't burn. He made sure the cardboard was a snug fit and then placed the bag on top of it. Sean looked over his contraption with great care until he was satisfied. He pushed the toaster's knob down and the heat went up the box and into the plastic. He waited with great anticipation and then the bag lifted off! Sean's young eyes grew wide with wonder and triumph. He had just produced his first flight. Thankfully he didn't burn anything down, such as his parents' kitchen or even the house.

Unbeknownst to the boy his father, who had heard a noise and decided to check it out, had been watching. He inwardly laughed, but was also amazed by his young son. Once he was sure Sean was finished with his contraption he hurriedly went back to his bedroom.

Sean, however, was much too excited to go back to sleep so he ran to his parents' room. He jumped on the bed and dove between the two people that had just been jolted awake. Well, they had pretended to be asleep.

"Hey, what are you so excited about, *a stor?*" Fiona asked, using an Irish term of endearment.

Sean was going to tell his parents about his dream, about flying to another land, about meeting wacky Joseph. And his plastic bag balloon! He had made it fly, just as the big ones did. *He* had done that! He was pretty sure they would be excited at his accomplishment, but then again maybe they would make fun of him. He thought about it for a moment, and then decided not to. "Oh, nothing, it's just a really nice day and I thought we could go riding."

Sean's parents looked at each other, smiled, and acquiesced.

"But before we go out we're having breakfast!" Fiona insisted.

Father and son looked at each other, and nodded in agreement. They knew there wasn't anything better than her breakfasts.

Fiona quickly went to the kitchen and started cooking. She also prepared some sandwiches for lunch. They would make a nice outing of it.

The Sandovals finished breakfast and headed toward to the stable. They past the chicken coop where eight hens gave them delicious eggs with orange yolks. Sean had carefully named each one of them with Navajo and Irish names—all boy names. His parents had helped him, but at the time he hadn't told them what he needed them for. One day Tibah and Fiona went looking for Sean. They found him in the coop feeding the girls, and talking to them as he called them by name: Ahiga *he fights* was rather feisty; Bidziil *he is strong*, Kilchii *red boy* who was completely red, Nastas *foxtail* seemed to have twice as many tail feathers as the other ones; and the Irish clan: Alroy *red* who Sean was sure was Kilchii's sister, Brian *strong*, Carney *victorious* who won all her pecking fights, and Lorcan *brave warrior* a fierce fighter. Tibah and Fiona's eyes grew very wide and they laughed harder than they ever had as they heard Sean talking to the hens and calling them by their boy names.

They proceeded to the stable where the horses stood at attention as soon as they heard the family walk in. Fiona went to one of the stalls.

"Ah, my lovely Nollaig, how are you this morning?" Fiona asked her beloved horse, the one Tibah had given her for Christmas a few years back. She had immediately fallen in love with the mare and named her for the holiday. She was a cream-colored appaloosa with a reddish-brown star on her handsome face, and a mane and tail of the same shade. It was the greatest gift Tibah could give his treasured wife, and he told her the horse reminded him of her—the red hair and the porcelain skin. The mare was gentle, loving and loyal, yet every once in a while she could be lively and strong tempered which would make Fiona tease her with "oh, Nollaig, you're so Irish!" The horse would answer back by nuzzling Fiona's hair and cheek, and was as sweet as sugar when presented with a carrot. Nollaig reminded Fiona of Donegal, her home back in Ireland, of her happiest memory as a little girl where she would look at her father sitting on his horse, and he in turn would stare back and ask: "Want to come with, lass?" Padraig of course already knew the answer. He would lift her up and sit his little darlin' in front of him. Oh, how she remembered his strong arms around her as he held the reins, the warmth of his chest against her back, and the inimitable feeling of complete well-being and happiness. Padraig gently squeezed his heels into the horse and the trio started walking. Fiona and her Da enjoyed this cherished time together, of a father and daughter who adored each other, a father she believed was the absolute perfect Da in the world. As they rode they breathed in the clean, crisp air that blew toward them from the sea. They followed the ribbon of country road along the craggy cliffs, and could see as far as the Iveragh Peninsula.

"Let's gooooo!" Padraig said, and spurred the horse into a gallop. Young Fiona held on tightly and screamed in delight as the cool wind flew into their faces and made their eyes water. They only stopped when the horse was breathing hard, its warm sweat smelling of wet hay and becoming a light steam that wafted up to the riders. As Padraig walked the steed to cool down they also smelled the wet grass, and took in the lush plains of different greens which gleamed and shimmered from the previous night's rain. It made the countryside a sea of brilliant emerald. An old man once told her that Ireland was the only country in the world that boasted forty shades of green. She believed it.

"Mam, are you and Nollaig ready?" Sean asked bringing her back from her childhood.

"Yes, my love, we are, she's all saddled up. How about you and Nizhóní?"

"We're ready too," the boy said, as he caressed the neck of his mount. Like Fiona he adored his horse, especially since he was Nollaig's colt, and witnessing his birth was something Sean would never forget.

On that particular day Nollaig was standing in her cubicle when she buckled a bit and went down on her side. Tibah and Sean had just finished cleaning out the stalls. He ran to the horse and shouted at Sean: "Get your mother! Nollaig is having her baby."

"Right now?"

"Yup, right now. Now go!"

And he did. Sean ran faster than he ever had. "Mam, Mam!" He screamed. "Mam! Nollaig is having her baby! Mam, Mam!"

Fiona heard her son's cries and came running out. "Is she on her side?"

"Yes. Dad told me to get you."

Mother and son ran to the stable and to Nollaig's stall. Tibah was petting her neck and talking softly to her. Fiona and Sean went in.

"Sean, *a stor*, you can stay against the wall, but be very quiet."

"Okay." He watched his parents, overjoyed that he would

be able to see the baby horse being born. He stood very still against the boards of the stall. He didn't want to scare the mare, and he certainly didn't want his parents to tell him to leave.

Fiona sat next to Tibah and put Nollaig's face on her thigh. She caressed her star, cheeks and neck. "Ah, lass, it's time to bring your little one into the world. We'll be here to help you through it." She turned to Tibah. "Is she alright?"

"Seems to be." He stood up and went toward her hind legs. And then it started. A bubble, the amniotic sac, began to appear beneath her tail. It kept getting bigger like someone blowing gum. When Sean saw a small head emerge inside the clear sac he held his breath. He watched as Nollaig's stomach heaved up and down. She was pushing, and every time she did more of the foal slid out with the fluid and the sac. When the miniature horse was almost completely out its snout broke through the pouch and it started breathing on its own. So did Sean. He had been holding his breath the whole time. The foal was completely black, the only white spot a star like his mother's. Tibah broke another part of the sac with his hands and pulled more of it out. He left it on the hay and picked up a blanket he had prepared for the occasion, and started to clean the foal with it. He watched carefully in case he needed to pull out the legs. Nollaig rose up a bit and looked behind her. Yes, she understood her baby was fine. Her nostrils flared as she whinnied a welcome to her newborn. She shifted a little and the rest of the sac and the foal's legs and hooves came out. It was a fairly easy birth. Mare and colt looked at each other, their heads gently moving from side to side.

"Oh, you're such a good girl," Fiona murmured to her beloved horse, "would you just look at your little beauty!"

The foal slowly tried to get up on its front legs. Nollaig wanted to get up too. Fiona understood this and carefully stood up. The mare in turn tried standing up, being mindful not to trample her newborn. She did finally get up, keeping one foot in the air so as not to kick the little one. She lowered her head and started licking the fluid off of her baby, who was now resting on its bent legs. The foal tried standing up again, but fell several times.

"Daddy, can I help?"

Tibah was watching. "Sure, son." He was going to add 'be gentle', but he knew his son would be—because of his character, or because he would naturally know what to do? Either way he was confident Sean would do the right thing. And Tibah was right. The boy gently went up to the foal and pet his neck. The slimy fluid from the sac didn't bother him in the least. He cleaned the little horse with the blanket like his father had, and started talking to him: "Hey, little baby, do you want to get up?" The foal stared at him. "Come on, I'll help you," Sean said, and put his arms around the tiny neck. He slightly lifted him, albeit carefully. Sean thought maybe he was still 'breakable'. Foal and boy tried a couple more times and when he finally stood on his thin outstretched legs he looked more like a spider than a horse.

"You did a fine job bringing your colt into this world, Nollaig, a fine *awéé* indeed," Tibah said.

In the background a loud whinny echoed through the stable. It came from the stall next to Nollaig's. It was Tibah's horse, Nízhánee.

"Oh, yes, just like your name, you are lucky big boy. Your Nollaig has given you a fine colt. You should be a proud father.

Nízhánee whinnied even louder. Had he understood?

Sean was awestruck by what he thought was surely a miracle, a miracle he wanted to witness over and over. He thought maybe he would become a veterinarian when he grew up. He loved animals and wanted to help them when they were hurt or sick. He was always surrounded by them— his cat when he slept, playing with his dogs, talking to his chickens, and now he was attached to the newborn foal. When the colt stood for the first time on his own Sean thought his heart would melt. It was the most beautiful sight he had ever seen. Tibah, who had been keenly watching his son, asked him what he thought. The boy could only speak one word: Nizhóní *beautiful*. And that is what they named him.

"I think that is a perfect name, he is definitely beautiful. And he's yours," Tibah ended.

Fiona smiled. Sean didn't react. But then it hit him. He looked at his father, and then at his smiling mother. He looked at the colt and whispered: "Really?"

"Really."

Sean who had been very quiet the whole time suddenly rushed to his father to hug him, but before reaching him the mare and her foal jumped. The colt, who was still trying to figure out how to stand without falling, fell down onto the hay as if he had been pushed. Sean's little heart stopped, completely devastated by what he was sure he had just caused. "I'm so sorry!" He exclaimed.

Tibah laughed. "It's alright, little man, Nizhóní is not made of glass. He'll be fine. Come, let's go help the little guy back up."

Nizhóní and Sean grew up together, and as close as brothers. If people didn't believe that horses had emotions all they had to do was watch these two best friends, and they would understand. They were inseparable, and just like two young boys they played together. Nizhóní's favorite game was pushing Sean down and nuzzling him in the ribs. He loved when the boy laughed, and Sean was so ticklish he was sure we would die from that laughter. The boy also found secrets about his horse. Nizhóní loved being scratched on the back side of his snout, in the soft spot right behind his lower lip. Whenever Sean scratched or pet him there the horse would rub Sean's cheek with his own, covering him with his mane as if they were kids in a tent at a slumber party. Sean talked to his Nizhóní, especially when he brushed him, washed him, cleaned his stall, fed him, and gave him carrots. In return he received an unconditional love as only a horse could give. The feelings were mutual.

Now a handsome full grown stallion, Sean kissed the soft nose of his four-legged brother before leading him out of the stable. The Sandovals were ready and headed out for the hills. Sean rode ahead, his parents right behind him. They were proud of their young son and they smiled at the joy of the boy on his mount. Tibah had put him on the back of a horse at the same time he started taking his first steps. Riding for the boy was as natural as walking. As his father watched him he marveled at how gratified his son made him, and had no doubt that he would continue to do so. It was in his character and his kind heart.

Tibah showed Sean nature's bounty, just as his ancestors had done for him. They hunted animals of all sizes: Deer, elk, rabbits, squirrels, reptiles, and ate them for the sole purpose of nourishment and never for sport. Tibah also showed his son how to end their lives with the least pain possible, and to always thank them for their sacrifice as he recited a prayer over the lifeless animal. Other animals Sean learned about, and more importantly how to protect himself from, were cougars, wolves and coyotes. Plants and herbs were also an important part of his education. Tibah explained to his young son their uses, whether as a medicine, or for helping food taste better. A favorite of Sean's was the bigberry manzanitas, a shrub that could grow as tall as a tree and produced large red waxy berries in clusters that looked like miniature apples. They could be used to flavor food, or be made into a juice. Sean always enjoyed his mother putting the flowers in vases around the house, and making cakes with the dried berries. Oh, how he loved his mother's baking. Blue dicks were also useful. Their lovely mauve flowers were a favorite of Fiona's, and its bulb could be eaten raw or cooked, and also used as a starch. Sean was also fascinated by plants like the yucca. Native Americans used their roots, which are high in saponins, as a shampoo. In its dried form the tough fibrous leaves with their sharp tips could be used to pierce meat, and then formed into a loop to hang and cure. But Sean was most interested in the ones used for healing, such as the prickly pear cactus that could keep blood sugar stable, or wild licorice that could be brewed as a tea to support the immune system. Another one he found fascinating was mesquite flour, which his father ground from whole pods and gave to his mother. It was sweet and Fiona used it mainly for desserts, but what captivated Sean was that it was good for diabetics because the sweetness came from fructose and the body could process it without insulin.

Whenever the Sandovals went out riding Tibah would show Sean more of the abundance of the nature surrounding them. He was proud to be able to show his son the bounty of the land, and the ways his ancestors revered it. He also always made sure the boy understood that he was only a part of it, and that it was his to share among all living beings, and never to be taken for granted.

The Sandoval family rode a little farther, marveling at the beauty of the high desert. They were surrounded by mesas of rose-colored sand that became cliffs, and continued into snow covered peaks at the top of Mount Taylor and the Sandia mountains. Fiona, who had come from a completely different countryside, albeit beautiful in its emerald splendor, was always enthralled by the American Southwest. She considered it more her home than Ireland had ever been, and never regretted her move to this part of the world. They stopped the horses at one of the highest points in the land with a view to the horizon that seemed infinite. They dismounted next to a large tree as the sun had reached its peak in the hazy, hot sky and was bearing down on them. They were grateful for the cooling shade of the immense branches, and Fiona proceeded to take their lunch out of a picnic basket. Tibah helped her and laid out a couple of blankets.

Sean was distracted by a little mound lying on the ground a few yards down the hill. He went towards it. As he got closer he realized it was a dead animal as he saw tufts of fur and some ligaments still attached to a few of the bones. He was a little nervous, but he crept up until he was right above it. The blood had dried on some of the fur and also seeped into the earth making it a dark brown. He was pretty sure it must have been a rabbit, most likely killed by another animal, maybe a coyote. He understood this, even though the only parts left were no longer attached to each other. He stared at it intensely and then placed his hands above the little body and said a prayer as his father had taught him in respect for the little creature. Sean was fascinated by the anatomy. He looked at it for a long while and then carefully picked up one bone and then another. He meticulously started placing them, trying to recreate the skeleton. He didn't mind the shredded sinew, the intestines that were still hanging over parts of the carcass, or even the pungent smell that reminded him of an old dirty, moldy sponge. He continued placing the pieces, sometimes moving them from one area to another, sometimes putting them where they had been originally.

Tibah noticed what his son was doing and was ready to yell at the boy to get away from the dead creature when Fiona gently put her hand on his arm and held him back. "Why are you stopping me?" He asked, "don't you see that he's playing with a carcass and not a toy?"

"Of course I do, but you're not seeing the bigger picture."

"What bigger picture?"

"Look beyond the carcass. Look at how his brain works."

"What does that mean?"

"He isn't afraid at all. On the contrary, he's fascinated, but not by the death. Humans have a subconscious intention, or a tendency, of what they would like to do with their lives. I would wager that our son, who not only is compassionate with animals, but even at this young age with humans, will head toward the medical field."

"So what you are seeing is that one piece at a time he is maybe trying to figure out how they all fit together, so that he knows how to 'fix' them?"

"I believe so."

The father watched his little son recreate the discarded carcass with no inhibitions.

"You're right, Fiona, he is passionate. It would be a noble profession, and I would be very proud of his choice, although the way he watches birds flying I thought he would do something with air."

"With air?"

"Yes. I'm not exactly sure, maybe a pilot?"

"May the Spirits bless him in their infinite wisdom, and

guide him toward his path and choices," Fiona said.

"Aho," Tibah nodded in agreement.

When Sean finished his 'puzzle' he went back to his parents. He was pleased with himself, pretty sure he had recreated the skeleton correctly. He was also ravenous. His mother washed his hands with some of the water she had packed and gave him a sandwich. He ate it quickly and asked her for another. He was still hungry.

"It's a good thing I packed extra for my growing boy," Fiona chuckled.

As soon as they finished their lunch gray clouds loomed above them and suddenly burst into a downpour. Fiona and Tibah ran from under the tree and stood in the rain, their arms open and their faces toward the sky.

"Come on, Sean!" Fiona beckoned, "stand under the rain with us."

"Aren't we going to get wet?"

"Of course, that's the idea," his father said.

"But why?"

"Well I think your mother does it because she probably misses the rains of Ireland. It doesn't rain too often here."

"And you Daddy?"

"When it rains I feel I am part of creation."

"What do you mean?"

"God is showering His world, blessing His garden, our crops, making everything grow and cleansing Mother Earth. He knows that like all beautiful women She likes to be clean and fresh. Look at how pristine everything is around you."

Sean did as his father asked and understood—the land had turned a darker shade, the plants and trees as well, and they all glowed as if a coat of lacquer had been sprayed over them.

"It's pretty," the boy said, "everything looks new."

"Yes, it is, my son. Now, close your eyes." Tibah wanted all the boy's senses to understand and to literally feel nature.

Sean did. His nose smelled the freshness of the earth, the aroma of nature. The water made rivulets on his little arms and matted his hair to his scalp. He opened his hands and held them out letting the rain fill the cups of his palms, then drank the pristine liquid. His ears heard the rhythm of the raindrops falling on leaves, on stones, on the ground at his feet. He listened carefully as nature produced its unique symphony.

A little while later, as the rains in New Mexico never lasted very long, the family stood together, hand in hand.

"Oh, look!" Fiona said, pointing toward the sky. "Look what God painted for us." They looked up at the magnificent rainbow above the mesa. It reminded Sean of Jack and Ryan's hot air balloon which also triggered thoughts about his 'trip' to France and shape-shifting. He wanted to know more, especially about the birds. He would ask his father about it. Would he become an eagle one day?

CHAPTER 3

Sean quickly fell asleep after the fun filled day. His dreams started immediately. He saw himself morph into a giant eagle and he traveled once again, as he had in his previous dream, to France. He spied Joseph Montgolfier in his atelier where he was building something.

Sean stood next to the Frenchman. *"Bonjour, Monsieur Joseph."*

"Ah, bonjour Jean, how are you today?"

Sean had given up trying to correct his name. "I am fine, and you?"

"Très bien, mon petit."

"What are you doing, Monsieur?"

"I am building a box. I'm making it out of very thin wood," Montgolfier said, "and then I am going to cover the sides and top with some taffeta."

Sean watched with great enthusiasm. "What's taffeta?" The boy asked.

"It is a very light material. I need this box to be light. I am going to make it fly."

"The box will fly?" Sean asked excitedly.

"That's the idea."

"How is it going to fly, Monsieur?"

"I'll show you. Are you ready?"

Sean nodded his head vigorously. "Oh, yes."

"Would you help me?"

"Of course!"

"Good." Montgolfier handed Sean a net that covered more taffeta, which in turn was glued to paper. The entire shape was oval. "Now hold this up, and be very gentle."

Sean was careful and followed Joseph's directions. "Like this?"

"Parfait! You're doing a wonderful job." Very gently Joseph inserted the box at the bottom of the net. "Ready, *mon petit ami?"*

"Oui, Monsieur!"

"Keep it straight."

Sean did. His arms were stretched up, holding the creation that extended from the floor to his hands. "Is this right?"

"Yes. Now, are you ready?"

"Oh, yes!" Sean answered, every nerve in his body heightened with anticipation.

Joseph crumpled some paper and put it in a metal plate which he placed in the box. "Get ready to be amazed."

"Ready."

Montgolfier lit the paper. It immediately turned to fire. The heat warmed the air and then it happened. The contraption started to rise. "Jean, let it go!" Sean did. Both man and boy watched the first *Montgolfière* slowly lift up toward the ceiling. They screamed in delight and watched as the little aerostat climbed on its own. It stayed there until the paper burned out and the air cooled. As it did it gradually came down. When it reached the floor it gently folded itself on its side.

"It worked! It worked!" Sean hollered.

"Yes, yes, it did!" The two embraced, grabbed each other's arms and danced around the very first hot air balloon that had just taken flight.

"Now we are really going to have some fun!"

What did he have in mind? What could be more fun that what they had just done?

In the next scene of Sean's dream he watched Joseph with another man. They were outdoors and looking over the apparatus they had built. It was similar to the original little one, but this one was huge, fully inflated and ready to ascend. Joseph and the other man each held a rope attached to the contraption and held it down. The boy immediately stood next to them.

"Ah, bonjour Jean."

"Bonjour Monsieur Joseph."

"This is my brother Étienne."

"How do you do, Sir."

"I'm well, thank you, young man."

"Jean helped me build the very first little one," Joseph said to his brother.

"Good work, *mon petit.*"

"Thank you, Monsieur Étienne."

"Jean, you are just in time to witness history. Are you ready?"

"Oh, yes, Monsieur."

"Joseph, ready?"

"*Oui.*"

The brothers let go of the ropes and the three of them watched as the contraption floated up.

"It works! It flies!" Sean screamed.

They started running after it. The hot air balloon soared for about a mile before it came down and crashed.

"Oh, no," Sean said, "it broke."

"That's alright, Jean. This was just the first test."

The brothers constructed another globe-shaped balloon of burlap with thin layers of paper on the inside. There were four pieces, the top and three sides held together by 1,800 buttons. They covered the outside of the envelope with a fish net of cord. Their invention weighed 500 pounds.

They tried it out, and as Joseph and Sean's original smaller one had, worked just as well. Sean clapped and jumped up and down, delighted that the larger one was successful.

Their next step was an even bigger contraption. The envelope was made of sky blue taffeta decorated with suns and signs of the zodiac.

"This one is going to go up pretty high," Joseph said.

"Yes, it's going to be fine, but what will the altitude do to humans?" Étienne asked.

"I don't know. How will we find out?"

"The King proposed to send up two criminals, but that doesn't seem right to me, not as far as history or even as human beings, no matter what these men have done."

"Nothing will happen," Sean said.

The brothers whirled around and looked at the boy. "How do you know?" They asked at the same time.

What was Sean going to tell them? That he was from the future? "I just know." The brothers laughed. "I'll prove it to you. *I'll* go up."

"That's very courageous of you, young man, but we wouldn't want anything to happen to you."

"Nothing will happen," Sean said with confidence, already thinking that he would be the first person to ever ride in a hot air balloon.

"*Non, mon petit*," Jean said. "We are going to send up a duck, a rooster and a sheep.

"Why?" The boy asked.

"Well, if there is a problem the duck can fly. The rooster, on the other hand can't, but hopefully will be fine. He is, after all, the symbol of France."

"And the sheep?" Sean asked.

"It's the closest thing to a human being."

Sean stared at the brothers and tried once again to convince them to let him go up, but they wouldn't budge.

"I'll tell you what, Jean," Joseph said, seeing how disappointed the boy was, "you can name the sheep." He would have to be satisfied with that.

"*Monte Au Ciel*, climbs to the sky," Sean volunteered.

"That is wonderful!" Étienne exclaimed.

"Montauciel it is," Joseph concurred, making a name out of it.

In September of 1783 the flight with the animals was held at the château of Versailles, in front of the French king and queen, Louis XVI and Marie Antoinette, as well as a crowd of curious onlookers. Among the audience many were politicians, French as well as diplomats from other countries. The king thought it would be a great coup for France if the brothers pulled this off. All were fascinated at this new invention. Would it fly? They wondered. The blue and gold hot air balloon was tethered to the grounds in front of the palace and the crowd. They watched as the Montgolfier brothers prepared their *globe aerostatique* for its maiden voyage. The animals in the round gondola were 'ready'. Montauciel's front legs were on the edge of the basket and he looked at the mass of people, wondering why these humans had put him this contraption when he could be eating some tasty grass. The rooster, the symbol of France, was sitting on top of the wooly shoulders and was *cocorico*-ing, the French version of cock-a-doodle-doo-ing. He seemed happy enough. The duck just sat on the floor, bored out of its mind. Why was he riding when he could just fly?

A canon boomed. It was time. The brothers looked at each other, their eyes conveying hope and success. They couldn't let the king down either. Would he punish them if their invention didn't work? Would the people see the monarch as a fool? The brothers thought positively—it was all they could do, and pray. They released the rope holding the hot air balloon. It lifted off gently as if it had done this a thousand times. The Montgolfiers let out a sign of relief. The astounded audience cheered and clapped, mesmerized and duly impressed by this invention. They wondered if they might have the courage one day to stand in such a basket and float in the air. The king was pleased. The flight lasted approximately ten minutes and flew about two miles at 1,500 feet. The balloon landed in a field of grass and wild flowers. It was a gentle landing which the animals surely appreciated.

A month later, Étienne Montgolfier was the first human to ascend in the *Montgolfière*, the name awarded to hot air balloons. The brothers also had a bottle of champagne on board, for a couple of reasons: When the military decided to explore hot air balloons as a weapon they decided to have champagne on board, in case they needed a peace offering as it was one of France's best products. The second reason was purely pleasure from the bubbly substance, for a delightful ending to a successful flight. To this day it is customary to pop open a bottle of champagne after a voyage. Étienne's flight was successful and the Montgolfier brothers celebrated their achievement. After clapping, cheering and jumping up and down they indulged in the champagne. No decent celebration was complete without the lovely bubbly liquid. They not only drank it they sprayed each other with it, and even poured it over their heads. They splashed around in it and danced and jumped up and down. It was a glorious day! They had made man fly!

Half a year later, in June of 1784, Madame Élisabeth Thible, a French opera singer, was the first woman aloft. She was accompanied by Monsieur Fleurant. They were in *La Gustave*, so named for the Swedish King, Gustav III, in honor of his visit to France. Thible was dressed as Minerva, the Roman goddess, as she was to sing a duet with Fleurant from Monsigny's *La Belle Arsène*, a popular opera of the time.

During their flight Madame Thible nourished the fire box in between arias. Fleurant stated that in addition to her lovely voice, it was thanks to her amazing courage that their flight was so successful.

CHAPTER 4

Only a few weeks had gone by since the *Rainboyws* had landed in the Sandovals' back yard. And now the day had come. It was time to go to the Balloon Fiesta. Sean could hardly contain himself. He ran to his father's pickup and waited for Tibah to *finally* come out.

"Ready, little man?"

"Oh, yes, Daddy, very ready!"

Tibah wasn't at all surprised that the boy hadn't complained about waking up so early, even though it was barely three o'clock in the morning. They drove off the Reservation and headed the few miles to the park where Jack and Ryan, and their hot air balloon, were waiting for them.

Once at the park they left the vehicle and headed for the field. Sean was duly mesmerized. Several balloons were lined up and ready to take off in the dark. He watched as they were being filled with fire from their burners giving them glows and making them into magnificent Chinese lanterns. Sean held his father's hand as he walked toward them, his only focus the multi-colored giant light bulbs illuminating parts of the ebony sky. They drew him toward them like magnets. As the pilots fired their burners the flames roared and the glows became stronger in the dark. Slowly and silently the globes rose toward the star-filled black canvas. It was an image Sean would never forget. As the balloons took off Sean held his breath. The boy was entranced and thrilled that he could walk among the majesty surrounding him.

Tibah gently pulled his son's hand and guided him toward the multitude of balloons preparing for the mass ascension. The colossal fabric swells lay flat on their sides on top of the cool grass. As they walked past them Sean could only wonder how beautiful their colors would be once they were inflated and in the sky.

"Hey Sean! Good morning to you," Jack and Ryan said at the same time.

Sean followed the voices. It came from the brothers that had descended on their land not too long ago. They were preparing the *Rainboyws*. "Good morning!" He called back, excited to see them.

"Are you ready for your first ride?" Jack asked.

"Oh, yes, Sir."

"That's great. Now come over here and let me show you what we need to do." He looked at Tibah who nodded. It was fine with him.

Sean ran over to Jack who started explaining. "The basket can hold up to eight people, and the balloon is a '150'. That means that the envelope capacity is 150,000 cubic feet."

"That sounds big," the boy said, trying to understand what that exactly meant.

"That means you can fit 150,000 basket balls in it." Jack said, clearing it up for Sean. The man laughed when the youngster's jaw dropped. "So, the first thing we need to do is to make sure everything is the way it should be."

Sean looked at the carefully spread out envelope with the cables attached to the basket. John and Adam said a quick hello to the Sandovals and continued their work. They attached the burners and the instruments to the top of the gondola. Jack and Ryan meticulously followed their progress, made sure everything was connected. Although their team had been with them for a long time they still double-checked everything themselves.

"How do you get the air in?" Sean asked.

"Ah, that's our next step, and we do that with an inflator fan." Jack turned to his crew. "Ready?" He hollered. They nodded back and positioned the case that housed the airplane propeller in the mouth of the envelope and started inflating.

"But it's not hot air," Sean remarked.

"That's right. Once the air from the fan is in then we heat it up with the burners."

"And that's what makes it go up. It's the hot air," Sean said, remembering his 'trip' to France and watching the laundry float up as he and Joseph sat together.

"Hey, very good! Where did you learn that?"

The boy shrugged his shoulders as in 'I just know'. He surely wasn't going to tell them about Monsieur Joseph, or even the toaster.

As the air filled the globe Sean watched as one of the crew held a rope attached to the top of the balloon.

"Why is he doing that?" Sean asked Jack.

"He's holding the crown rope. It prevents the envelope from rolling from side to side and keeps it straight with the gondola."

Ryan went up to the boy. "Hey, Sean, come with me," he said.

"Okay."

Ryan started walking into the now almost completely inflated envelope. "In we go."

"In there?"

"Uh huh."

The boy followed him into the heart of the balloon. "Wow, this is big!" He exclaimed standing in the middle of the immense globe surrounding them.

Ryan chuckled at Sean's incredulity, and he knew the child was definitely not afraid and loving every moment. As he watched the man understood that the boy was falling in love, just as he had, and knew this would not be Sean's only flight. He would mirror the twins' passion, of that he was certain.

When they came back out Sean caressed the wicker gondola. It reminded him of a really big basket similar to what his father put produce in. Over the edges soft suede covered the padding between the uprights. Inside, the row of instruments and two fuel cylinders adorned the side of the carrier.

Jack stepped into the creel and fired the burners. As Sean watched he smiled as the fire making machine reminded him of a face. He could see the mouth, the eyes, and the flames that went through the coils were the hair. As the air heated up the envelope started to rise and shifted the gondola into an upright position.

"Okay, Sean, we're upright," Jack said, "in you go." The boy obeyed and put his feet in the stepping holes of the wicker. He climbed over the padded side and stood up. Only his head was visible. Ryan and Tibah followed. John and Adam held the aerostat by the handles on the sides of the gondola.

"Ready to fly, Sean?" Ryan asked.

"Ready!" The boy's little heart was beating faster than it ever had.

Ryan nodded to the chase crew and they let go of the basket. They gently lifted off the field with a practiced ease and expertise. The crowd, who had been watching around them, clapped and shouted. The boy waved to the people, but the only thing he could hear were the squeals of joy inside his chest.

If Tibah could hear his son's happiness he would tell Sean he didn't have blood in his veins, rather hot air ran through them.

"What do you think, son?" Tibah asked.

Had his father been reading his thoughts? "Nizhóní."

"You're right, Sean, it is beautiful."

Sean looked around. The sky had lightened up and was now a soft, inviting baby blue, filling up with the multitude of iridescent hot air balloons that bobbed up and down. They reminded Sean of exquisite holiday tree ornaments, and he was one of them.

Jack continued his explanations: "Once the air cools, the balloon will lose its lift and will start to descend." Yeah, Sean knew that too. "The reason we have so many balloons and pilots that come from around the world is because of the wind pattern that exists in Albuquerque. It's perfect for flying hot air balloons."

"What do these do?" Sean said pointing at the instruments.

"This is the altimeter, it measures the height that we are at. We have a rate of climb indicator, called a variometer, which tells us the speed of the climb or descent," Jack answered.

"Also important to watch is the envelope temperature, we wouldn't want it to get overheated."

"And this instrument is for fuel quantity and its pressure. And of course a radio," Jack continued.

"For music?"

"No, not for music, to communicate with air traffic control and other balloons. And of course in case of emergencies. But you know, Sean, we do make a kind of music with the burners."

Sean nodded. He thought that was brilliant. He listened to the burners as it came on and off, spouting flames. Jack was right. It had its own rhythm, its own cadence. The boy looked down and marveled at how high they had climbed in such a short time. He also now knew how birds must feel, how they saw the beauty of the earth from above—the trees, the rivers, the land, the people and the houses. He wanted to stay in the balloon forever.

Ryan clicked the button on the side of the radio. "Good morning, this is hot air balloon 18045, the *Rainboyws*. We'll be on 118.8. *Rainboyws* out."

"It seems we're being steered toward where you live. It's unusual, but it does happen every once in a while." Ryan said.

"I don't think Sean minds," Tibah said. "As I mentioned before, if you want to practice from our land I will make sure that you are allowed to."

Sean was thrilled. His Dad was the best! And oh, he hoped the winds would always steer them to him. Sean watched how Jack handled the burners. The liquid propane entered the silver coils which heated it up and turned it into a gas. It produced the fire needed. The boy understood it was the way Jack governed the balloon, especially the altitude.

"So how much control do you have, Jack?" Tibah asked.

"We are at the pleasure of the winds. They blow in different directions at different altitudes. Albuquerque has perfect winds for hot air balloons. It's called the Albuquerque Box. You ascend to a certain height and the wind changes direction, and you go with it. It's possible to make a perfect box and land close to where you originally took off from. Of course it's never a sure thing, and the winds will carry you off to wherever they please. It's kind of fun not knowing where you're going. And as you know that's how we came to meet you."

"I understand, and you are always welcome to repeat it any time you wish," Tibah said.

"Thanks, Tibah," Ryan said.

"Do you know who the very first passengers on the first ever hot air balloon flight were?" Jack asked Sean.

"The sheep Montauciel, a rooster and a duck," Sean answered.

"Hey, very good, where did you learn that?" Jack asked.

Sean raised his shoulders as he had before.

Ryan mouthed 'TV' to Tibah over Sean's head. He responded by lifting his shoulders like his boy had. He didn't know either.

"Why do balloons fly so early in the morning?" Sean asked.

"Good question, little man," Ryan said, "they fly better when it's cold, less heat to expend."

They flew for a little over an hour, admiring the beauty around them—the clear blue, the mesa, the mountains and the hundreds of hot air balloons making the sky their personal canvas. Sean didn't want this ride to *ever* end.

Jack announced they would be landing fairly soon.

"Sean, look up," Jack said. "Remember the valve, do you see it?"

"It really does look like a parachute."

"That's right. It lets the heat out. Now, when we land we

might tip over to one of the sides. If it's a little rough the wicker from the gondola will absorb most of the impact so it won't be too bad, but make sure to keep your hands and everything else inside. Okay?"

"Okay, the boy answered."

"You're not scared, are you?" Ryan asked.

"No." *Was he kidding? That would be so much fun.*

They came in gradually for the landing and didn't tip over, although Sean would probably have loved it. The chase crew, who had been following in the van and communicating with the brothers on the radio, was right at the spot where they landed and held down the basket. They were close to the banks of the Rio Grande. The pilots and passengers got out of the basket and started dismantling and packing up the flying contraption. They looked as if they had been doing it as a team for years.

"Now this is what I call a first class chase crew!" Jack said with pride.

"I'm with you, brother. Maybe we should do this again. What do you say, little man?"

As Sean vigorously nodded his head he was sure it was the best day of his young life.

CHAPTER 5

Sean enjoyed school, especially the library. His favorite subject was anything that had to do with air, hot air balloons and flying. By the end of the year he had checked out and read everything and anything pertaining to his favorite subject. He begged his parents to take him the public library in the city. Again he checked out everything he could and kept this up for a couple of years. His birthday and Christmas gifts consisted of anything pertaining to more of his favorite obsession.

Sean, who was now twelve years old, voraciously read everything he could find on hot air balloons. He loved the Montgolfier brothers, they were his idols. He always remembered his boyhood dreams where he would visit the Frenchmen in their native land. How had those visions been so vivid? Why did he feel that he had actually been there? Had he shape-shifted?

Ever since the first landing of the *Rainboyws* and the first balloon ride, Jack, Ryan and the Sandovals had become good friends. With Tibah's blessing the twins could come out as often as they wanted to practice. Sean was of course ecstatic. Jack and Ryan immediately understood the boy's passion for flying and they invited him the first few times they took off from the Sandovals. And then Sean was a regular. He went up with them on every flight. They knew that one day he would be a great pilot and they were thrilled and honored to be his mentors. At every occasion they taught him details about every aspect of hot air balloons and flying them. Sean loved every moment.

The conditions that morning were perfect for a flight and as the *Rainboyws'* crew drove up Sean was immediately out the door and running toward them.

"Hey Sean," Jack and Ryan hollered.

"Hi Uncle Jack, hi Uncle Ryan."

"Are you ready to go to work?" Jack asked.

"Ready!"

The five of them, which included John and Adam, started taking the equipment out of the trailer. They laid out the envelope, the uprights and the gondola. They then proceeded to fill the *Rainboyws* with the inflation fan. They were ready to ascend.

"Okay, let's get up in the air," Jack said. "Ready to fly, Sean?"

"Absolutely, let's do it!" He said, as excited as ever.

"Sean?"

"Yes, Uncle Jack?"

"Take her up, you're the pilot today."

Sean just stared, dearly wanting what Jack had just told him to be true as a thousand butterflies danced in his stomach. "Really?" He whispered.

"Really, young man, you are more than ready. Now go for it!"

"Yes!" Sean hollered as he pumped a fist in the air. He fired the burners and slowly maneuvered the basket off the ground. The chase crew let go of the handles and jumped into the van and took off.

Jack and Ryan could not be prouder of their protégé and they hollered right along with Sean as he piloted his first ascension.

Jack, Ryan and Sean climbed effortlessly into the sky, the only sound an intermittent burst of the burners.

"The boy's a natural," Ryan said.

"Yes, we always knew that."

"Does that mean I'm doing alright?" Sean asked.

"Yes, Sean, more than alright," Jack answered.

"Thanks, guys."

"You're welcome."

"I love you guys."

"We love you too, as if you were our real nephew," Jack said.

Jack, Ryan and Sean continued flying together from the Sandovals' 'field'. A couple of years later, on his fourteenth birthday, Sean took the tests and received his coveted FAA hot air balloon pilot's license. Jack and Ryan had of course accompanied him, and were as proud as parents.

"Sean passed with no problems whatsoever," Jack said to Tibah and Fiona when they brought him back home.

"With flying colors—all puns intended," Ryan continued.

Sean looked at the two men and shook his head. His 'uncles' were a little strange, but oh, how he loved them.

CHAPTER 6

At eighteen Sean and his two childhood friends, Charlie and Joe, were riding the yellow school bus. They had been a trio ever since they could remember. They were leaving the Navajo Reservation, just on the outskirts of Albuquerque, and were on their way to a Friday night basketball game. It would be their last, as this was the year they would be graduating high school.

"Hey, Sean, I've been meaning to ask you, what kind of name is Fiona?" Joe asked. He was the stockiest of the three, a great devotee of his mother's delicious fry bread.

"Yeah, that is kinda weird," Charlie said.

"It's no weirder than any of the Navajo names," Sean retorted.

"Does it mean anything, like our names?" Joe asked.

"It does," Sean said, but didn't divulge anything more.

"Well?" The two buddies asked at the same time.

Sean paused for a moment before speaking. He knew he was different. He was half Navajo, half Irish, a combination he was proud of. It also made him a good-looking young man. "It means white and beautiful." Sean stared at the boys. They were his friends, but they had better not a say a bad thing about his Mam.

"That makes sense. She is white, and I guess she's pretty too," Charlie said. The woman was beautiful, even though she was old (anyone older than nineteen was old), and they all knew that, but he wasn't going to say that to his friend. It would be embarrassing, and he especially didn't want Sean getting mad.

"Of course she's pretty, dumbass," Joe said.

Sean smiled. "She's beautiful."

The boys didn't say anything, not wanting to offend their friend, although they had marveled at her beauty too.

"She talks kinda funny," Charlie said.

"That's because she's not like us, stupid. She's from Ireland. That's how they speak over there."

"And that's what I like best about her," Sean said with defiance. "I like the way she talks, I like that she's from a different place and loves to cook different foods from around the world. She even makes really good Navajo food," Sean said thinking about the bigberry manzanita cakes and the blue dick flour she used in it. She's different from other moms, and my Dad says I have the best of both worlds," he said with finality. His voice had grown louder with each phrase. His look dared the other boys to say anything negative about his mother. And they knew better than to anger him. Although Sean was a little different than they were, he still had proud Navajo blood. They also knew of his temper and remembered when he had gone after some boys who were bullying girls. When one of the boys roughly pulled on their pigtails to the point where the girls screamed in pain, Sean ran up to them fists swinging and bloodied a couple of noses. No, they knew Sean's temper as well as his athletic prowess, and did not want to mess with him in any way. But they also knew that he was a true and loyal friend and would always have their backs, as long as they hadn't done anything mean or hurtful. He constantly took the side of the underdog, whether it was human or animal, especially if they had been hurt.

"We like all that about her too, Sean, really we do! She's a really cool lady." Joe said, trying to keep Sean calm.

"And she's really cool as a Mom too," the other boy hurriedly added.

Sean's kind heart came from his mother and he inherited his athleticism from his father. His good looks were a combination of western European and Native American, although his features mimicked his mother's more than his father's—green Irish eyes slightly almond shaped, a nose that was slightly upturned, and full sensuous lips. His strong jaw and tough body were inherited from Tibah. He also had a perfectly and permanently lightly tanned skin, and a blend of his parents' black and red hair that had come out as a rich shiny auburn.

The last basketball game of the season ended and their team was victorious. A celebration was, of course, in order. Sean, Charlie and Joe, as well as many from their school wound up at one of the houses where they participated in an evening filled with food, laughter, dancing and too much drinking. Alcohol was easily accessible. Someone always had an older sibling that would help them out. They wanted to be 'cool' so they drank as much as their big sisters and brothers. They also indulged in loud music and smoking weed and cigarettes, until someone accidently knocked over a candle. Unfortunately it was too close to a curtain which immediately caught on fire and quickly spread over to the furniture. Some tried to put it out, but instantly realized that the flames were faster than they were. Although the home didn't have too much in it, just the bare necessities, it was enough to feed the frenzy of the fire that was swiftly engulfing the house. They ran out coughing and screaming, heading for clean air and safety. Once outside of the now smoking adobe they lay on the ground protected from the danger. They watched in horror as the fire meticulously destroyed the house.

Sean looked at Charlie who was sitting next to him. "You alright, man?"

"Yeah, I'm good," he said, coughing.

"Where's Joe?"

The boys looked around and then went pale when they realized their friend hadn't come out.

"Oh, my God, here's still in there," Charlie whimpered.

Sean jumped up. "I've got to get him!"

"No, Sean, no, it's too late!" Charlie screamed after him,

but Sean was already heading into the house.

Joe had lost control of his senses from over-drinking, and even though he understood there was a fire and needed to get out, his limbs were not responding to the weak suggestions from his brain. He tried vehemently, but his legs gave out from under him. When they did Joe landed on his head and blacked out.

Sean ran into the burning house. "JOE! JOE! Where are you?" He screamed. There was no answer back. "JOE!" Sean hollered over the roar of the fire. The flames were licking the walls and crawling up to the ceiling. Sean started coughing, barely able to see anything from the thick smoke. Sean was still screaming and trying to locate his friend when he stumbled into him and fell. "Joe! Joe! Are you alright?" He shook him, trying to wake him up, but wasn't getting any response. "Joe! Wake up, damn it!" He tried again. Sean knew they had to get out, and *right now!* His eyes were watering and he was coughing, the smoke creeping into every orifice of his body. The flames were consuming what once had been a home. Soon it would only be ashes. "Come on, Joe!" He tried to lift him, but the teen was a hefty 250 pounds and complete dead weight. Sean started pulling him, but it was no use, he wasn't getting any farther than a few inches and they were seriously running out of time. He coughed some more and the tears mixed with the smoke smeared his face. He tried again, pulled Joe up by his belt, got him into a standing position and crouched under him letting the heavy body fall on his shoulders in a fireman's hold. Sean thought his own frame was groaning from the stress and thought for sure he would have a few hernias when they finally got out. No matter, Sean was not leaving Joe behind—they either both came out, or they both would perish together. *I'm too young to die, and so is Joe. We're getting out of here!* Sean insisted to himself.

"Come on, Joe, we can do this!" He hollered reassuringly. Was he saying it to Joe or to himself?

Sean hobbled toward the exit with his load as fast as he could. The fire was all around them and the smoke was so thick Sean couldn't see anything in front of him. He was going by memory of where the door was, trying to find it so they could finally get out. Thankfully Sean remembered well because as soon as they passed the threshold the roof collapsed right behind them. It caused the house to buckle and Sean stumbled forward and fell, Joe right along with him. A collective cheer came from the crowd when they saw the boys. Charlie and some of the others ran up to them and helped carry Joe and Sean away from the house and the lethal flames.

"Are you okay?" Charlie asked as he watched Sean sitting on the ground with his head between his knees, trying to cough the smoke out of his lungs. Sean nodded.

"Is he alright?" Charlie asked, as he realized Joe wasn't moving.

"I don't know. I found him passed out on the floor," Sean answered. "Hey, Joe, can you hear me?" He asked the body lying on the ground. "Joe! Answer me!" Sean moved closer to his friend and knelt down on his knees next to him. He put his ear near Joe's nose and mouth. Nothing was coming out. "Oh, my God, he's not breathing. Get an ambulance!" he screamed.

"Somebody call an ambulance!" Charlie yelled at anyone who might have a cell phone.

Sean took his shirt off and quickly put it under Joe's neck. He then proceeded to give him mouth to mouth and started CPR. It had been a class in his school and Sean was now glad he had taken it, but Joe wasn't responding. Sean continued. "Come on, Joe!" He said in between breaths. "Come on, brother!" Suddenly Joe started coughing and tried to get some more air in his system.

A collective 'YES!' went up from the crowd and from Sean as well.

Joe opened his eyes and looked around him. He quickly understood what was happening. "Nílchi Deesdoi," Joe whispered as best he could using Sean's Navajo name, "you saved my life, man."

"Hey, what are friends for?" Sean said and smiled, overjoyed that Joe was still with them. He flopped onto his back, exhausted from his efforts and the lack of clean air in his lungs. He also realized that he loved what he had just done—pushed his body and his brain to save a life.

"I owe you, man."

"I'm just glad you're still with us. That's plenty."

Sean knew what Joe meant, but he just brushed it off. Joe, however, would never forget what his friend had just done for him.

CHAPTER 7

After the fire Sean was dropped off at his house. He opened the door, entered and tried to be very quiet, but his mother was up and waiting for him. She was sitting on the sofa.

"Hello, Sean," she said dryly.

"Hi, Mam." Did she know? Why was she up so late? Of course she knew.

"Are you alright?"

She wasn't going to kill him! "I'm fine."

"Good. That was a very brave thing you did."

Sean lifted his shoulders. "It had to be done."

"I'm glad Joe's alive and I'm very proud of you. However, I hope this sort of thing won't repeat itself."

Sean didn't know what to say. He thought it best just to let his mother do the talking.

"Wash up and come back. I need to talk to you."

"Yes, Mam." Sean took a quick shower and changed. He went back to his mother, although what he really wanted to do was take some pills for his headache and go to sleep.

Fiona was waiting for him. "Here take these, Sean." She handed his some aspirin and a glass of water. Ever since he was a little boy Sean always marveled at how smart his mother always was.

"Thanks, Mam," Sean said, drinking down the pills.

"I'm going to tell you one thing, Sean. If I ever see or hear about you drinking again I will pound you into the dirt until you are invisible!" Fiona exploded.

Sean had never seen his mother this angry, and truth be told he was scared. He knew she had a temper, a 'good Irish one', his father used to kid her when she didn't get her way, but nothing like what he was witnessing now.

"Come here!" she commanded.

"Yes, Mam," Sean whispered. He went to his mother, albeit reluctantly.

"Sit down next to me, Sean," she said patting the cushion next to her. Sean did as she asked. "Listen *a stor*," she said calmly, "I'm sorry I yelled at you, but you have to know that drinking is the absolutely worse thing you can do to me."

"How do you mean?" The teen inquired curiously, not understanding.

"I think now is the right time to tell you a few things about my side of the family." She started with a heavy heart: "I saw what the drink can do..."

Fiona could see her youth through the glazed eyes that were staring off in the distance, as if she were trying to better focus her mind. She slowly started relating the story of her young life to Sean as best she could, while fiercely holding back tears of pain and sorrow.

CHAPTER 8

Fiona's father, Padraig, was the most charming individual that walked the earth. He was a gentle, soft spoken man who loved people and animals. He was tall and good looking with dark hair and green eyes. His handsome Irish features and jovial personality made him even more amiable. Everyone in the county loved the man. But when financial problems stalked his happy home he couldn't get out of the predicament, so he turned to the only thing that didn't want anything from him—alcohol. The liquor was his friend. It never demanded payments, never talked back, turned his lips into a smile and made him happy—until the proverbial one too many. And then Padraig became a monster, a drunk, foul-tempered alcoholic who would become a violent wife and child beater, oblivious and totally out of control to what he was doing to the family he actually adored.

Fiona remembered her father bursting into their secluded little home on the outskirts of Ardara, on the Donegal shore, after an evening of drinking. She would wonder how he made it to the house through foul weather, rain and bitter cold. Apparently the alcohol must have insulated him from the elements. Somehow he would always manage and, God forgive her, Fiona wished when he was in this state he wouldn't find his way home. As he barged into the house he screamed for her mother at the top of his lungs. Fiona, who was sixteen at the time, was hiding behind a curtain.

"Molly! Where the devil are you?" Padraig screamed. He saw the shadow of a body in a corner, turned and faced his young daughter. "Why are you hiding behind the drapes?"

"It's me, Da," Fiona whispered. She was petrified. Her legs had turned to jelly. She couldn't move.

Padraig looked at the girl, but she could tell the image wasn't registering. "You know, Molly, you always were the prettiest one in the county. Come here now, lass, make your man happy," he said, reaching for her.

Fiona rushed under his outstretched arm and ran to the kitchen, grateful that her legs were responding.

"MAM! MAM!" She yelled. Where was her mother?

Molly seemed to manifest out of thin air behind Fiona. She pushed her daughter out of the way. "Go to your room and lock your door, no matter what you hear!" She commanded.

"Now aren't I the lucky man, there's two of you!" Padraig exclaimed, overjoyed.

"Padraig, that's Fiona."

"Fiona? Who's Fiona? Your twin?" He asked, slurring every word.

"For the love of God, she's your daughter," Molly said. Padraig's stare was blank. He had no idea what she was saying. The older woman turned to the girl. "Go to your room, now! Do as I say and lock yourself in," she repeated to Fiona.

"But Mam, I need to help you, to help Da," she retorted.

"There isn't anything much we can do. It's the same every time. I'll handle it. Now go!"

"Yes, Mam," Fiona answered. In the pit of her stomach she could feel a knot starting to form. That was always a bad sign. She did as she was told, ran to her room, bolted the door and hid under the blankets. The screaming started. She covered her ears and the tears ran down her cheeks. The young woman thought her heart would turn to stone. She couldn't quite make out the words from the commotion coming from the kitchen, but she could guess. This wasn't the first time. She knew her father was getting his way with her mother and surely turning her delicate white skin into ugly black and blue welts. As much as she wanted to help she didn't know how, and she fervently prayed that her mother would come out of her predicament not too badly hurt.

Fiona heard a horrific crash and then nothing, just complete silence. That wasn't good either. She waited a few minutes. Still nothing. Something wasn't right, and she had to find out. At least when there was noise she knew, or could imagine, what was going on. She slipped out of her bed and slowly ventured down the staircase. On the last step she could see the kitchen had been destroyed—plates were shattered, pots and pans had been used as weapons and the table and chairs were overturned. Fiona looked over by the stove and screamed. She covered her mouth and held the bile that was racing up to her throat—her parents lay in a pool of blood. Their bodies were side by side, not as the love birds they once had been, but grotesquely positioned on the floor next to the overturned table. Their limbs were askew and intertwined at the same time, and their blood flowed from the evident wounds from the gashes in their skulls. They had fallen head first together on the cast iron stove and sustained their fatal blows. Padraig probably had been holding Molly and she couldn't get out of his embrace. When they tripped and fell they connected with the stove. They both died instantly.

CHAPTER 9

Fiona was sent to live with her aunt and uncle, her mother's brother and his wife. She was miserable. She didn't like her uncle and remembered her mother mentioning that her brother was useless, and always up to no good. They had given her a small room which was always cold, and fed her just enough food to keep her from getting sick. They lived on a farm, and Fiona helped with the chores from the very early morning until late into the dark of night. They made her work very hard and long hours for the bit of food and the roof over her head. The girl was always kind and polite, but she didn't get any respect from either her aunt or uncle. The older woman was worn out, probably because of her incompetent husband and her boring, insignificant life. Fiona was not going to endure years on a farm doing all the work her uncle should be doing, and turning out old and beaten down like her aunt. But how could she get herself out of her predicament? How could she get away? And where would she go? She had no money, and didn't know anyone outside of her immediate circle. She had finished school and knew she wouldn't go any farther in any studies, not that she really wanted to. She didn't have a great longing for a specific subject or profession, but she definitely knew she had to do something better with her life. Fiona missed her parents, the lovely, loving couple they once were. She longed for the kindness in her mother's heart for her only child, and the cozy home she kept for her family. Her mother had been like a sister, young and still fresh, to the point that people joked about who the oldest was—until the troubles with her father started. Then she quickly faded, from the color of her skin to the glow in her heart. She seemed to age in months instead of years. People who hadn't seen her in a while wondered if she had a terrible illness. Fiona also remembered how Molly had taught her the art of the Donegal sweaters, perhaps the most beautiful in Ireland. She lovingly showed her all the intricate details of the knitting, the different designs and so many different stitches. She and Fiona would make sweaters together sitting by the fireplace. Padraig would watch them, amazed at their quick fingers and fiercely proud of his lovely girls. She missed the man who once was the best Da in the world, the one that would take his little girl riding and show her the beauty of their land. What a sad waste. And now would she waste away as well in this godforsaken house with these cold people? How was it they were even related?

That's it! Fiona exclaimed one night as she was under the harsh blankets—the sweaters! Oh, thanks, Mam. That same night Fiona heard her uncle coming back from the local pub. Her door was closed, but she feared he might come into her room. She quickly put on some clothes and one of the two sweaters she managed to knit in the rare moments she wasn't working. The other one she tied around her waist and listened from behind the door. The last item she tucked in her back pocket was a picture of her Mam and Da, their arms around each other's shoulders as Fiona, then a little girl, sat on a horse behind them.

The man stood right outside, and Fiona could actually smell the fetid odor of the alcohol coming from the other side of the door. The bile rose to her throat as it triggered the horrific memories of her father, and the last time she saw her parents. Her uncle opened the door and entered her room and went after her. Fiona ran past him and out of the house, without waiting to find out what he wanted. All she knew was that the intentions were immoral, and she certainly wasn't going to endure the same predicament as she had with her parents. She ran across the meadows, those green fields she had ridden across with her Da. The tears streamed down her young, frightened face, but as terrified at the unknown that lay ahead of her she didn't stop running until her lungs were screaming that they were unable to continue. Fiona finally stopped. Her legs trembled and her body heaved as it gasped for air. She looked around at the blackness of the sky and hills. As scared as she was she realized that for the first time she was in control of her own destiny, whatever that would be.

Fiona's aunt and uncle never saw her again. She left county Donegal and the only corner of the world she had ever known.

Fiona managed to get herself to Dublin by selling one of her sweaters for just enough money to get a bus ticket, and for a few meals. When the young woman arrived in the city she found a job washing dishes late at night in a restaurant. The cuisine was Mediterranean, and as she worked she also watched the chefs prepare the meals. During the day she would knit wool into beautiful sweaters. She lived with another young woman who worked as a secretary. They pooled their resources together and managed to live in a studio apartment. Sheila worked during the day and Fiona at night. It was a convenient arrangement, especially for the size of the flat. They hardly saw each other, except for a few minutes when one of them was leaving for work, and on weekends. Every once in a while they would splurge and take in a film at the local cinema, but the occasions were few and far between. They were just barely surviving. Fiona also brought food home from the restaurant, food they would have thrown away. She chose well, always picking out uneaten items like cheese and bread. Every once in a while there were soups, salads or meats that would go bad and would be thrown away. Fiona was allowed to take them, and she was grateful.

One night after Fiona arrived at the apartment she sat on the sofa, the one she used as a bed. It was late and she couldn't sleep. She stayed there for a couple of hours, just thinking. Her roommate on the other side of the room woke up to go to the bathroom. She saw Fiona, awake and crying.

"Oh, my God, Fiona, what's wrong?" She asked, worried.

"I have a problem."

"What kind of problem?"

"Terry."

"Has he been bothering you again?"

"Yes, and it's getting worse. I can't get him to leave me alone. Oh, Sheila, as soon as I left the restaurant he came after me."

"But doesn't he leave earlier? I thought all the waiters left before you did."

"They do, but he was waiting for me. Once I stepped outside he came up behind me and pushed me against the wall."

"Oh, my God. Did he hurt you?" Sheila asked, fearing the worst.

"He pinned my arms against the bricks and started kissing me," Fiona said shuddering. "I could smell his foul breath. He'd been drinking."

"Oh, Fiona."

"I swear I thought he was going to rape me, so I managed to kick him in the balls and he fell to his knees. I ran away as fast as I could."

"We have to go to the police."

"And tell them what? That he tried to rape me, or that I'm pretty sure he's *going* to rape me. Ah, they won't give me the time of day. And it would be my word against his. And anyway, how would they help? Post a policeman outside my door, or follow me around? Hardly."

"We could at least make a report. That should scare Terry off."

"That won't keep him away, besides, he'll make a fuss at the restaurant, find a way to get back at me and get me fired. I'll lose my job and I can't afford that."

"Alright then, I'll come pick you up every night, that way there will be two of us."

"Oh, Sheila, you're all heart, but I can't impose like that. And you have to work too." Fiona took her friend's hands in hers. "I've made up my mind. I'm leaving."

Sheila gasped. "The apartment? Dublin?"

"Both."

"Oh my God, where will you go?"

"Somewhere where they don't drink, where they don't become savage monsters and lose control of their faculties. Somewhere where they don't just see me as a piece to take and do anything they want with. I'm fed up, Sheila. I'm going where the land is big and I can lose myself in it. I'm leaving this island."

"But Ireland is your home."

"Yes and no."

"What does that mean?"

"That means that yes, I was born here. I have loved it and always will. I am loyal to it and will always be, but it is also bad for me. Wherever I turn people want to hurt me, even my own bloody family. It's time for me to go, to spread my wings toward a different horizon."

"But where will you go?" Sheila repeated. "It sounds to me that you're heading for a Muslim country with no booze."

"No, Sheila, there might not be much drinking in those countries, but I'll feel just as sequestered there. I don't want to be a third class citizen, I want to be free, and most of all safe."

"I understand, but I'll still miss you like crazy."

"Oh, so will I! The time we spent together has been very dear to me. You'll always be the sister I never had." The two woman embraced and their tears flowed down their cheeks.

"You too, dearest Fiona, I love you too. Promise you'll take care of yourself."

"I shall."

Sheila looked at her friend. "Have you thought of where you'll go?

"Like I said, somewhere big where I can get lost and feel safe."

"Like...?"

"Australia or America."

"But Fiona, they drink there too, and just as bad as they do here!"

"Yes, they do, but they have a bigger country, and for some reason I know I'll find a safe haven there. Somewhere out there in the wilderness I will find happiness."

"Oh, Fiona, you're such a romantic. It sounds like you're going to the most remote place in the outback, or the far west. Aren't there crocodiles and snakes? All sorts of wild animals?"

Fiona laughed. She would miss Sheila. "I'm sure there are, but animals attack you only if they sense they are in danger or to survive, not to get in your pants. It's the human animals I want to get away from."

"You have a point." Sheila didn't want to tell Fiona that she was so damn beautiful every man on the planet wanted to get into her pants, no matter what country and nationality. She could have been a model, she was absolutely exquisite. Her hair was a dark red and her creamy white complexion hardly had any freckles, and the few that she did have just made her more endearing. Her body was flawless, with curves in perfect proportion. Fiona had considered modeling, but as she discovered more about the business she hated it. Just more people wanting to take advantage of her—in every way. There was also a problem and that was her height. Fiona was petite and just barely over five feet. She would have been limited, but she could still have made a career out of it. "You'll let me know where you are, where you wind up?" Sheila asked.

"Of course."

"And you're planning to leave when?"

"Well, I wanted to give you enough time to get another roommate, and I still need some time to gather funds. I figure I'll need money for at least three months. I also have to get a passport and a visa."

"Wow, I can see you've been thinking about this for a while."

"Yes, Sheila, I have, and I feel good about it. I know it's the right decision. Somewhere in my soul I know this to be true."

"Alright, but we're still walking home together every night."

Fiona smiled and wished she could take Sheila with her, but she also knew her friend would never leave the emerald isle. "Agreed, and thank you."

"Now, go somewhere really exotic where I can visit you. That'll give me something to look forward to."

"I'll try my best."

"Good enough."

CHAPTER 10

Fiona worked tirelessly at the restaurant, and asked for even more hours of overtime. She also diligently knitted her sweaters for at least eight hours every day on her days off. Those were over eighty hour weeks, and her determination fueled the energy she needed to keep going. She immediately applied for a passport and a visa. Once she got those she went to a travel agency. The office was small and a little dark. The agents were assisting the people across their desks and Fiona waited for one of them to finish. She looked around and saw posters from different countries. The white-washed Greek isles, the Norwegian fjords, and the Polynesian cabanas in the water all looked beautiful, but the one that caught her eye was the one with the brownish-red mountains in a sun-filled exquisite blue sky. It said: 'Land of Enchantment'. Fiona stared at the poster, transfixed. That was it, that is where she was supposed to go. Her eyes fell in love with it, her gut pushed her, and her heart confirmed it. When the next agent was available Fiona went up to the desk and sat down in front of her.

"Hallo," the agent said. She was an older woman with an endearing smile who probably had been with the agency for decades. She had probably used her benefits and traveled to many places around the world. She seemed pleasant, and Fiona immediately liked her. If anyone could help her it probably would be this woman. "Please, have a seat. How can I help you today?" She asked.

Fiona smiled and pointed at the poster. "Where exactly is that?" She asked.

"Oh, lovely isn't it, that's New Mexico."

"*New* Mexico?" She had heard of Mexico, but not New Mexico.

"Yes, it's one of the fifty States, between Texas and Arizona."

"Have you ever been there?"

"No, I haven't, but it does look lovely."

"It does. Do you know anything about it?"

"Well, if I remember right it's the fourth largest state."

"Really." This was getting better and better Fiona thought. She had told Sheila that she wanted to go to a bigger country. "Is it very populated?"

"Oh, no, the population is pretty spread out among two cities. The largest are Albuquerque and Santa Fe, the capital. I hear they are beautiful and are known for their art colonies."

"How do you mean?"

"It's an artist's Mecca. Santa Fe boasts the most galleries after New York and Los Angeles."

"Very interesting. And the rest of the population?"

"Spread out in other smaller cities and throughout the state."

Fiona had said to Sheila that it was time for her to go, to spread her wings toward a different horizon. She smiled at the older woman—she had found the horizon that awaited her. "How can I get there?"

The day had come. After hugs, tears and goodbyes Fiona left her dearest friend and took the green double-decker bus to the international airport. Her luggage consisted of a small carry-on suitcase with wheels Sheila had given her as a goodbye present. She didn't take too many things with her, not that she had that many. Whatever she didn't want she either gave to Sheila or to some charity. She just had a few clothes and two sweaters she had knitted. She thought maybe they would come in handy. She wasn't sure why or how, but she almost always followed her instinct and it had so far steered her well. In any event if she got cold she would be able to cover herself up with them.

The only other item she brought with her was a travel book on the United States that the travel agent had suggested. Fiona had gone straight to the first bookstore and picked it up.

She arrived at the airport, got off the bus and looked at the sign on the building: *Aerfort Bhaile Átha Cliath,* Dublin Airport. Fiona had never flown before, or for that matter been to any airport. She looked at the immense building and didn't quite know what to do, just that this was the place where she would take a plane to the United States. She entered the building and saw an older man wearing a uniform. She decided to ask him for help.

"Excuse me, could you help me out please?"

"Certainly, young lady, what can I help you with?"

"I've never done this before, this is my first time flying and I'm not sure what to do," Fiona said honestly.

"Ah, I can help you with that. Where are you going?"

"Albuquerque."

"Where?"

"It's in the United States."

"Ah, so you're probably going to either New York or Boston."

"Oh, yes, I'm supposed to change planes in Boston."

"Do you have a ticket?"

"The travel agent gave me a printed piece of paper."

"That'll work, let's take a look." The older man took his glasses out of his pocket and put them on. He looked at the electronic ticket. "Okay, so you're on Aer Lingus to Boston. All you need to do is check in with your printout. Go to that counter and they'll help you from there." The man showed her where the counter was located.

"Thank you so much, you've been a great help."

"My pleasure, young lady, have a good trip and have fun."

"I'll try, thank you again."

Fiona went over to the counter and the agent checked her in for the flight and put a small note in the computer stating that the passenger was a first time flyer.

Once on the aircraft the flight attendants were extremely

attentive and explained a few details to Fiona. They put her at ease, and the novice flyer was grateful for the attention and the kindness of the crew. Although Fiona was not one to scare easily she was a bit apprehensive that she would spend six hours in a metal sausage over the Atlantic Ocean. She paid close attention to the instructions about the seat belts and the emergency procedures. Fiona was a quick learner. The plane left the gate and taxied onto the runway and stopped. Why had they stopped? And then the pilot revved the engines. She hadn't expected the noise and held her breath. The aircraft slowly rolled forward and gained speed. Fiona squeezed the armrests until her knuckles turned white and didn't let go the entire length of the runway. She looked out the window and saw the tarmac and the airport building rushing past her. She had never gone so fast in her life. And then they lifted off and her shoulders sank into the back of her chair. Her stomach also churned a little. When they smoothed out she finally took a breath and was ecstatic as she imagined that birds did this all the time. She became more at ease and realized she was headed toward a new life. She found that she actually enjoyed the plane ride. She had always wondered, and was envious, of what the birds were able to see and now she felt blessed that she could as well. As she looked out the window she was amazed at the beauty and the immensity of the island below her. She tried counting all the different greens the old man had told her about. Would she reach forty? With every mile she became more fascinated by the scenery, and was more and more anxious by what awaited her on the other side of the ocean. Fiona was at the moment too excited for regrets and concentrated on her new experience in the sky and the life that lay ahead. She envisioned it as an adventure, and forced herself to believe that she would be happy. At some point she reminisced about her parents, their unfortunate demise and the life she left behind. Although when she thought more about it she could only picture sadness, misery and painful survival. Her only regret was Sheila, she had been a good friend. Maybe if everything went well she could visit.

About an hour into the flight one of the crew brought Fiona her meal. She didn't know they served food on the flight. She had been thrilled when they offered her a drink, and it was *free,* and was amazed when the flight attendant placed it on the table that came out from the back of the seat in front of her. Now the kind lady was placing a tray with hot food on it. She was ecstatic when the smells tickled her nose and could hardly wait to try the meal. She was hungry and hadn't figured out where or when she would be eating. This was a really nice airline. Did all airlines do this? Fiona finished everything on the tray and thought the corned beef, potatoes and cabbage, along with the little piece of cake was excellent. Even the bread and fruit were delicious. Now she didn't know if she was supposed to get up and give the flight attendant her tray. She would ask as soon as one of the pretty girls walked by. Fiona didn't have long to wait as the efficient attendant took her tray.

"How was it?" The flight attendant asked.

"Oh, excellent, thank you very much. By the way, how high are we?"

"We leveled off at 30,000 feet."

"Ah, yes, thank you." She shouldn't have asked.

"Would you like a headset?"

"A headset?"

"It's for the film." What was she saying? How could they watch a film in here? "It's free of course," the flight attendant continued. "Unfortunately the one we were going to show broke, but thankfully we always have a classic for the North American route we can show, *McLintock!* I'll be right back with your headset."

"Oh, uh, yes, thank you very much," Fiona said, anxious to discover how this film thing worked. She was going to watch a movie, in plane, at 30,000 feet! She wasn't sure if she was in heaven, or if she was a queen.

True to her word the woman returned with a headset and showed Fiona how to use it, and how the film would be projected on the screen in front of her.

"I haven't heard of that film."

"Oh, it's an oldie, with John Wayne and our very own

Maureen O'Hara. Come to think of it you look a lot like her. Now, let me show you how to work the buttons on the armrest."

When Fiona was settled in she took in the movie. She had never seen it before and thoroughly enjoyed the big, handsome American, and of course the lovely Maureen. She laughed with the rest of the passengers when the actors slipped and fell in the mud, and had an amusing free-for-all. The young woman was not yet aware that her final destination was nicknamed Duke City after the Duke of Alburquerque in Spain, although many thought that it was name after John 'Duke' Wayne. Had Fiona known she would have sworn it was a sign, a positive one of course.

The crew on Fiona's flight prepared for their descent into Boston. Fiona listened attentively to their instructions and followed the procedures, although she was wondering and a bit apprehensive about how the metal sausage was going to land on a little strip of tar.

The green aircraft with the Aer Lingus shamrock logo on its tail descended from the southeast over Massachusetts Bay. The little boats looked no larger than big white dots in the water around the city. Fiona marveled at the large metropolis at the edge of the Atlantic, and was amazed at how many skyscrapers there were in the city of Boston. Dublin boasted a couple, but they didn't compare to how many she could see outside her window. They descended some more and were right over the water which, she thought was *really* close, so close that she was sure they would land in the bay. Oh, I'm going to get very wet! she feared, but suddenly the wheels were over the runway and they touched down. She finally exhaled when the pilot taxied toward the gate. She marveled that in only six hours she had traveled from Ireland to the United States of America.

Fiona thanked the crew profusely and followed the other passengers through customs and immigration with no problems as she had been cleared in Dublin. She found her way out of the terminal and stepped onto American soil for the first time. It was busy with people of all nationalities leaving the international airport. Fiona liked being one of the travelers, was even proud that she traveled from one continent to another on her own. The agent from the Dublin travel agency, Caitlin, set everything up for her, and also meticulously wrote every step of the trip out. Fiona followed the next step and found an airport shuttle that would take her to her motel near the airport. She sat down in the van and looked outside into her new world. Oh, Lord, they were driving on the wrong side of the road! She had known about this and found it a bit disconcerting, but she was sure that at some point she would get used to it. As she held the back of the seat in front of her Fiona believed, perhaps for the first time in her young life, that she was safe. When the shuttle arrived at its destination Fiona checked into the motel without difficulty, and when she saw her room thought this was the most pleasant place she had ever been. The people, starting at the airport in Dublin, the Aer Lingus crew and everyone up until this moment, had been kind and helpful. When she sat on the bed, something she hadn't slept on in a couple of years, immediately fell asleep.

Very early the next morning Fiona took the shuttle back to the airport and flew to her next destination. Her adventure continued. She took another flight for a few hours and once again enjoyed the view, crossing several states from New England to the magnificent Rockies in Colorado. She connected in Denver, on her way to her final destination. On her third and last flight she concluded that she had traveled and seen more of the world in two days than she might ever have, had she stayed in Ireland. She mentally recalled what she had seen, and as a bird would.

When Fiona landed in Albuquerque the sun was just setting, and she gasped as the Sandia Mountains next to the airport turned red. It was the live poster from the travel agency. Somehow the 'Land of Enchantment' had beckoned her from the other side of the world. She smiled, more than that her entire body glowed.

CHAPTER 11

Fiona had enough money to stay in a small motel for about a month. She rested in her room for a day, just relaxing and being lazy, and also understanding for the first time the meaning of jet lag. She would wake up in the middle of the night and lay awake for hours and then during the day she would sleep. She finally figured out that she had to either sleep extra hours or stay awake longer. She decided she had rested enough, and when she became sleepy during the day she would keep herself occupied. Fiona's little motel was close to Old Town in Albuquerque, so she decided to go and discover everything she could about the city. She would start with the oldest part. With a little help from the woman at the reception she found her way into the old section of town, which was in walking distance. She wanted to learn the history of the city and the state, wanted to know everything about it. She looked at the store windows on the plaza and was captivated by the southwestern memorabilia. She especially liked the cowboy hats. On a whim she decided to try one on. She walked into the store and put one on over her fiery red hair.

"May I help you?" The older sales lady asked.

"What do you think?" Fiona asked coquettishly. "How do I look?"

"Well, I think you look just lovely. And you're such a pretty girl, anything would look good on you."

"That's very kind of you."

"Oh, I just love your accent!"

"Really?" Fiona had never thought about her accent.

"Oh, yes, it's endearing. Where are you from?"

"Ireland."

"It must be beautiful there. I've never been, but I hear it's very green."

Fiona laughed. She liked this woman. "Yes, it is. That's because there are two seasons."

"Really?"

"Yes, the wet season and the rainy season."

The older woman thought that was the funniest thing she had ever heard. "Oh, you are too funny! And I love that sweater you're wearing. Irish?"

"Well, yes. I made it myself."

"I'm impressed. It's beautiful."

"Thank you."

"Are all the sweaters in Ireland as gorgeous?"

"Well, I think so. But the ones from where I'm from in Ardara, county Donegal, which is in the northwest, are of course the best."

"No doubt. So, are you here on vacation?"

Fiona and Gladys, who turned out to be the owner, talked for over an hour. By the time Fiona left the shop she had a job with the condition to produce at least two sweaters a week—the cold season was getting closer. Fiona was ecstatic. She was very fast and could definitely knit the two sweaters. And what Gladys offered her as a salary, in addition to the sweaters, was more than she ever made in Dublin. Her new boss also introduced her to a friend who rented her a small, furnished studio apartment very close to the store. Her monthly expenses were less than her share had been with Sheila in Dublin, and she would be in walking distance of work. Fiona was happier than she had been in a very long time, and was sure she had found her heaven on earth.

CHAPTER 12

Young Tibah Sandoval was driving his pickup back to the Reservation, which was located just a few miles from Albuquerque. The Navajos were pretty much in northeastern Arizona and northwest New Mexico, and there were a few Reservations scattered around the state. He turned onto I-25. He had just finished delivering his produce to the Yeibichai casino which was on Navajo land as well. He thought about his business. He was happy with it and made a good living. He looked at the road ahead. Something wasn't right. He was going south instead of north and he was almost downtown. He normally would have gotten angry with himself as he was pretty well organized in his ways and his work. But then he thought about it. There was a reason. There always was a reason, he didn't just 'go the wrong way'.

Tibah decided to let himself be 'guided'. He followed a sign to Old Town. He usually didn't frequent this part of the city, but he found himself there now. He parked and started walking. He still wasn't sure why, but he continued. He looked at the shop windows and then just went into one. *What was he doing in this store? Did he need something in it? Did he come to buy something?*

It was the store Fiona worked in. The Irish woman walked up to Tibah. "May I help you with something?" She asked.

Tibah looked at the pretty woman. *Why was he here? And where did this stunning creature come from?* He immediately knew she wasn't local. "Uh, yes, I'm looking for a sweater, it's getting colder at night." *What? Where did that come from?* He let it be, divining that the Spirits were doing the directing, and possibly playing with him. They had a sense of humor, and Tibah was very familiar with their ways.

"Well, you've come the right place. I think I have just what you want. Would you follow me?" Fiona said.

Hmm. She knows what I want and I should follow her. "Okay." Tibah followed her and noticed her lovely curves. She was petite and exquisite. And she had magnificent red hair!

"Come this way, I have a couple over here."

Tibah looked at the sweaters. They were really nice, so nice that he actually wanted one. These were the ones Fiona knitted for the shop. "This is perfect. Which one should I get?" He asked her.

"Do you prefer green or blue?"

"I think the green one." *It matches your eyes.*

"Good choice, I like that one best too."

Tibah's chest was expanding. Was his heart telling him something? "May I ask where you are from?"

Fiona looked at the man with the natural tan. He was tall with dark eyes, high cheekbones and a mane of jet-black hair pulled back in a sleek pony tail. His jaw was square and powerful, and his smile was warm and endearing.

"Are you Indian?"

"Navajo. And you're not American."

Fiona shook her head. "Irish."

"Now I understand."

"What is it you understand?"

"Where your beauty comes from."

Fiona's eyes darkened. Was he like all the other men?

Tibah saw the immediate shadow covering her eyes and knew he had hit a raw nerve. Had something terrible happened to this woman? "Please, I didn't mean anything, just that you are a very beautiful woman. I'm sorry, I only meant it as a compliment." His eyes were pleading. He didn't want to hurt this lovely creature. "I'm afraid I've gotten myself in trouble before, I tend to speak my mind a little too easily."

Fiona was intrigued. "How do you mean?"

Tibah inwardly let out a sigh of relief. She didn't leave, and didn't seem mad, so he still had a chance to try to make things right. "Well, good or bad, I believe in saying things like I see them. If you're being an ass I'll let you know about it, if a child is being nasty I'll tell him to settle down, if I see a horse I'll pet him and tell him he's beautiful..." Tibah bit his tongue. "Uh, that didn't come out the way I meant it to."

Fiona could only laugh. Tibah had found a way to tickle her Irish good humor. "Are you calling me a horse?" She asked.

"See what I mean? I get myself in trouble all the time."

"I see what you mean."

"Can I at least make it up to you over lunch?"

Fiona looked at him. She thought he was magnificent, a beautiful horse too. She smiled. "Would you show me the local cuisine? I don't know anything about it. I just moved here."

"Absolutely! I know everything about it. New Mexico has amazing food and is famous for its chile peppers. We'll start with Christmas."

"Christmas? It's not even close to that time of year."

"No, no," he chuckled, "that's a chile sauce, combination of red and green chiles."

Fiona was intrigued. The one good thing that came out of working at the Mediterranean restaurant in Dublin was that she acquired a love of cooking, and she wanted to discover cuisines from around the world. New Mexican food was definitely at the top of her list. She also thought there were many things she would enjoy learning from this man. She knew deep down that this person was genuine, that he cared intensely about many things, and she wanted to know what they were. It was also the first time that she didn't feel uneasy around a man, on the contrary.

This Irish woman was stunning, Tibah thought as he stared at her face. Her eyes were the color of emeralds and her naturally rose-colored lips begged to be kissed. Oh, he so wanted to oblige. And he especially wanted to run his fingers through that glorious red hair.

"Would you like to try it on?"

"What?"

"The sweater?"

"Oh, yes, please." No, not really. He just wanted to spend more time with her. He wanted to know everything about this woman. And if that meant trying on every item of clothing in the store he would.

Fiona helped him into the sweater. As his arm went down into the sleeve her hand brushed against his back. Oh, the muscles were as hard as rocks! "So what do you think?" She asked, trying to keep her mind occupied, and off of what she was sure was a stunning and sculpted body. Fiona realized that she had never been interested in any man before. Her past had shut out the natural enthusiasm and curiosity of a young woman wanting to discover her own sexuality, or the yearning of two bodies toward each other. But something about Tibah seemed to be awakening the emotions that had been buried for so long.

"So what do you think?" Tibah asked, holding his arms out.

Fiona 'straightened out' a wrinkle or two on his arms as she brushed her hands down the sleeves. "I think it was made just for you. It fits perfectly, and you look very handsome." Fiona bit her lip. Was that too forward? What had gotten into her?

"Like a beautiful horse?"

Fiona roared with laughter. The tension was broken, and although they wouldn't admit it *yet* they were very much attracted to each other.

Tibah purchased his sweater. Fiona took her lunch break and they walked to a restaurant that was close by, a typical New Mexican hangout with smells that immediately welcomed them. It was tastefully decorated with local pottery and paintings, and patrons regaling themselves with large plates of food. Red and green chiles appropriately adorned the walls.

"This looks lovely, Tibah, and the smells are incredible!" Fiona exclaimed.

"And wait 'til you taste the food."

"I can hardly wait."

"Good."

They sat down in a booth and looked at the menu.

"You'll have to explain most of these dishes," Fiona said.

"It will be my pleasure." Tibah really liked this beautiful woman, and was looking forward to explaining anything she desired. And he did.

A waitress in a colorful dress came up to them. "Hi y'all, are you ready to order?"

Tibah had meticulously explained each and every item on the menu. "Yes, thank you. We'll have the enchiladas with rice, guacamole and refried beans."

"Red or green?"

"Fiona, your preference?" He asked.

"Christmas," she said proudly.

"You got it."

The waitress left and Tibah saw Fiona staring at him. "What is it?"

"I'm having a wonderful time, and the food sounds so exciting! How could it not be with 'Christmas' in the middle of all that?"

Tibah laughed. "I'm glad you think so."

"Thank you, for everything."

"You're very welcome."

They enjoyed their food and when Fiona had eaten every morsel on her plate Tibah announced that they were going to have dessert.

"Dessert?"

"Of course."

"I don't think I could."

"Ah, there's always a little corner for something sweet. We're having *sopapillas*."

"I guess I could find a way."

"That's my girl."

Fiona liked the sound of that, *my girl*. She liked the idea of being Tibah's girl. "By the way, what is sopa…"

"Sopapilla. It's a kind of uh… puff," Tibah said, trying to describe it to her.

"A puff?"

"Well, like a little air cushion."

Fiona still wasn't quite sure what it was. "Sounds fun," she ventured.

As soon as the 'puffs' arrived the man looked as if he had returned to boyhood. "Oh, yeah," he crooned.

"You have a sweet tooth!" She chuckled.

"You found me out, I most certainly do." He picked up a small bottle filled with a thick amber-gold liquid. "Here, let me fix it for you and put some honey on it."

"Okay." She watched his hands as the gooey substance cascaded over the hot pocket.

"Ready!" Tibah said boyishly. He cut a piece off with his fingers and put it close to her face. "Try it." He watched her lips as her mouth opened.

Fiona bit into it and her lips brushed his fingers. "Oh, that is so good!" She said, her mouth full of the airy 'puff'. It was delicious, but she kept thinking of the fingers her lips had touched.

Tibah took the rest of the piece and put it his own mouth. "Good, isn't it?" He mumbled.

Fiona nodded. "Amazing."

"You're becoming New Mexican very fast," Tibah laughed.

"And I think that's perfectly wonderful."

Once their tummies were satiated they had a coffee and relaxed. They enjoyed each other's company and also talked about serious things. Fiona explained how she wound up in New Mexico, about the circumstances with her parents and the time she spent in Dublin.

CHAPTER 13

"You will see that my story is not so different from yours," Tibah said.

Fiona wondered how that could be possible, but she listened attentively, appreciating the openness in which he conveyed his story to her.

"I was a teenager in high school. We had just won a football game and everybody was celebrating. My whole family was there, my parents, brother and sister. I asked my father to drive me home. I was a bit nauseous. I had gotten hit by a couple of guys, and I thought my brains had been shaken loose from my skull."

"Did you get into a fight?" Fiona asked.

"How do you mean?"

"Why did you get hit?"

"It's part of the game."

"But why?"

Tibah grinned. "We were playing American football." Fiona stared at him blankly. "It's not like the football they play in Europe, it's more like rugby."

"So you don't play, uh, European football in the United States?"

"Oh, sure we do, we just call it soccer."

"I see. Please go on." Fiona knew she had a lot to learn, and she also knew that she would enjoy discovering all the new things that would come her way. So far everything had been a lovely journey. She hoped Tibah would guide her some more. She would like that.

"My family dropped me off at the house," Tibah continued, "and then they went off to celebrate. It was the highlight of the week—a football game, food and booze, especially booze. I later learned that I had a pretty bad concussion. When I got home I immediately fell asleep." Tibah's dark brown eyes became almost black as he thought about that night. "At around four o'clock in the morning the Sheriff woke me up. There had been an accident."

"Oh, no! What happened?" Fiona cringed. She knew it wouldn't be good.

Tibah's jaw clenched tight. "Everybody had too much to drink. You must understand that Indians are extreme with everything we do, whether it is loving someone, fighting for a cause, a war, or drinking. There's no middle ground, and my family was no exception. That night my father, brother, sister and four other people were killed. Two cars. Head on collision. No one survived, but my mother."

"Oh, Tibah, how terrible. I'm so sorry," Fiona said, truly distraught for this man. "At least your mother survived. Thank God for that."

"No, not really."

"What do you mean?"

"When my family died it was if she had as well. She was like an empty shell, on 'automatic' mode, just going through the motions without any kind of emotion. One death is traumatic, but losing a husband and two children is more than a person should have to endure."

"But she had you."

"I don't think that mattered very much. I know she loved me, but a few weeks later my mother left me as well. She had lost the will to live. Life had no meaning for her anymore. She wanted to be with the ones she loved. I was seventeen, and losing my entire family like that did something to me."

"Oh, Tibah, I should think so. How terribly traumatic for you."

"Of course, being a know-it-all hot-headed teenager who was in pain I stupidly turned to the bottle."

"Oh, no," Fiona said, wincing.

"At first the alcohol made me feel better, made me forget the agony in my heart. But when I overdid it, which became all the time, then I would turn wild. And that's a real crazy Indian for you." Tibah laughed harshly, but Fiona shuddered, remembering only too well what the drink had done to her own family.

"One night I wandered off into the desert. I couldn't see much. The moon was hidden somewhere and I just walked right into the blackness. Some stars were out, but that was about all I could see. I didn't care where I was going. I just thought that the farther I could walk the farther I would get away from the pain and grief. I kept going until I stumbled, fell and passed out. When I finally woke up, and the only reason I woke up was because I was completely dehydrated. Of course I didn't have anything to drink. I remember looking around and trying to get my bearings. I had absolutely no idea where I was, just somewhere in the middle of the mesa. The only thing visible was an infinite horizon of red earth, a few berms, dead branches, tumbleweed, and a cactus here and there. If I had been in my right mind I might have been able to squeeze some juice out of the prickly plant."

"Cactuses have juice?"

"Cacti," Tibah said, gently rectifying her mistake.

"I have so much to learn," she said, not minding the correction in the least.

"I will gladly help." *And it would be my great pleasure.*

"That would be lovely, thank you Tibah. But please tell me more."

"The prickly pear cactus is very useful and the blooms are just beautiful. And then the fruit comes out and seems to be standing on top of the pads next to each other. The pads, or leaves, are also known as nopal, and you can eat all of it."

"Really?" Fiona asked fascinated, the cook in her awakened. "What color is the fruit, and how is it used?"

"Oh, it can all be used in many ways and it's healthy too. Full of vitamin C. The fruit is quite delicious, and you can eat everything including the seeds, but not the skin. It also makes a wonderful juice. The color ranges from a rose to a red to a purple, depending in what part of the country you're in."

"That sounds delicious and very pretty."

"And then of course you have the pads."

"Don't they have thorns?"

"Oh, yes, nasty spines, but you can cut them off with a sharp knife and use the rest of it in many ways. You can leave it as is and grill it, chop it up, cut it into thin strips and cook it like vegetables."

"What does it taste like?"

"Like a lemony green bean."

"Oh, that sounds delicious."

"Yes, and here in the Southwest they make many dishes with it. The nopals are put in soups, rice, salsas, stuffed with cheese, added to chicken dishes, even served with eggs. Of course there are many more." *And I'll be glad to help you discover all of them.*

I have to find a local cookbook, Fiona thought. "Go on, Tibah."

"Well, as I was saying, if my brain had been clear I could have found a cactus and survived from it. But my mind wasn't thinking about surviving, on the contrary I had lost my desire for living. I was literally all alone. I had no family, no money, and no foreseeable future. What did I have to live for? And for whom? Certainly not for myself. So, after thinking about this for quite a while I leaned up against a rock and sat or slept there for two days, waiting to fade away. I just didn't want to be around anymore."

"That is so sad, Tibah. I so glad you're still very much alive."

"Actually I am too, but I probably would still be out there, and very dead of course, if our local Sheriff hadn't found me. He tracked me down, gave me some water, put me in his car and slapped me really hard."

"He slapped you?"

"Uh, huh, best thing anyone ever did for me."

"How do you mean?"

"He told me to get my act together and not try to kill myself. Uh, those weren't his exact words, trust me. He tried to make me understand that what I was doing was definitely not my path in life. And that I shouldn't leave my family, who were supposedly watching me from the heavens, without a legacy. He went on and on, telling me how disappointed they would be that the last child had died, and most of all in a cowardly way. The man was relentless. He talked, well, more like lectured me, for over an hour. He told me that I still had a roof over my head, that I wasn't alone, that the entire tribe was behind me, that my family had been well liked and respected. That I had to prove to my people, and even more so to myself, that I wasn't just a deadbeat, that I could make something of my life. His words were powerful, and he was able to reach my heart. It also sobered me up, literally. I stopped drinking, well I do have a beer once in a while and I enjoy it, but I will never go back to that hot-headed soul-less teenager. I finished high school, enrolled into an agriculture college and learned everything I could about this land. I had a little piece I called my own and do what I wanted with it, so I figured I would use it to grow things. When I wasn't in school I washed cars and made some money for food and necessities. One day I talked to my professor, told him my predicament, and we came up with an idea."

"What did you do?"

"The man was a wonderful mentor, and to this day I consider him a great friend and as close a family member as I could have. Oh, and the Sheriff of course is probably one of my best friends."

"Definitely."

"During the course, which was basically learning how things grow, the entire class would go to my property. We first prepared the land, then planted little chile pepper plants, corn, and other fruits and vegetables. Once a week the students would work the land and take care of everything we were growing. In just a short time we saw results. It was amazing. I was fascinated by the way Mother Nature worked and marveled at the production. I loved everything about it, and more importantly I loved my land."

"Sounds like the perfect combination."

"It was. I had my crops and a small business where I

would sell at local farmer's markets. Whatever I didn't sell I would give to the people on the Rez. We helped each other out. A couple of years later the casino on the Reservation asked me to supply them with my produce. It has been a happy relationship ever since. As a matter of fact I was just coming back from dropping off a few baskets to them."

"Is the casino close by?"

Tibah laughed. "Not too far, but I took a wrong turn and wound up in your store. I usually don't come to this part of town."

"Well I for one am very glad you took that wrong turn. It has been a pleasure meeting and talking to you, Tibah. And I'm glad everything turned out for you."

"Yes, it did. What once started as a necessity turned into something wonderful. I realized how much I truly loved producing food. Each piece of corn or baby chile pepper was beautiful, like a little miracle. And when you see rows and rows of it, well, it's paradise." He looked at Fiona. "Would you be interested in seeing it?" *Say yes, please say yes!*

"How could I resist a piece of paradise?"

CHAPTER 14

Fiona and Tibah's relationship bloomed from that day on. They had been together for several months. She knew Tibah was the man for her, and that he loved her too, but she needed a sign. As they sat on the sofa in the living room of Tibah's home she knew she wanted to spend the rest of her life with him.

"Tibah, I love your name, but I've never asked you its meaning."

"If I tell you what my name means I would have to either kill you, or marry you."

"Seriously?"

"More or less," Tibah said, grinning.

"What am I supposed to say?"

Tibah looked into the shimmering emerald of Fiona's eyes. *How could the Great One have created someone so beautiful and brought her to me?* "You are supposed to give me an answer. Will you marry me?"

"Will you tell me the meaning of your name?"

"Absolutely."

"Then, yes, *M'fhíorghrá*, I will," Fiona said, beaming.

Tibah took her hands in his and kissed them. "God's gift."

Fiona smiled. "Are you telling me I am God's gift?"

"No, I am."

"I know that."

"That's my name."

"What's your name?"

"Tibah."

"Yes, I know."

Tibah started laughing and it just escalated. "Fiona, listen to me," he said between breaths. Fiona didn't know why he was laughing, but she started as well. It was infectious. Was there anything better than two people who loved each laughing together? Tibah tried again. "Fiona," he gasped trying to form words, "God's gift..."

"Yes, I know, that's you. You said that," she said, now hysterical.

Tibah was laughing so hard he couldn't form any words. They looked at each other and roared, fell into each other's arms, crumpled to the carpet and slowly settled down without saying a word. They lay next to each other, Tibah gently caressing Fiona's face. "Tibah, it means God's gift," he said.

"Well, I'm glad that's finally cleared up. So Fiona, it means white and beautiful," she answered back.

"My beautiful white dove, you are my *Tahnee Ligaíi Hasbídí.*"

"That's my Navajo name?"

"Yes, and my name for you."

"All that means Fiona?"

"It means my flame-haired white dove."

"Oh, I like that." She looked at Tibah. "And now that I know our names does that mean I can kill somebody?"

"Well, you can't marry anybody else."

"Good to know."

"It seems to me the Spirits have brought us together."

"The Indian ones or the Celtic ones?"

"All of them," he answered, "definitely all of them." Tibah smiled and inwardly thanked them as he remembered his 'detour' to the shop where Fiona worked.

They held each other and he kissed her passionately.

"By the way you mentioned that you wanted to show me something."

"I did. It's directly in front of you. Look at the mountains. It's one of my favorite things to do, watching the sun go down right over them."

Sitting in Tibah's home, leaning against the sofa and holding hands, they watched the sunset make the Sandia Mountains turn red. He was right. It was one of the most beautiful views in the world and the living poster she had first seen in the travel agency in Dublin that brought her to the land that had enchanted her, and allowed her to meet the love of her life.

CHAPTER 15

The purple and peach sunset followed Tibah as he raced his pickup to the hospital. His wife was next to him, writhing in pain with contractions.

"What do you see, my love?" Tibah asked.

"What do I see? Right now?" She asked incredulously.

"Yes."

Fiona opened her eyes. Even that seemed to hurt. The desert looked blurry, but even in all her pain she loved the land around her. "I see…"

"Yes?"

"Beauty."

"Yes, it truly is, but be more specific."

"Tibah, why do you want to know, and why right now?"

"Please, do me this favor, it's important."

"Hot air. The wind, it feels hot." Whether it was hot or not Fiona wasn't sure, but it sure felt like it.

"Yes, my love. Thank you."

Tibah's smile was one of the biggest Fiona had ever seen on the man she loved.

Another pain shot through her, but she held the scream back and bit her lip instead.

Tibah was in the hospital waiting room reserved for expecting father. There was a television, some books and magazines, coffee and beverages. Three other men were either biting their nails, perspiring or just sitting in one of the chairs staring straight ahead as if in a daze.

"Is it taking too long?" Tibah asked any or all of the others waiting.

"It can take a few minutes to several hours," the most relaxed of the four men said. "I gather this is your first?"

"It is."

"Yeah, I figured. Well, this is my fourth, so relax, man. Babies have their own time schedule. When they're ready to come out they will. We're at their mercy."

"Yeah, and just wait 'til they're older. It just gets worse," another said. He was the oldest of the men in the room.

"What do you mean?" Tibah asked.

"I have a couple of teenagers, a boy and a girl. Just wait and you'll see what I mean. The more their brains develop the more demanding they become. Then suddenly they know everything, and parents are dinosaurs and know nothing."

"Sounds like you've got your hands full. I know what you mean," the most relaxed of the men said. "And you decided to have another one?"

"This one was a surprise," he groaned.

The men laughed.

"Oops."

"Yeah, but you know I can hardly wait. There's nothing like kids."

Now Tibah was confused. He knew children took on a life and personality of their own, and he swore he would try to be the best father and caregiver possible. Hurdles would surely arise and he would try to resolve the problems as best he could. But right now he was worried about Fiona and the unborn baby. He was antsy. He didn't know what to do with himself, so he went to the hospital's gift shop and looked around. He picked up some cigars and found a charm for Fiona, a lovely dove made of turquoise. He bought a gold chain to go with it. He went back to the waiting room hoping he would have news soon.

Tibah hadn't been there more than a half hour when a nurse came in. The men all stared at her. Which one was a new dad? A couple of them stood up, Tibah was one of them. She looked at their faces. This was one of the best moments of her job. "Mister Sandoval?"

"Yes, that's me," Tibah said, slightly apprehensively. "Is everything alright with my wife, with the baby?

"Your wife is doing well and you have a healthy, beautiful baby boy. Congratulations!"

Tibah picked up the nurse, twirled her around, kissed both her cheeks and once he let her go jumped up and down. "I have a son! Thank you! Thank you, Miss."

"You're very welcome!" She answered, laughing. She loved happy outcomes, and the new fathers always became cheerful little boys.

"When can I see them?"

"In about half an hour. Your wife needs to rest a little and we're cleaning up the baby."

"I understand, thank you, thank you again."

The nurse left the room and Tibah turned to the others. "I have a son!" He shouted, lifting his arms toward the heavens. Before the men could congratulate Tibah, the new dad started hugging and lifting them up as he had the nurse. This was probably the happiest day of his life. The other expectant fathers didn't complain, on the contrary, they were just as excited as he was, and smacked the new dad affectionately on his back. He handed each one of them a cigar. "Good luck to all of you," he said, before leaving the room.

Tibah left the hospital, lit a cigar and started walking. He stopped after about half a mile. He looked around. There wasn't much there, just a field of red earth and several bushes scattered around. It was a pretty deserted area. His cigar was down to about half its original size. He held it in his hand as he lit another one, and then another. He put the longer ones on the ground in an X, the smoking ends pointed upward. With the half smoked cigar he made shapes in the sky just above his head and prayed. Tibah was performing his own ceremony with his mini fire in honor of his newborn son. He thanked the Great One for his blessings. He looked at his 'fire', prayed and started dancing and singing around it. Deep, passionate sounds came from his throat. He wasn't sure if they were coming from his mouth or his heart. Probably both. The only thing he knew for certain was that at that moment he was the luckiest and happiest man alive.

When Tibah walked into his wife's hospital room he thanked the Spirits once again for his glorious gifts—his beautiful and amazing wife, his precious son, his land and his happy life. Fiona looked radiant, albeit exhausted. She held the baby close to her chest. He was of course beautiful, a combination of his father's strong features and his mother's gentle expressions. Even though the little human had only just arrived there was no mistaking whose child this was.

"How are you feeling, Fiona?"

"Like the happiest woman in the world."

"I know what you mean."

"Would you like to hold him?"

Tibah nodded and gently lifted the boy out of his mother's arms.

"A father. I'm a father!" Tibah whispered joyously. "Have you given him a name?"

"I thought we would do it together."

"No, you are the one that gave him life and light."

"Well you had a little something to do with that."

"I guess so," he chuckled, "and I enjoyed every minute of it. Don't ever say that I'm an ungrateful man."

"You are a wonderful man, Tibah, with a caring soul. I wish all women could be as lucky as I am, and I am sure little Sean will have just as wonderful a father."

"Sean. Yes, that is a good name, strong."

"So it's okay?"

"Of course. Does it have a meaning?"

"It means Tibah."

The new father started giggling as he remembered the first time they tried explaining each other's names and laughed until they fell to the floor. "I'm not as confused as the first time we tried to figure our names out."

"Sean means gift of God, just like Tibah."

"You have named our son perfectly, and in my honor."

"I have. You are both perfect and God's gifts to me. Thank you for being my husband… and a beautiful horse."

Tibah laughed and gently kissed his wife's sweet lips. "Now let me tell you his name in Navajo."

"He has a Navajo name?"

"Of course."

"What is it, my love?"

"Nílchi Deesdoi."

"That's beautiful! What does it mean?"

"Does it have to mean something?"

"No, of course not, but being the wife of a Navajo man I've learned a few things. I know all names have a meaning."

"Have I told you that I love you mainly because you are so smart?" Tibah asked his wife.

"You have, and I'll never get tired of hearing it."

"Good, because I intend to tell you an entire lifetime." Tibah bent over to kiss her again, the baby cradled between their chests.

"So, Nílchi Deesdoi, what does it mean?"

"Hot Air."

Tibah lifted the baby high above his head. To their surprise the baby gurgled with delight.

"He likes it!" Fiona said, laughing.

"Of course he likes Nílchi Deesdoi," his father said proudly. "He likes hot air."

"And now I know why you asked me what I was seeing in the car."

"Yes, my Tahnee Ligaíí Hasbídí."

CHAPTER 16

Sean had listened to his mother relay her story, from her youth in Ireland to her meeting his father in New Mexico, up until the day he was born. He was impressed by their love and appalled by what the alcohol had done to both sides of the family. He knew the Indian population had a serious problem with alcoholism, and he swore to himself right then and there that he would not follow in their path. He also really didn't like how it made him feel, especially the aftermath. He had a monstrous hangover and was having a terrible time remembering much of what had happened, although the fire had definitely sobered him up.

"Mam, I'm really sorry, and I promise you I won't ever drink again."

"Oh, Sean, please understand that I don't want you to stop anything. I can't control what you do, nor do I want to. I do, however, want you to have fun and enjoy life. It can be done without alcohol, or just in moderation. There's nothing wrong with enjoying it, but I find it ridiculous when it is consumed in excess. It defeats the purpose of appreciating something tasty. The drink is wonderful for a while, it makes life fun and makes you feel good. It also alleviates certain pains, but that is only a temporary fix. It is devious, it slowly destroys and kills you, and usually those around you who love you as well. I don't know what you will do with your life, but what I do know is that it will have meaning. You are destined to be special, even more special than you are now."

Fiona opened her arms and Sean hugged her tightly.

"You are the special one, Mam, and I promise I will make you and Dad proud of me."

Fiona looked at the color of the eyes that mirrored her own and smiled. "I already am, *a stor*, my treasure."

Tibah had entered the house from the back. Mother and son hadn't heard him, and he had stayed in the kitchen listening. He overheard their conversation with tears in his eyes, fiercely proud of his family. He adored them. Tibah washed his face and went into the living room.

"Hey Dad."

"Hey Sean." Tibah went to his wife and kissed her.

"Hello, *M'fhíorghrá*" Fiona said.

Tibah went to sit next to her. He so loved the shine in her eyes whenever she saw him. He hoped his love for her was somehow just as powerfully displayed. *"Meergrah,"* Tibah repeated phonetically, "my true love."

"And soul mate," Fiona added.

Sean smiled at his parents' amorous *tête-à-tête*. He wished that one day he would find someone to love and who would love him just as much.

"Uh, Dad, sorry to interrupt, but could I ask you a question?"

"Of course, what's up?"

"I know you work the land and how much you love it."

"Yes, I do." Tibah was wondering where the young man was going with this.

"And I guess you would want me to do the same."

"You mean help me out?"

"Yes."

"Well, you do that already."

Sean dutifully helped his father as much as he could. "Right."

Tibah looked at him, patiently waiting for him to get to his point. "What are you trying to ask me, Sean?"

"Well, would you be really upset if I wanted to do something else?"

"You mean as far as work?"

"Uh, yeah."

"Why would I be upset?"

"Well, it wouldn't be what you want."

"Sean, listen to me carefully. If you want to do the work that I do on our land I would be thrilled. However, if you have visions of other things I would be just as happy because you would be following your dreams and your heart."

"Really?" Sean asked, incredulous and ecstatic.

"Absolutely. A man must find his way, walk the path he was meant to follow." Tibah looked deep into his son's eyes. "And I have a feeling it has to do with air, hot air." He had observed his son's obsession with air and flying. He inwardly smiled and knew that the boy would somehow include his other love, medicine.

Sean's eyebrows shot up and his eyes grew very wide. "How did you know?" He exclaimed.

"An eagle told me about all this a long time ago."

"That sounds very Indian."

"I am *Diné*," Tibah said, using the Navajo word for his people.

"And when and how exactly did this happen?"

"When you were nine and saw your first hot air balloon. What you perhaps didn't see was the eagle circling above you." Sean smiled as he remembered the momentous balloon. "You confirmed it by trying to burn down the house," his father continued.

"I never tried to burn down the house."

"The toaster."

"Oh." Sean never knew his father had been watching.

"So you see, I knew before you even did."

Sean looked at his mother. She had a smile on her face, the one that said 'I'm happy for you, go live your dreams'. He went to his parents and hugged them, thinking he had the best mother and father in the world. He also sensed that in the last twenty-four hours he had matured from a boy to a man.

CHAPTER 17

Sean graduated high school and followed his dreams. He wanted to be a Marine, to follow in the footsteps of the brave Navajo warriors who had served gallantly in many wars, and even now in Afghanistan. He respected them immensely, and many of them had been from his part of the world. He thought long and hard about which branch to enlist in, and after thoroughly researching decided to enlist in the *Air* Force. He wanted to be a Pararescuer, an elite member of the military. The training would be one of the toughest in the world and would take two years, and only a very small percentage made it through the rigorous curriculum. The Pararescuemen were fierce warriors when they had to be, but their main objective was rescuing wounded military personnel, and usually in the most difficult circumstances. Thinking about it Sean knew he had chosen well. His Navajo warrior legacy was in his blood, his love for medicine was just as strong, and his passion for all things related to air was in his soul. He had absolutely no doubt that his choice would be accurate.

Once Sean finished his basic training he signed up for the PJs. The Air Force approved his request. That of course did not mean that he would automatically be a Pararescue Jumper, it just meant that he was being given a chance to *try*. He arrived at Lackland Air Force Base in Texas.

Sean knew the first part of the training would last ten weeks, and he confirmed to himself that he would endure and make it through. As he walked onto the base he noticed the Pararescue logo and gasped as he realized he hadn't really taken a good look. It was of an angel, a beautiful woman with wings holding a globe. Hanging above her was a parachute that looked like a hot air balloon! The ribbon on the bottom had an inscription: 'So that others may live'. In his mind's eye he saw himself wearing the emblem on a coveted maroon beret, and in his heart he knew he had chosen the right branch of the military service. A hot air balloon, a beautiful woman and a globe of the earth. Perfection.

Over sixty young men stood at attention in their green and khaki fatigues as the sergeant walked into the room.
"Good morning!"
"GOOD MORNING, SIR!" They answered back in unison.
"Pull up some floor."
"YES, SIR!" They sat down.
"There are almost seventy of you here today. By the end of the day that number will have changed. There will be less. By the end of the ten week training there will only be about twenty percent of you left, maybe less. Pararescuers have the unique distinction of having the highest dropout rate in the entire U.S. specials ops community." He eyed each of them, knowing that in their minds they firmly believed that they wouldn't be the ones leaving. He appreciated their sentiment, but also knew that no matter how much they wanted to be a Pararescue Jumper it took a special breed of man to make it all the way through. He continued: "A Pararescuer is part combat soldier, part doctor, and a member of a special operations command. PJs are the most highly qualified medical rescue teams in the world, trained extensively in survival and trauma care. You will become a highly trained medical specialist, a formidable warrior ready to go into the harshest terrains, the wildest seas, the coldest mountains, the hottest deserts, and even into a hell called war. And you will go in not so much to fight, but to save your fellow warrior from a possible certain death. You will be

trained hard and relentlessly, until you either crack or maybe move on." He looked at the young men in front of him. They were listening attentively. "Anyone want to leave yet?" He asked them.

"NO SIR!" They shouted.

"Preparation and training to become a PJ will last two years. The first ten weeks will be here in the scorching Texas heat." He grinned as he looked at them. He was the only one in the room who truly knew what was in store for them. He would be one of the trainers wreaking havoc with muscles and stamina their bodies never knew could be pushed to the extent they would put them through. He would inflict a good deal of physical and mental rigors that were part of the training.

The young men didn't utter a sound.

"*If* you pass the first part of the preparation then you will continue, *if* you are still with us," the sergeant continued, as his voice kept rising, "and right now YOU BELONG TO ME! ON YOUR FEET! MOVE!"

The rookies did as he asked and jumped off the floor. The butterflies in their stomachs were becoming the size of lemons, but they were excited. Their training would be unlike anything they could have ever imagined. The young men were about to begin a training that would push their minds and bodies farther than any of them would have thought possible.

CHAPTER 18

At 0400 hours the young men put on their PT clothes, threw a rucksack full of gear and food they would need throughout the day on their backs, and lined up in formation. They stood in front of a large warehouse and the instructors wasted no time with their physical training and endurance. They started with what they were sure would at some point total a million push-ups, pull-ups and exhausting calisthenics they were sure they would have nightmares about. And that was just the beginning.

At 0600 they continued to the pool. They thought that would be a bit of a respite since the bodies would carry their weight. They couldn't have been more wrong. Their first exercise was swimming the entire length of the training tank, as the instructors lovingly called it, in one single breath.

Sean felt the fire in his lungs about two thirds of the length and thought his body would quit, but his mind refused. He certainly was not leaving in the first few hours. The men continued, their hearts persevered, but some of their bodies couldn't. They watched as fellow trainees walked away and picked up an air horn. As soon as they blew it they were out. The dropout percentage had started.

There were many punishing exercises and they were pushed to their limits. Day after day there were more dropouts. They trained from four in the morning until nine at night. Sometimes when they were finally in their cots ready to fall into an oblivious state of sleep the instructors would come back in and extend their training for several more hours.

They were drained and would have to endure, if they could handle the exhaustive program, another ten weeks. Sean firmly believed that flames of pain were crawling under his skin and searing every part of his body. His legs were weak and shaky and were not taking orders from his brain which is why, as they subconsciously put one foot in front of the other, ran into another man before he had time to stop them.

"Wow, sorry, man," Sean said, "legs aren't obeying too well right now."

"No problem, I'm doing about the same," he chuckled.

"Name's Sean Sandoval," he said putting his hand out.

"Hey, good to meet you, man, I'm Nicolaos Katsopoulos," he answered, shaking Sean's hand. You can call me Nico or Kats, I get it all the time."

"Tough time pronouncing your name?"

"Yeah, most people have a problem with Greek names."

"Where are you from?" Sean asked.

"From Albuquerque."

"No kidding!"

"Something wrong with that? Did you think I would have said Athens, Sparta or Astoria?" Nico asked, perturbed.

Sean chuckled. "No, man, relax. "I'm from the Rez right outside of Albuquerque."

"Wow, talk about a small world! Navajo?"

"Actually half Navajo, half Irish."

"No fucking way!" Nico said excitedly.

"What? Something wrong with that?" Sean asked, repeating Nico's question. It was his turn to feel the heat creeping up under his collar.

"Oh, no, man, on the contrary," Nico said, grinning.

"What does that mean?"

"It means you've probably got one hot temper, you can drink anyone under the table and you're undoubtedly one hell of a fighter. The best of all worlds."

Sean laughed, relaxing. "Maybe."

"How could you not? Although I've been known to be pretty badass myself."

"Of course, you're Greek." Both men laughed and took an instant liking to each other. They would become good buddies. "Your family is there?"

"Yeah, although you'd think Dad just came over from the old country."

"Why's that?"

"As American as he is he still has old fashioned thoughts. One thing he said to me was to find a nice Greek girl, marry her and have Greek babies."

"Holy shit! Did you?"

"Not yet. I did find a nice Greek girl, Sophia, and I asked her to marry me."

"Sounds like my Big Fat Greek Wedding," Sean laughed.

"Exactly, however, the good thing is I'm actually in love with her."

"I'm glad for you, man. I'm curious about something."

"What's that?"

"How or when do you know you're in love?" Sean asked, thinking about his parents.

"Oh, you haven't been there yet, huh."

"Well, I've had my share of girls, but no, I've never been in love."

Well, it's not science or planned. It just happens."

"But how do you know?"

"You'll know, my friend, you'll know. It kind of hits you."

"Yeah?"

"Uh huh. Just don't worry about it."

"Oh, I'm not. And definitely in no rush at all."

"That's my boy. You just go out and have fun. I'm sure the ladies will oblige."

"I've had pretty good luck so far."

"I don't doubt that, you handsome bugger," Nico said, slapping him on the back. "Ready for dinner?"

"I think I'm too tired to even eat."

"I know what you mean, but we have to."

"Right behind you."

Hundreds of butterfly kicks and dozens of pool lengths started to become 'normal'. When they were pushed to their limits many of the trainees would find an 'automatic mode' or zone out place to a place where they became robotic. The less they thought about the pain and torment twisting their bodies the easier it was to get through the throbbing agony. They became stronger, excelled physically and mentally. It made their minds agile, showed them a way of thinking faster—lives would depend on it.

The indoc course was also where they learned teamwork and the trainees became close. Of course that didn't mean they would miss an opportunity to have some fun with their peers. One morning Kats woke up and still half asleep noticed the other guys watching him. He immediately knew they were up to something. He tried taking off the blanket and getting out of the bed, but he couldn't move. They had completely duct taped him, including the blanket, to the cot.

The guys laughed and walked off without helping their fellow colleague, who looked more like a roll of tape than a human being.

"I'll get you for this, you sons of bitches!" Nico hollered.

They knew he would, and really didn't mind. It was in good fun and gave them much needed laughs. It released the stress and tension of the training.

CHAPTER 19

The ten week Pararescue indoctrination course was coming to an end. Sean and Nico had distinguished themselves among their peers and their superiors, were well liked and respected. So far they had survived weeks of punishing physical training, to include conditioning in running, marches, weight training and extensive swimming exercises. They also learned CPR, medical and dive terminologies, qualified in weapons and leadership. The graduation from the past ten weeks was 'the ticket to ride the pipeline' which meant that the future PJs were eligible to begin learning special skills that would make them elite special operators.

All the young men who had made it this far were looking forward to the next phase of their training. They went on to the Army Airborne School in Fort Benning, Georgia.

Sean and Nico looked at each other and grinned, buddies on the adventure of their lives, yet they were very serious when it came to their training. They were focused on becoming Pararescuemen. When they arrived at Fort Benning they were amazed at the jump towers, some of them 250 feet tall. They formed their own unique skyline, and could be seen from anywhere inside or outside the post. Sean and Nico also learned that this was where all military personnel who are airborne start from, including the elite branches such as SEALS, Rangers, Delta Force and every special operations team, including some international forces.

During their first week of parachutist training Sean and Nico spent a lot of time learning, practicing and perfecting their landings after jumping from towers and platforms of different heights into sand or rocks. Their second week concentrated on taller towers and mock jumps. Although it was hard work Sean was enjoying himself. As he practiced jumping, steering parachutes and learning skills in case of a malfunction, he could hardly wait for the real thing— parachuting out into the air. He wanted to be as close as possible to being that noble eagle. He had missed being 'in' the air, communing with the sky and seeing the world from above.

The third week finally came, which meant that they would practice jumping out of an airborne plane. The Lockheed C-130 Hercules stood at attention on the airfield waiting for its jumpers. The first-timers were excited, and understandably a bit apprehensive, but their excitement and confidence in their instructors, 'the Black Hats', who were given the nickname because of the black baseball caps they wore, overrode their anxiety. They were some of the best instructors and leaders of any military branch. They knew their responsibility included teaching the novices everything they needed to know about parachuting, but even more so they wanted to make them perfect. Mistakes could cost them their lives. The C-130's engines revved and then taxied down the runway. It amazed the men how effortlessly the big steel bird lifted off and climbed to 1200 feet and flew at about 150 miles per hour. It was time. Sean could hardly contain himself as he firmly believed he would finally understand what birds of all sizes had the privilege of experiencing every day.

The large ramp in the back of the plane opened and the Black Hat signaled to his rookies. "On your feet!" He hollered over the engine noise.

"Yes, Sergeant, Airborne!" They yelled back, using the appropriate title.

The soon to be jumpers attached their hooks to the cable just above their heads. The instructor checked each jumper's gear. And then the green light came on. It was the signal they were waiting for. Sean felt his loins swelling. This always happened when he was taking off or landing in airplanes, when he was ascending in a hot air balloon, or anything that put him in the air. This was no exception. This was *really* it—he was going to fly. The Black Hat signaled and each person held the strap attached to the hook. GO! That was the signal they were waiting for. Sean and the others jumped forward and let go of the cable as they exited the back of the Hercules.

Sean screamed in delight as the wind took him into the great ocean of the sky. He looked up and saw the chute automatically opening above him. The force pulled him forcefully back up and then he gently drifted to earth. It was as quiet as the hot air balloon, save for his breathing and the rhythmic pounding of his heart. As the air rushed into his body he felt the closest to being that eagle of his boyhood dreams. Sean was in paradise. When he was ready to land he remembered the technique. As the balls of his feet touched the ground he immediately bent his knees, tucked his chin in and fell to his side. Sean and his fellow jumpers gathered their parachute and waited for the bus to take them back to the airfield to get ready for their next jump. To their delight they would do it many times over.

Sean, Nico and the others jumped throughout the week, during the day and at night. The morning after the last jump the trainees were awarded the basic parachutist rating and were allowed to wear the Parachutist's Badge. Immediately afterwards they left for their next destination.

CHAPTER 20

Sean and Nico traveled together to their next destination in Florida. They had just finished the 'air' training and were now on their way to 'water' training, to the Combat Diver School in Panama City. They would spend the next five weeks jumping out of helicopters and learning the intricacies of recovery and special operations waterborne missions.

They further learned techniques and procedures on how to safely escape from a sinking aircraft that has crashed in the ocean. That took one day at the Naval Air Station in Pensacola. Sean and Nico were loving every minute of their training.

Their next stop was in Washington state to take part in the SERE training program—Survival, Evasion, Resistance, and Escape. They were close to landing at Fairchild Air Force Base where they would spend several weeks learning survival techniques in remote areas of the northwestern wilderness, using minimal equipment. Sean was ahead of the game thanks to his father's Navajo teachings, and wasn't worrying too much. For Nico, however, as tough and indomitable as he had been so far in the previous trainings, Sean thought that maybe this kind of training would be a struggle. He chuckled to himself as he knew Nico's idea of survival was a snack in the middle of the night in a twenty-four hour diner, or raiding the fridge and heating up his mother's leftover moussaká. On the other hand he had no doubt that his buddy would pull through—Nico was as tough as his Spartan ancestors.

"Holy shit!" One of the passengers and a SERE candidate exclaimed as he looked out of the window and took in the northern landscape.

"What's wrong, Johnson?" Nico asked.

"The trees are huge, and everything is white!" The man's eyes had grown so big and round that they seemed to take up most of his face.

"That's called snow," Nico answered.

"Where you from, man?" Sean asked.

"Florida."

"That explains it. I guess you've never seen mountains either then," Nico chortled.

"Nope. The highest peaks we have in Florida are sand dunes."

"Oh, you're in for a treat, Florida boy."

"I'm looking forward to it. One of the reasons I joined the military was to travel."

"Well, welcome to the another part of the world." Nico laughed.

"This is going to be fun," Sean added.

"Yeah, wait 'til he sees real mountains."

Sean, Nico, Ted Johnson and the rest of the new group were awake and ready for their first day of SERE training. They went outside and Johnson screamed.

"What's wrong?" Nico asked.

"It's as cold as a fucking freezer!"

The fun's starting, Sean thought.

"You better get used to it. This is just the beginning." Nico looked up. "And it's not even snowing."

"Aw, shit," Johnson grumbled.

The group of a dozen men were driven deep into the rugged Washington forest. When they came off the truck Johnson jumped off the back end and sank in four feet of snow.

"This is fucked!" Johnson swore. He was stuck and couldn't get out of his predicament. It was his first encounter with snow. "And fucking cold and wet!"

"Uh, huh, sounds like snow," Nico said.

"Get Johnson the fuck out of there!" The sergeant bellowed.

"Yes, Sir!"

And they did. They helped the Floridian out of the hole and back onto his feet. Johnson was a tall man, standing at least six foot four and seemed almost as square. Sean looked at the big man and pictured him with a beard and lumberjack clothes in the middle of the forest. He could pass for Paul Bunyan, the giant of American folk tales, and make a living as a lumberjack.

"Never seen snow?" The sergeant cooed.

"No, Sir!"

"Well, get used to it! Because you're going to live in it, breathe it, eat it, and even play with it!"

"Yes, Sir!" Johnson answered.

"You're from Florida, right?"

"Yes, Sir!"

The sergeant turned to the formation. "Sixty-five percent of you will quit. That means only one out of ten will make it." The sergeant turned back to Johnson. "Will you be my first one to go?"

"No, Sir!"

"Anyone else want to volunteer right now?"

"No, Sir!" They hollered.

"Any other of you ladies never seen snow before?"

"No, Sir!"

The sergeant nodded, but he had a peculiar grin on his face. He was going to have fun with Johnson. He loved taking these young men, who sometimes had never ventured any farther than their state or even county, and turn them into smooth military machines who could get themselves out of difficult situations, and survive the most challenging conditions. His greatest reward was when they came back alive because of what he was able to teach them. It gave him an immense sense of accomplishment and pride. He looked at the men in front of him. They each wore an eighty pound rucksack.

"Can any of you ski or snowboard?" The sergeant asked.

Nico and Sean and several others raised their hands. They knew that volunteering in the military almost always had its consequences, but this was more of an answer to a question.

Sergeant Smith, and of course the men questioned if that was his real name, stood in front of one of the men who raised his hand. "Where did you learn?"

"Utah, Sir, I'm from Salt Lake City."

The sergeant nodded. He continued to the next man. "How about you?"

"New England, Sir, I'm from Boston."

"Bahston?"

"Yes, Sir."

Sergeant Smith knew he was going to have fun with this bunch. "And you?" He asked Nico.

Nico was certainly not going to tell the sergeant that he learned in St. Moritz, in the Swiss Alps. "I'm from New Mexico, Sir."

Smith nodded again, continued and stopped in front of Sean. He looked at his name. "Sandoval? You ski too?"

"Yes, Sir."

The sergeant nodded and continued down the line. When he finished with his questions he looked at his newbies. He knew a percentage would not make it through the training, but he would do his best to keep as many as possible in the program. It they did that meant that if the occasion ever presented itself they could survive or help someone else. It never was an easy task. He looked at each of the individuals in front of him. He didn't care if they knew how to start a fire in the wilderness, what he did care about was the will to not give up, and not let the stress get to them. No one could teach them to have that kind of drive. Everything else, though difficult and demanding, the candidates could learn. Humans could live forty days without food, seven days without water, three minutes without air, but not a second without hope. This is where these men would find out if they had the heart and perseverance of a warrior.

Fresh snow started falling.

"Johnson? Get over here," The sergeant bellowed.

"Yes, Sir." The big man tried running but fell. He got to his feet and hurried over to the instructor.

"Open your mouth."

"Sir?"

"Are you hard of hearing?" The sergeant yelled.

"No, Sir."

"Well then open your fucking mouth and stick your tongue out."

Johnson did as he asked. Snowflakes gently landed on his tongue. His eyes slightly grew at the new sensation.

"When you're thirsty you don't wait for things to melt, understood?"

"Yes, Sir!" They answered.

Nothing seemed to intimidate the big man. Once he had been shown what to do with skis he put his heart into it. He wanted to excel and be as good as Sean and Nico and the others that seemed to have been skiing since they could walk. Johnson could tolerate an incredible amount of pain. Every time he fell his peers would cringe as he would go down hard.

"The bigger they are the harder they fall," the sergeant said.

It didn't bother Ted. He just got up and tried again and again. In the beginning he couldn't seem to master a turn to the left and all the trees that had the bad fortune to live on the right side of the slope were mowed down or crushed by the abominable snowman named Johnson.

"Hey, Johnson, what did that poor tree ever do to you?" One of the men hollered.

He didn't pay any attention, he didn't mind. They were just having fun and besides, he wasn't the only one falling all over the place. He looked around and saw that the novices looked like rigid spiders. Ted was sure that they would all get the hang of it. It was just another sport and they were athletic and in shape. After the tough training they had endured learning to ski was like a vacation.

What the others didn't know was that Johnson was

enjoying himself and had fallen in love with snow. He like everything about it. He could play with it—yes, someone had started a snowball fight and Ted excelled at the new sport and was victorious. He also liked that when he was thirsty he could just put some in his mouth and it would melt. It was better than ice. He found it fascinating when the sergeant showed them how to make snow shoes so they wouldn't sink and could better walk on the white mass. He also liked that when the snowflakes fell and covered the ground it absorbed sound. To Johnson it made the world a different place, and when he really looked at the snowflakes he marveled at their structure and realized that no two were alike. Of course it was also wet and it could make the atmosphere cold, but Johnson was getting used to that too. By the end of the day the novice skiers were sliding down the slopes. A few more days and they would be as good as their teammates. The big man was looking forward to another day of skiing.

CHAPTER 21

Sean, Nico and Ted Johnson sat around the campfire they built in the heart of the forest. They sat on logs and stretched their hands out over the flames to warm them up.

"So why did you join?" Nico asked the big man.

"My parents died when I was really young, some truck driver ran a stop sign and crushed their car. They didn't come out alive."

"Wow, sorry man," Sean said.

"I didn't really know them and my aunt and uncle raised me. To me they're my real parents. Anyway, they won a trip to New York for a week. You know, everything included, hotels, shows, food and so on. It was the first time they traveled out of Florida. They were really excited. They called me from every place they went. On one of those calls they told me they were eating at a restaurant in a high rise with the most amazing view of the city."

Sean could feel a stone forming in the pit of his stomach. He didn't interrupt the man.

Johnson continued: "We laughed because I was at a donut shop myself and I told them that my view was of the gas pumps… and then the line went dead." The big man's blue eyes turned several shades darker. "I watched them die," he said solemnly.

"What do you mean?" Nico asked.

"There was a TV in the donut shop. I saw the towers

crumble. That's where they were, at the top, eating at the restaurant in one of the towers."

"Fucking 9/11," Sean said. "Shit, really sorry, man."

"Yeah."

Ted Johnson took the first flight up to New York. He knew he would never find his aunt and uncle, but he also knew that he had to help. And that's what he did. He spent three weeks with any group or organization that went into the rubble, at first looking for survivors, then just trying to find remnants of what once were human beings. He wanted to help families find closure. It was his way of helping others and of fighting his own demons and the fury toward the monsters who had destroyed so many lives, whether they had died in the buildings or were family members. He also realized that he loved what he was doing. When one of the firemen Johnson had been working with noticed the enthusiasm in the big man he immediately understood the passion in his heart. He suggest the Air Force PJs. Standing in the debris and ash at Ground Zero Ted Johnson's light slowly brightened. He had found his calling.

CHAPTER 22

The SERE training that Sean, Nico and Ted, among other military specialists, included procedural instruction of equipment and techniques that would help them to survive and return home, regardless of unfriendly environments or harsh climatic conditions. They were training to become experts in methods to survive the dangers of not only natural habitats such as jungles, deserts, oceans and arctic arenas, but also human threats and capture.

One of these escape exercises was in the water, in a rigid inflatable boat. Half a dozen men sat immobile above the water. They were far enough from the coast that they couldn't see any lights from the shore. The black sky and ocean were so dark they melted into each other. They were completely immobile, except for a gentle rocking back and forth, just enough to make the men queasy. Nico could feel the bile starting to make its way up to his throat.

"Oh, shit!" Nico whispered.

"What?" Sean asked.

"I'm getting sick to my stomach."

"Now?"

"Don't you think this would be the perfect moment?" Nico asked sarcastically.

"Take some deep breaths and throw some water on your face," the instructor whispered. Although most of the people taking the course had strong stomachs, every once in a while even the best seafarer could get sea sick.

Nico followed the instruction, but suddenly he lost the contents of his stomach to the sea. He felt better, but was mortified.

"Feeling better, Kats?" Sean asked.

"Yeah, but totally fucking embarrassed," he whispered.

"Ah, happens to the best of us."

"Not me, I've got all this Greek blood, remember?"

"And that means what?" Sean asked.

"There's water in that blood. Greece is surrounded by the sea with more than two thousand islands, for Christ's sake. Greeks don't get sea sick."

"Kats, you are so full of shit, man," Sean said, trying hard not to burst out laughing.

"You say a word of this to anyone…"

"I promise, I won't tell a soul," Sean whispered and crossed his heart.

All the men in the dinghy were dying to laugh, but had to keep silent. Sergeant Smith nodded to Johnson and the big man grabbed Nico from behind and pulled him overboard. He held him by his neck under the water. After a few seconds the big man pulled him back into the boat with one hand.

"What the fuck?" Nico spattered, aggravated.

"Guess what, Kats," Sergeant Smith asked.

"What, Sir?"

"You'll never be sea sick again, a little cold maybe, but your stomach will always stay down."

Nico realized that the instructor was right. He was no longer feeling sick to his stomach, and he was most definitely freezing his ass off. As he trembled on the side of the boat he smiled at the men who were grinning back at him.

The sergeant looked at his candidates. He liked this group. They were good guys—tough, dedicated, great athletes and they had that special drive. They also had a sense of humor and that was a great asset in difficult situations. If a prisoner could think of a joke while in captivity, and put a smile on his own face, he could find the strength to survive another day and more.

The men stood at attention in the woods in front of Sergeant Smith. They were worried. The trainer had a sly grin on his face. To the candidates that was not a good sign. And they were right. The instructor had a sense of humor that he directed toward the trainees.

"Men, today is going to be a fun day."

That was definitely not a good sign. "Yes, Sir!" They answered bravely.

"We are going to learn how to survive in the wilderness from what the earth has to offer."

The men's hearts sank. Sean smiled as he thought that this would probably be Nico's biggest challenge.

"You will not die from starvation, ever! Is that clear?"

"Yes, Sir!"

Smith pointed toward the ground. "Do you see this rotten log?"

"Yes, Sir!"

Sean cringed. Shit. Bugs. He didn't like them at all. They tasted like dirt.

"When a tree has become rotten the main reason is that it has been attacked by insects such as earth worms, wood grubs, mealworms, termites, and my personal favorite weavels.

Sean grimaced and looked at the men. They had turned pale. Nico was the worst of them. Sean felt bad for him, but he knew that since he had come this far he wouldn't give up because of little bugs.

The sergeant continued: "When you're in survival mode you need protein and fat. Insects will give you enough protein to keep you living. Don't think too much about what you're putting in your mouth. Just eat it. And don't just swallow, chew it. They are also great for bait, to catch fish. So first you find them."

The instructor went to the most rotten part of the log and broke off pieces that had several holes in them.

"The more holes you see the better your chances at

finding the critters. Aw, look," he said lovingly, "there's some cuties now." He pulled out an earth worm. "Okay, so this guy isn't the best tasting. He actually tastes like dirt. Probably the reason they call them earth worms." He laughed. The candidates didn't particular share his sense of humor. The sergeant held out the worm for them to see and then placed it in his mouth. Half of it was still sticking out over his lips and wiggling back and forth.

Sean thought Nico was going to pass out.

"Remember, make sure you chew it," he mumbled, as he bit down on the squirming worm. The men could hear the crunch. "Ah, not bad. Okay, your turn. Find yourselves some grub."

The trainees did, albeit reluctantly, as they knew the critter would eventually wind up in their mouths.

"Kats, try to find mealworms, they don't taste like much."

"I don't even know what the fuck that is."

"Chickens love them."

Nico stared at his friend. Sean read Nico's face without too much trouble: *I'm from the city. Do I look like a fucking farm boy?*

Sean handed a mealworm to Nico. "This is what it looks like. Now show the Sarge."

"Lovely," Nico grumbled. "Uh, Sergeant, I found one."

"One what?" The instructor asked.

"A worm, Sir."

The sergeant looked at it. "You've got a mealworm there. Excellent. Your first try?"

"Yes, Sir."

"Very good. Now go ahead and enjoy."

"Yes, Sir." *Oh, fuck, here goes nothing.* Nico put it in his mouth and started chewing. His mind kept repeating: *It's a delicious really small baby octopus tentacle from the beautiful clear water of the Aegean. The fucking cook should be fired. It's a baby octopus tentacle from the Aegean. The son of a bitch should be fired.*

"Well?" The sergeant asked.

"Needs some lemon, Sir," Nico said, swallowing the last morsel as fast as he could.

They all laughed, and the instructor did as well. It was an answer he hadn't yet heard.

Throughout the day the men discovered where to find insects, earth worms, mealworms, slugs and more 'natural' items—berries, wild grapes, maple seeds and acorns. They also learned how to build snares from vines and trapped several small animals which they cooked and ate. The worse item on the menu had been the weavel. It not only tasted foul it looked like a cockroach.

After several weeks Sean, Nico, Ted and the rest of the candidates proudly received their survival training badges. Sean looked at the SERE logo. He thought it was beautiful, as it depicted a gallant eagle positioned behind barbed wire. Sean was sure the raptor was one of his power animals as he had been captivated by the giant birds since he was a child. As with all badges there was an inscription. This one read 'Return With Honor'. Sean hoped he would never find himself in a position where he would have to survive or escape from, but if he did he truly would do his best to live up to the motto.

CHAPTER 23

Sean and Nico were excited as they flew toward Kirtland AFB in their hometown of Albuquerque for the Pararescue EMT Paramedic training. It would be the longest at twenty-four weeks.

As soon as they landed they left the base and headed to their respective families. When Fiona saw her handsome son in his uniform she fell into his open arms.

"Oh, Sean, you look so good! How are you?"

"Really good, Mam, and so happy to see you!" He lifted her up and swung her around.

"She's right, Nílchi Deesdoi, and even though you've lost a few pounds it suits you, you look real sharp. I'm very proud of you," Tibah said.

"Thanks Dad, I'm proud too. I'm really glad I chose the PJs. And right now the best part is that I'm going to be here in town for several months."

"That is so wonderful," Fiona said.

"Yeah, Mam." Sean looked at his parents. "Do you know what I want to do right now?"

"What?" His parents answered in unison.

"New Mexican food!"

"Christmas?" Fiona asked, remembering the first time Tibah had mentioned the dual salsas.

"Absolutely!"

"Let's go!" Tibah said, leading the way toward the pickup truck.

The Sandovals went to their favorite restaurant. When Sean had eaten enough for at least two people Tibah asked him about his training. The couple listened, fascinated, at what the young man had accomplished. Their pride glowed in their hearts and on their faces, and Sean was happy. It gave him an amazing sense of accomplishment, and was thrilled that he could please his parents.

"So why is this next training so much longer than the others?" Tibah asked.

"We're doing the EMT Paramedic training and then the Pararescue recovery specialist course."

"So more in the medical areas," Fiona said, remembering the little boy who had pieced back the rabbit so many years ago. She had been right, medicine was in his blood.

"Exactly. This course is about how to manage trauma patients prior to evacuation and provide emergency medical treatment. There are two phases. The first one is four weeks of EMT training. Phase two lasts twenty weeks and provides instruction in minor field surgery, pharmacology, combat trauma management, advanced airway management and military evacuation procedures. Once we've accomplished that we go to Tucson and work with fire departments, paramedics, and local hospitals. And then we get our EMT certification." Sean's parents were thrilled that their son would be at the Air Force base for several months.

"I'm really proud of you *a stor*," Fiona said, holding back tears.

"And I'm impressed, Nílchi Deesdoi," Tibah added.

"Thanks. Oh! Here they are, sopapillas!" Sean exclaimed, delighted at seeing the waitress bringing them a large tray with his favorite desert.

"Ah, yes," Fiona grinned, "the little cushions." She had lovingly called them that ever since Tibah introduced them to her, and continued it when her son was a little boy. It was a family favorite.

"I invited Kats over to the house to meet…"

"Cats, as in kitties?"

Sean laughed. "No, Nicolaos Katsopoulos, Kats for short, and he's no pussy cat. He's been a great friend since the first day of training in Texas."

"We'll be very happy to meet him, Sean," Fiona said.

"Absolutely. Any friend who's been through what the two of you have is like family to us too," Tibah added.

"Thanks, I'm sure you'll like him."

Sean introduced his best friend to his parents and they did immediately like each other. They talked about their training, Sophia, Nico's fiancée, and their future dreams. It was a quiet, relaxing evening they all enjoyed.

"Thank you for a lovely evening. It was a pleasure meeting both of you," Nico said, as he was leaving.

"Thank you for coming and for being such a good friend of Sean's," Fiona said. She hugged Nico goodbye and Tibah shook the young man's hand.

"You come back and see us anytime you want, and do bring your fiancée," the older man said.

"I will. Thanks again."

Sean accompanied Nico to his car and whistled when he saw the striking metallic beige Porsche. "Where did you steal this from, Kats?"

"Gift from my parents."

"Oh. Guess that means they might be rich."

"Filthy."

"That's nice. By the way, how come you didn't tell me about it?"

"I was going to, Sandoval, really I was, but I didn't know how."

"Uh, I'm rich. See, simple as that. Come on, Kats, this is me," Sean said. He was a little hurt.

"I'm really sorry, Sandoval, but it's something I try not to advertise. People see you differently and all I want is to be one of the guys."

"Well, you're definitely that, and I'm proud to be your friend. As far as being different because you're rich I personally don't give a damn. I know the real Kats and that's all that counts."

"Thanks, man, I appreciate it."

"Although I might have to borrow that pile of scrap metal

you call a car sometime."

"Anytime, my friend."

"Oh, and I figured out why you joined the Pedros."

"Do tell."

"You wanted a fast-paced lifestyle, without the prestige of course, combined with a profession that didn't pay too much."

"You did finally figure me out," Nico laughed. "Well, I should get going. I really enjoyed your parents."

"Yeah, they're cool."

"It's going to be good being around our families for a while."

"I agree. Home cooking, Land of Enchantment and close to the ones we care about, and all while doing what we love."

"And I just love your Mom's Irish accent, *and* she's drop dead gorgeous. Now I know where you get it from."

"Are you saying that I'm pretty?"

"Yeah, asshole, you're pretty," Nico said as he pinched Sean's cheek.

"Aw, Sophia will be jealous."

The two men teased each other and laughed, the laugh of youth with a lifetime in front of them, a life of hope, love and adventure.

CHAPTER 24

Nico left the Sandovals in his Porsche and thought about how happy he was at this moment in his life. He was in the military and damn proud of it, especially the elite team he was a part of. It was physically grueling and mentally challenging, and he thrived on it. When he was a teenager he had no idea what hard work meant, either as a job or how much a body could be pushed. He laughed out loud as he thought of why and how he joined the Air Force. It was, however, the best thing he had ever done in his life, and firmly believed that everything happened for a reason.

At the tender age of eighteen Nico found himself staring at the front of the Air Force recruiting office in a typical strip mall off of one of Albuquerque's main boulevards. Before opening the door his young life flashed before his eyes.

Nico's earliest memory was of playing in the back of his parents' home on a swing set, his mother lovingly pushing him as he flew through the air, squealing in delight. He was a happy child. His mother, a stay at home mom ever since his father had become wealthy, loved her house and taking care of her family. Her favorite pastime was cooking delicious meals. Many of the recipes had been hers, and now people across the land could taste them in any of their restaurants. Dimitri adored his son as well, and as modern in his ways as he was, he was still very traditionally Greek. From the day

Nico was born he already knew what would become of his offspring. The boy would inherit the chain of restaurants he had meticulously grown from one little mom and pop shop. He and his parents had started the small restaurant when they arrived from the old country when Dimitri was ten years old. They had worked hard and long hours, and the older man knew they could achieve the American dream. Dimitri went to college and returned with a business degree. Twenty-five years later the stores had multiplied into an empire that rivaled all the big restaurant chains. It had made Dimitris Katsopoulos a very wealthy man. Nico was to jump into his father's shoes and continue his dream, adding a wife and children. But, as in many cases, father and son did not have the same desires. Nico really didn't know what he wanted to do other than have fun, drive hot cars, play with even hotter girls and travel the world. Basically be a playboy, and live the good life. The older man knew this, had seen right through him, and gave him an ultimatum. Since Nico had finished high school he could go to any of the best business universities in the world, and Dimitri would have no problem whatsoever paying for it. The other choice was to work at one of the restaurants and learn about every position, starting at the bottom and making his way to the top.

Nico rebelled. He believed the restaurant business, well, business in general, was definitely not in his DNA. He tried to convince his father, but the old man wasn't buying it. He had no doubt that one day his son, and only child, would see it his way. The only thing he was pleased about is that Nico had found a young and beautiful Greek girl he had fallen in love with, and were engaged. On that front Nico had his family's blessing, but the friction between the two men was getting unbearable and causing problems in their home. It was also making Nico and Sophia's relationship stressful. On one occasion, when the four of them were having dinner, the two men were having such a disagreement that they were practically at each other's throats. Nico stormed out of the house. If he hadn't he knew he would have probably punched his old man. Even in his heated state he kept himself from hitting his father. He still respected him as his elder, but right at the moment he didn't even want to see him. His father was the most stubborn mule he had ever known.

Nico didn't return for three days. He of course kept Sophia informed and asked her to be patient with him. She understood and was very good at keeping the peace in the family. Nico wound up hanging out with some high school buddies, drinking too much, smoking pot and watching movies at a friend's house. One of the films was *Black Hawk Down*, the true story about a downed helicopter under heavy enemy fire in Mogadishu. The movie changed his life. He wanted to be Ty Burrell, not the actor, but the man he was portraying—PJ TSgt (at the time) Tim Wilkinson. The next morning, after a night of overindulgence, Nico found himself at the Air Force recruiting office and enlisted. As soon as he signed the paperwork he walked out of the office, spread his arms out to the world and closed his eyes. Nico stood in the parking lot, his face turned to the sky and smiled. He had never felt this good, ever. For the very first time in his young life he knew what he wanted to do, what he wanted to pursue. He would make something of himself, something he would be proud of. His *Babá*, however, was going to be mad as hell mad!

CHAPTER 25

At the Kirtland air base Sean and Nico had additional training in combat tactics, mountaineering, field medical care, and helicopter insertion and extraction. They were of the very few that had survived all the demanding preparations and trainings. They would be graduating right there at the base in Albuquerque. It had taken them about two years.

The respective families of the graduating young men came to watch their sons receive their maroon berets with the coveted Pararescue emblem in the front. The Sandovals and the Katsopoulos' were among the assembled parents and siblings and could not have been prouder. It had taken Dimitri a while to calm his wrath at what his son had done. Not only had he gone into the military, which of course wasn't bad and he respected immensely, but it wasn't the path he envisioned for his only child. The younger man would of course still be the heir to the fortune, and Dimitri shuddered at the thought of anything happening to his boy. He wouldn't let his mind go there, no, he would *never* let his mind dwell on negative and macabre thoughts. Dimitri adored Nico. He was proud of his son, no matter what he chose in his life. He would always have his back. That's what fathers did, even after disappointments. Seeing his son in uniform, receiving the coveted badge and beret for his achievement, made the older man's chest expand. Deep down the Greek warrior heritage glowed with pride.

The audience heard 'you may put on your berets'. This was the moment the PJs had struggled so hard for. This was it, this was their moment. After months of learning, of intense physical conditioning and training, of sweat, blood and even some tears, they had accomplished their mission. And they were damn proud of their accomplishment—and deservedly so. Every person in the room was just as proud, from their military superiors, their trainers and their families.

The young men donned their berets, stood at attention and together recited the Pararescue Jumper's creed. All present couldn't help but think how handsome and distinguished the PJs looked in their blue uniforms and their maroon covers.

The families and graduates listened attentively to an invited speaker, a local celebrity from the Albuquerque area, with ties to the community and a sponsor of many charities, especially military.

"I know of no braver individuals than the Air Force's elite Pararescuemen. Other special operations teams are very well known, such as the Navy SEALS, Rangers, Marine Reconnaissance, Delta Force and Green Berets. The PJs, the Pararescue Jumpers are just as amazing and belong in that elite group of warriors. They deserve to be just as well known. However, they have an additional asset, they are accredited EMTs, coveted field doctors. They are elite rescue specialists. In the worse terrain and weather conditions, on the sides of frozen mountains, in deserts that melt the soles of boots, or in a hurricane in the middle of an ocean they somehow rescue and mend fellow warriors or civilian citizens in any part of the world. And there are only about three hundred PJs. They are the elite few. They jump out of an aircraft at 30,000 feet, hang on a rope from a helicopter while being shot at, or salvage a pilot from a downed fighter plane in ten foot waves. They rescue wounded in wars, civilians from earthquakes and cyclones, and I'm sure they have probably saved falling kittens from trees." The speaker smiled at the new PJs and continued.

"Their fingers are delicate enough to insert needles and

perform minor surgeries, yet strong enough to handle weapons and to survive in the wild without any equipment. PJs disregard all personal safety to follow the motto they live by: 'so that others may live'. They put their own lives on the line in the most treacherous conditions, from minus fifty degree weather to a scorching over one hundred degrees in the most savage terrains around the world. As warriors they are fierce and incredibly well trained, but their main objective, their mission, is to rescue wounded and bring them back alive and home to their loved ones. They are the most qualified rescue medical teams in the world. There is no questions they love the job they do, although it is more than a job, it is a calling, a dedication to their fellow humans." The speaker continued. "Their reputation precedes them, and they are respected by the military as well as the civilian community. These new PJs will continue this legacy with honor, as they have already proven themselves by earning the angel badge. They are our guardian angels. When they are needed they will always be the first ones present."

The speaker turned to look at the audience. "One would think that with such a pedigree they would be quite the snobs, and who could blame them?" The listeners laughed. "But, no, on the contrary, these Pedros are amazingly selfless and true gentlemen. We salute you, brave and incomparable Pararescue Jumpers. Thank you for your dedication and for all you do. Congratulations to each and every one of you on this very special day, and on this well-deserved accomplishment. We are indebted to you."

The audience clapped profusely, agreeing with everything the speaker had said.

After the graduation ceremony the Sandovals and Katsopoulos' followed each other to Dimitri and Irini's home in an upscale Albuquerque neighborhood.

"Come on, let's go in. My mother has cooked a feast," Nico declared.

"Oooh, Greek food! I can hardly wait. I'm right behind you," Sean crooned.

Once in the house the women congregated in the kitchen

and Dimitri beckoned the younger men to his den.

"Gentlemen," the older man said handing each of them a snifter, "*Metaxa*, this is the brandy Alexander the Great drank, and Napoleon did not." He chuckled at his own joke.

"Thank you, Sir," Sean said and took a sip. "It's excellent."

"Of course it is, it's Greek," Nico said.

"So, tell me something boys, are you planning to make a career in the military?" He was addressing Sean more than Nico. He of course had plans for his own son.

"When I'm not in the military I'm a hot air balloon pilot. My dream is to someday own my own balloon and make a business out of it. I'll probably stay in the service for a while and get out after a few years."

"That's very impressive, Sean, and also a good plan. Personally, however, I prefer to keep my feet on the ground."

"I understand, Sir, it's not always for everyone, but I really love it."

"I can see that. And of course no better place for hot air balloons than Albuquerque."

"Absolutely. I grew up with the Balloon Fiesta, and I want to always be a part of it."

"It all sounds great. I wish you only the best in all your endeavors," Dimitri said.

"Thank you, Sir, that's very kind of you."

Sophia walked in. "Gentlemen, dinner is ready," she announced.

"Ah, perfect, come boys, let's eat."

They followed the older man to the dining room.

Irini truly prepared a feast. The table was covered with appetizers, each *meze* lovingly made by hand by Nico's mother and Sophia, his future wife.

The two women adored each other, a rather unusual event for mothers and daughters-in-law, but Irini understood the love her son had for the younger woman, and he was right. Sophia was a pretty girl, from a good family, and she had brains. Most of all she had a good heart and loved her son, and not for his money, but for his own heart. When

Sophia met Nico she didn't know he was the heir to the Katsopoulos fortune. She only saw the man. That he would one day be very wealthy didn't matter to her. What mattered was the quality their life would have, with money or without. What was important to Irini was that she make her Nicolaki, her little Nico, happy. They were a good couple, young, ambitious and caring. And she would be producing their grandchildren. Why shouldn't she like her? Irini would be the best mother-in-law any woman could wish for. In the two years Nico had been training Irini and Sophia had become as close as a mother and daughter.

Dimitri had also been paying attention to Sophia. He liked the choice Nico made, and she was a pretty thing, but the older man had detected something fascinating about his future daughter-in-law—she had a brain for business! She had graduated school at the same time Nico had. When he left for boot camp Dimitri took her to their restaurant in town. Sophia was amazed by the machinery in the kitchen and carefully watched how the people went about their work. When she asked what happened to the leftover food Dimitri told her that they threw it away. She immediately suggested food recovery programs. He hadn't heard of this. Sophia explained that restaurants donated the uneaten food, like fruits and vegetables, and also meals that were prepared but never consumed. These organizations made sure people in need received these items, and wouldn't go to waste. It meant more for the needy and less discarded food. Dimitri was impressed and wanted to know more. Sophia found all the information he needed. The two of them set the idea in motion. He was pleased. The restaurants across the country had less waste and helped the less fortunate enjoy good food at the same time. They became a good team. Dimitri started grooming his future daughter-in-law and sent her to business school while Nico was doing his military training. After a short two years Sophia had become his right hand. Dimitri was thrilled. He had found a way to keep the chain of restaurants thriving, and Sophia would play a large role in maintaining its legacy. The business would stay in the family, and would continue on to the next generation. At some point he realized that Nico was not the man for the job, his future wife was. Everyone was happy.

The families and invited friends sat at the long dining table. The waiters, who loved working extra time for Dimitri at his home whenever he had parties, served the appetizers. It was a Greek feast. There were platters of spinach and cheese folded in fillo, dolmades, shrimp, taramosalata, salads, stuffed peppers with feta cheese with oil and oregano, octopus, zucchini patties, small meatballs and different kinds of bread. The last hors d'oeuvre they brought out was several dishes of saganaki, flaming cheese in ouzo.

"Hey, Sandoval."

"What's up Kats?"

"Doesn't this remind you of the woods in Washington?" Nico asked mockingly.

"Totally. Now don't think about it and just eat your food," Sean said between mouthfuls, repeating the words he had spoken to Nico in the cold forest during their survival training. "Maybe your mom can accompany us the next time. Everything is just delicious."

"Now there's an idea. I'll have to ask her. Of course knowing her she'd jump at the idea of being with her little boy."

"I can see that. Mothers are the best."

"That they are."

The feast continued with the next course. Avgolemono soup, racks of lamb, moussaká, pastichio, stuffed eggplant, souvlaki of different meats, roasted lemon chicken with potatoes, a variety of fish and more salads.

Fiona, who had been sitting next to Irini, begged her to explain all the food she had prepared. The Greek woman was more than happy to. They became good friends and saw each other often when their sons were away. They would swap recipes or make the dishes. Irini was amazed by Fiona's knowledge of international cuisines, and the women had fun cooking together and for each other, and their husbands were thrilled. The two couples visited quite often.

"Anyone ready for dessert?" Irini asked her guests.

A collective groan rose from the table. They were completely full, but if the desserts were any indication from the divine food they had just eaten they would certainly find a way to enjoy some of that too. Irini did not disappoint as the waiters brought out the last course: Platters of baklava, loukoumades, galaktoboureko, kataïfi, semolina halvah, different varieties of ice cream, and last but not least, Greek coffee, cookies and chocolates.

All present who attended the graduation would remember the ceremony with pride, and the grand meal as well.

CHAPTER 26

Tibah looked at his son relaxing on the couch in their living room. Fiona was in the kitchen preparing one of the international dishes she had learned from working at the Mediterranean restaurant in Dublin. She loved to cook, especially for the men in her family. They in turn were thrilled to be her 'guinea pigs' as she truly would turn out delicious, creative dishes. It was her favorite hobby, and she continuously tried new recipes from around the world. They also knew what to get her for Christmas and her birthdays—cook books, the more exotic the better—and Fiona squealed in delight every time.

"Sean?"

"Yes, Dad," he said looking up from a book he was reading.

"You're leaving us in a couple of days, right?"

"That's right, five week training."

"I think it's time we did a sweat."

"Why not?"

"Tomorrow," Tibah said.

"Sounds like a plan."

Tibah had built a sweat lodge a couple of miles from the house on the highest spot of his land. It overlooked the mesa, and in the distance Mount Taylor majestically stood in the middle of the desert. Every once in a while when he felt his energy draining or just needed time to think, he would go for a sweat. Tibah built the lodge right after his family died and used it quite often. It helped him through the dark and difficult times. He would drift into a place of blankness and peace, where his mind would float soothingly in a tranquil space.

The skeleton of the hut, which Tibah built in a round formation, was made of small juniper trees, branches and boughs. The structure was sealed with mud and cedar bark and there was an opening in the top for the smoke. There was a large hole right below in the center of the lodge that would hold the embers and hot stones. He also left an opening to go in and out, framed it with wood and built a door. Although it was a bit of a modern touch he figured it was easier than throwing a blanket over the opening and the purpose was the same.

Sean and Tibah rode Nizhóní and Nízhánee, now older but still in great shape, to the sweat lodge. On the way they stopped to cut sage and pick up branches. It was just before sunset and the Sandoval men soaked in the magnificent crimson and peach-colored sky. When they arrived at the lodge they tied up the horses and built a fire. When the flames were at their zenith Tibah took out a round drum, one he made himself. It was exquisite, a piece of art he had worked on right after the deaths of his siblings and parents. He had steamed a wood ply hoop and bent it by hand, then stretched a meticulously scraped rawhide skin for the drum head. He also used the hide for the lacing, making a traditional pattern of the four directions of the earth—north, south, east and west, which formed a handhold in the back. It had taken him several days to make, and for the last twenty years Tibah always used it for the sacred sweat lodge ceremonies.

"Spirits of the North, Spirits of the South, Spirits of the East, Spirits of the West," Tibah invoked, each time he turned in the direction of the cardinal points. He made an offering of tobacco to the Creator, to the Grandfathers and

Grandmothers, as he held hands with his son above the fire they had built. He prayed for protection, for peace, for healing, for wisdom. Tibah then picked up a shell made of mother of pearl that contained burning sage. The men could smell its sweet aroma and Tibah brought the container above Sean's head. With an eagle feather he fanned the smoke all around the younger man and started chanting. Sean in turn smudged his father and then both men continued the ceremony around the fire with drumming, singing and dancing to the beat of the drum which guided them toward a trance-like state.

As the fire turned to embers Tibah transferred the hot coal to the fire pit in the lodge with a shovel. He also took the glowing stones and placed them one by one on top of the embers. The first stone he placed facing west, the next one north, then east and south, and in the center a few more for all people. Sean watched as his father performed the ritual his tribe had done for so many centuries. He would retain the customs and traditions of the Navajo to the best of his ability. The younger man fed the outdoor flames with more wood. The Sandovals sat around the fire until the sweat lodge was hot and steamy. Their eyes watched the flames until it was time.

"I brought you something, Sean."

"What is it, Dad?"

"It's an American flag that has been in my family for almost a hundred years. I want to explain."

"Please do," Sean said, intrigued.

Tibah pointed at the faded, soft material he held. "The red is for the Indians. The white is for the conquerors. The stars (which counted forty-eight) are for all the fallen. We are now one nation, we must live side by side. We must unite all the races of the world and make Mother Earth and her people a Sacred, Infinite Hoop. Each day we love each other more, that is the best we can do. You have both in your blood, Nílchi Deesdoi, the red and the white. Be proud of yourself, of who you are, as we are of you, for you portray the best of both worlds." Tibah handed him the flag. "This is now yours, and to be handed down to your own children and grandchildren. Do not forget our ways, and teach the next generations as our ancestors have done in the past."

"Yes, Father, I will not forget."

"Come, it is time."

Sean put the flag in his saddlebag and both men went into the lodge. They sat on the earth with their bare backs against the body of the hut.

Tibah dipped a cup into a bucket of water, poured it over the hot stones and called forth the Spirit Guides from the four directions. The steam whistled and undulated in the red glow of the lodge. Tibah put some cedar leaves and sage over the embers. It smelled sweet and Tibah explained that it had medicinal properties. The smoke filled his nostrils. His sinus passages opened and his lungs expanded. The two men started to perspire after only a few minutes. In just a short time Sean was sure that every ounce of liquid was coming out of his body. Tibah seemed to read the younger man's mind.

"When you bathe you are cleaning the outside of your skin. When you do a sweat you are cleansing the inside of your body, both physically and spiritually."

"I understand."

"Sky Father, cleanse our spirit, guide us on our paths, send forth your love and mercy, protect us from evil and from small-minded enemies of peace," Tibah prayed.

Tibah recited the first verse of the Navajo sweat lodge song. Throughout the night they would go in and out several times. After each time they reentered he would sing another verse. He repeated the ritual until the entire song had been sung.

Sean's meditation began with his young life. He watched himself grow and saw all the momentous events, from Jack and Ryan's landing to his military endeavors. The last thing he saw in his mind's eye was of himself becoming an eagle. Sean never realized how many hours had passed.

Tibah and Sean spent the entire night in the lodge. Every once in while they would come out, let the cool air hit them. They covered their wet bodies with sand and let it dry with the air. Before going back in they would rub it off. Tibah remembered a time when Fiona had joined him and remarked at what a fantastic exfoliation this was, as her skin had become silky smooth. At some point during the night Sean came out coughing and firmly believed the tears from his eyes were gushing the very last of the liquid left in his body. His lungs and body were releasing the toxins and negativity.

"A sweat lodge is like the womb of a mother," Tibah said. "It is dark and hot, and when you come out you cough and cry. What we are recreating is a rebirth, a spiritual rebirth."

"Makes a lot of sense," Sean said.

The last time they came out they splashed themselves with cold water. Sean thought that everything about that night was absolutely thrilling, not to mention amazingly cleansing. When he looked out from the highest point and saw the sun making its first appearance of the day over the incredible beauty of the mesa he swore the land was whispering to him.

CHAPTER 27

Sean and Nico said goodbye to their families and went on to Fort Bragg in North Carolina to the Free Fall Parachutist School. Sean was of course excited as he knew he would gain more control of his 'flying'.

The training consisted of instruction focusing on stability, aerial maneuvers and parachute opening procedures. They started out with wind tunnel training. Sean thought life couldn't get any better as he floated and bopped up and down above the powerful air lifting him. He learned quickly, and was master of his body and movements. He knew he would have no problems with the free fall jumps.

The course lasted about five weeks. During that time Sean and Nico excelled and made over thirty free falls, including night jumps and specialized jumps with additional oxygen and heavy equipment.

Sean was once again in his element. He was becoming more of an expert with each jump. When he was free falling he could have sworn the wind was singing to him.

Although the PJs went through arduous training sessions they loved what they were doing, firmly believed they would make a difference, and hopefully save lives.

Sean and Nico added the Free Fall Parachutist Badge to their uniform, but when they went out to celebrate at the end of their training they put on civilian clothes.

They walked into Sammy's, a bar within walking distance of the base that was the preferred hangout of the military in the area. They were looking for what all young men looked for—girls and a good time. Sean never had a problem with women, his good looks and Irish charm always facilitated his task. They sat down at the bar and ordered a couple of beers.

Sean looked around. His buddies were reaching out to some pretties who looked alone.

Having just finished his drink Nico asked Sean if he wanted another.

"Sure."

Nico waved to the bartender who brought them another round. "Here you go."

"Thanks. Uh, Kats, I have a question for you."

"What?"

"It's a little personal."

"Go ahead. If I don't want to answer I won't."

"Fair enough. You're in love with Sophia, she's beautiful, has a heart of gold and the two of you seem perfect together. So why are we looking for girls? I mean I know why I am, but what about you?"

"Ah, Sean, I do love Sophia and once we're married I will be faithful and try to be the best husband in the world. But right now I'm still young, in my prime and in the military, which is a world of its own. Whatever happens with another woman won't mean a thing. And 'little Nico' is Greek, and just loves to dance."

Sean roared. "You're too much, Kats, but I get it."

"It'll be our little secret," Nico whispered slyly.

"And safe with me." Sean lifted his glass. "Cheers."

"*Yássou, fíle!* Cheers, my friend!" Nico said, as he brought his glass to Sean's.

On a small stage at the end of the room a woman was sitting on a stool, tuning a guitar and getting ready for her performance. She was a solo show and the entertainment for the evening. When she was happy with the way the instrument sounded she nodded to one of the employees and a solitary spot beamed down on Angela Moreno. She lightly strummed the chords. Some people turned to the stage, others didn't notice. Sean did. Angela was an accomplished guitarist. As the music tantalized Sean's senses an inner peace he hadn't felt since the sweat lodge enveloped him. And then he really saw what Angela looked like. The woman on stage took his breath away and reminded him a little of Jennifer Lopez. Every sense in his body was heightened and every muscle was at attention. He had never had such a reaction to any woman before.

Sean nudged Nico in the ribs. "I think I just understood what you were talking about," he whispered.

"What do you mean?"

"About being in love."

Nico followed Sean's eyes. They were staring at Angela. "Ah, the beautiful singer," he chuckled. "Yes, my friend, you and every guy in here."

"No, man, I'm serious."

"Uh, huh."

"Do you know her name?"

"I heard somebody say 'Angela'. I think she's Hispanic and pronounces it *Anhela*."

Sean felt his chest constrict—in Navajo *Ajei* was the word for heart and used as a girl's name. The sounds were similar. This was a sign, he was sure of it.

And then Angela started to sing. Her voice was mesmerizing and Sean was not prepared for the sounds emanating from the woman's mouth. Each syllable was crisp and clear, and seemed to flow through warm honey before coming out of her lips. It was the most sensual voice he ever heard, and knew she was a silk glove slowly enveloping his heart.

"Oh, man, she's magnificent!" Sean exclaimed quietly.

"She sure can sing."

No, there was more to her than that. He just knew it. He continued to listen while Nico went over to a group of women. A little while later he came back to Sean.

"Hey, Sandoval."

"What's up?"

"If you don't mind I'm going to leave," Nico said with a glow in his eyes.

Sean looked at his buddy, saw the grin on his face and returned it. "Which one, Kats?" He simply asked.

"The blonde."

"Good choice. See you in the morning?"

"Uh huh."

"Bye, bye, little Nico, or should I say hello?"

Nico playfully smacked his friend on the back and took off.

Sean watched Angela. He couldn't get enough of her—of her singing or her beauty. He stayed late into the night until she finished the last song of her performance. The bar had pretty much emptied, but Sean waited. He had to talk to her. The singer came off the stage and headed for the bar. She sat on a stool not too far from Sean and asked the bartender for a soda.

"Ms. Angela?" Sean asked, pronouncing it the Spanish way.

"Yes?"

"My name is Sean Sandoval and I would just like to compliment you on a wonderful performance. You are very talented."

"Thanks, that's very kind of you."

"I really mean it."

"Yes, thank you again."

"I like to think of myself as a kind of musician."

"I'm not sure I know what a 'kind of musician' is."

"I whisper in the wind."

"You whistle."

"Not exactly."

"You play a wind instrument? Sax, clarinet. No, I think maybe the flute."

"None of the above. Come on, try to guess."

Angela was enjoying herself. Sean was not the usual military guy that came in for just the one reason, and to get drunk. He genuinely seemed to be interested in her as a person, and she liked that he was a musician. Just what kind of instrument did he play?

"Alright, but help me out a little, I need a clue."

"I make rhythm with fire."

"You play the drums, and your hands move so fast they turn to fire," she laughed.

Sean laughed as well. "That's a good try, but no, I only turn a knob."

Angela continued to play along. "A knob, hm, let's see, a guitar."

"A guitar?"

"Well, the knobs I was thinking about are actually the tuning pegs."

"Nope."

"Ah, I know," Angela said triumphantly.

"You do?"

"You're a DJ, you play the knobs on your mixing console, and you have a light show that makes things look like they're on fire."

"You are a very smart lady!" Sean exclaimed.

"I figured it out?"

"No."

"What? Oh, I give up."

"I'm a hot air balloon pilot."

"What?" She repeated. "Now, I'm totally confused. What does that have to do with music? Please explain."

"Piloting a balloon is similar to being a musician. You have to find the rhythm, and I find it with the fire."

"I'm still not sure what you mean, but it seems interesting, go on."

"Hot air balloons are basically at the mercy of the winds, so you have to keep adjusting the fire that goes into the envelope, and that's the rhythm. When you get it just right it's a perfect flight, like a finely tuned instrument that plays smooth and sweet."

"As a musician that is fascinating, and makes me want to go hot air ballooning. You make it sound like there's music, or a song in the sky."

"That exactly how I feel when I'm there!" Sean exclaimed, amazed that this beautiful creature sitting next to him managed to describe exactly how he felt about the air.

"Being suspended above the earth and in the sky makes me think of what a magnificent eagle with a 360 degree view gets to see every day. But the funny thing is when you're piloting a balloon and the burner isn't firing there is absolutely no sound whatsoever."

"That's amazing. There is always some sort of sound, whether you're sitting in your car or in a chair in your house you can always hear something, like a bus outside or people talking, or even a fly buzzing around."

"You're right, but when I'm up there, even though there are no sounds, it is a symphony in my heart. At least that's how I perceive it."

Angela liked this man. He wasn't like all the others, and she loved that he was enamored with his passion about the air, especially the way he described it with all the 'music'. His heart spoke, she knew that. She also wondered how much he liked 'real' music. Did he know about his namesake, Arturo Sandoval, the great Cuban Latin Jazz musician and composer? "That sounds really fascinating, Sean. On the other hand if that's a pick up line it's pretty damn unique, and the best one I've ever heard," she giggled.

Sean laughed. He loved the way she giggled and laughed. It was whimsical, even sensual. "It wasn't meant to be a pick up line, but I do find everything about you really lovely, and I would love to spend some time with you. Even just as a friend." Sean smiled, trying to mask his faux pas. Had he gone too far? And had she picked up on his slip? "As far as ballooning, it would be my pleasure to take you up for a ride," he added quickly.

"Are you full of hot air, Sean Sandoval?"

"I am hot air."

CHAPTER 28

Sean went back to Sammy's the next night and just as the previous evening waited until Angela finished. He really liked her, or was it more? Whatever it was Sean was a really happy guy around her, and wanted to spend as much time as possible with the stunning woman.

As in the night before they sat at the bar and talked. Angela explained that her parents had been killed in the big 1985 Mexico City earthquake. She was only three at the time (Sean quickly calculated that he was two years older) and came to live with her only other relative, her aunt, who lived just outside of Fayetteville. Sadly she passed away a couple of years back.

"I'm really sorry, Angela, that is always very difficult."

"Yes, I know. Anyway, I should be leaving, it's getting late."

"May I walk you home?"

Angela laughed. "Oh, you are a gentlemen, Sean Sandoval. If I lived close by I would be delighted, but if we walked it would take us several hours."

I'm game. "Are you here tomorrow night?"

"I am."

"May I come see you again?"

Angela looked at him. She liked the guy. He was different and interesting, and he had manners. As a bonus he was gorgeous. "Sure."

"Great, I'll see you then."

"Are you going to Fort Bragg?"

"I am."

"How about I give *you* a ride, I'm the one with the car."

Sean was sure his heart was bursting out of his shirt. "I would very much appreciate that," he said as calmly as possible.

It didn't take long to reach the base. Angela stopped the car and waited for Sean to get out. He turned to her and caressed her face with his eyes. He decided he was going to be a gentleman all the way. "May I kiss you?" He asked.

Angela had somehow felt those caresses and shuddered. When he asked she didn't refuse. He kissed her delicately and confirmed to himself how he imagined her lips would be soft and sweet as nectar. When she responded he kissed her passionately. The woman didn't resist and responded back. Sean knew that if he wanted more he could have all of her, instead he put his hand on the door handle and pulled it open. "I'll see you tomorrow, thanks again for the ride."

"You're welcome," she said and waved as she drove off. Oh, she wanted to taste his delicious lips again, and so much more.

Sean waited until the car disappeared and then yelled at the top of his lungs as he jumped in the air and clicked his heels. The guard in the shack at the gate, who had seen the display, gave Sean a big smile as he checked his credentials. Neither man said a word. Sean left the sentinel and headed toward the barracks. As the guard followed the happy man with his eyes he couldn't help but laugh as he watched Sean do what he thought was an Irish jig. Or were they merengue steps?

CHAPTER 29

Sean and Nico's training at Fort Bragg came to an end. They were free for the next ten days before reporting for duty. Nico went back to Albuquerque to see Sophia and his family, Sean stayed on. He wanted to spend more time with Angela.

Sean walked into Sammy's, but didn't see Angela on stage. Where was she? he wondered. He sat at the bar, willing the beautiful woman to appear.

"What'll it be?" The bartender asked.

"Beer."

"You got it."

"Hey, where's Angela tonight?"

"Not sure."

She stood behind him a few minutes later.

"Hey, Sean."

"Hey yourself. How are you?"

"I'm good."

"Not singing?"

"I told the owner that I had some sort of stomach bug and that I wasn't feeling very well."

"Something you ate?"

"Yeah, hooky."

"No!" Sean exclaimed in mock horror.

"Uh huh. Want to go?" She asked.

"Uh huh," he answered back.

They jumped in her car and took off. Sean was thrilled and was sure she had done that for him. "This means we can spend the night together? Oh, God, I'm sorry, that's not what I meant..."

Angela laughed. "I know what you meant, but yes, the evening is ours." Had he really made a mistake, she wondered.

How about a nice dinner?" Sean asked.

"I'm not that hungry," she lied.

"Oh, okay, well, what did you have in mind?"

"Are you hungry?"

"Not particularly," he lied as well.

Angela had been driving for about ten minutes and stopped in front of an apartment building. "This is where I live," she said.

"Looks nice."

"I have some snacks upstairs, would you care for some?"

"Sure, sounds good."

They parked and walked up a couple of flights of stairs. Angela unlocked the door and stepped in. Sean was right behind and followed her in. She turned around and he was standing right in front of her, so close their noses were almost touching, her breasts slightly pressing his chest. The light pressure was all they needed and suddenly they reached around each other and pulled at the same time, hungrily kissing each other's lips. Sean held her with one hand and closed the door behind them. They moved as one through the living room. Angela guided him to her bedroom, their lips and bodies still together. They tore each other's clothes off and Sean swiftly entered her the moment they touched the bed. It was over for both of them in moments. They lay next to each other holding hands, trying to catch their breath. Sean turned to look at her. They hadn't turned any lights on, but he could see her beautiful features from the street lamp shining through the curtains of the window. He delicately kissed her lips, her nose, her forehead. He nibbled on her ear, continued down her neck to her stunning firm breasts where he lingered for a while playing with them—with his hands, his lips, his tongue. Angela moaned in delight. She let Sean discover her body inch by inch, savoring every moment. His fingers caressed the skin on her stomach and his mouth followed them until they found the most exquisite and delicate flower her body possessed. He tenderly tantalized her. He wanted this to be one of the most specials moments of their lives, and for Angela, it was.

Her cries of fervor thrilled him. He knew they were coming from the amazing voice she possessed, but he also knew the beautiful sounds came from somewhere deeper. He was sure it was from her soul.

As they became one rhythm Sean was sure his own soul was singing to their perfect harmony.

Sean and Angela spent the week together. While he was in North Carolina his orders came through. He was to be deployed to Afghanistan in the next few days.

They were lying in bed together, in each other's arms.

"I'll write to you all the time," Angela said.

"That means a lot. I'll write to you too, I promise."

"I'm glad. I'll look forward to your letters, Sean."

"Yes, Ajei, I will too," he said and kissed her with all the passion he possessed.

Before leaving for the other side of the world Sean went to see his parents the few days that were left of his leave.

CHAPTER 30

"Babá?" Nico said as he went to his father's den. The man was always at his desk.

"What's up?"

"I just got my orders."

"Oh?" Dimitri looked at him, waiting for the younger man to tell him where he was being sent. When Nico didn't divulge anything his heart skipped a beat and simply said: "Afghanistan?"

Nico nodded. "Yes. But I want you to know that I'm not scared."

"No, I know that." *But I am! Oh, my God, my boy is going into the lion's mouth.* "You are probably the bravest person I know and I'm very proud of you, my son."

"Thanks Dad. There's something I want to talk to you about."

"Of course, what is it?"

"I would like Mom to be here too."

"Well, let's get her in here."

Nico nodded and went to get his mother. When the three of them were sitting down he looked at his parents. There wasn't anything dumb about either one of them. They knew he was about to drop a bomb on them. He hoped they would take it well.

"What is it, Nicolaki?" Irini asked.

"I just told Dad that I'm being deployed to Afghanistan."

"Oh," the woman gasped, but held her composure.

"There's something else, and I wanted to tell both you at the same time."

"And what would that be?" His father asked.

Nico looked at his parents. Maybe it would be okay. "I want to marry Sophia." There, it was out, he said it.

"We know that, you're already engaged," Irini said.

"Yes, we are. What I mean is, before I leave. I want to get married before I deploy."

"But you're leaving in just a few days," Dimitri said.

Irini was the calm one. "Is there a problem?" Nico didn't answer. "Is Sophia pregnant?" She asked as delicately as possible.

Nico smiled. "Not that I'm aware of."

"So why the rush, my son?" Dimitri asked.

"I know I'm not the son you wished for..." Nico started.

Dimitri leaned forward. "You are much more than I could have hoped for. You turned into one hell of a man, and I am the proudest father in the world."

"Thanks, *Babá,* I really appreciate that, but what I meant was that I didn't follow in your footsteps and take over the business. I'm sorry, but it's not my dream. I had different ones than you did."

"I realized this a while back. Whatever you want to do with your life is fine by me."

"I know you and Sophia have been doing great things together. The business is thriving, better than it ever has."

"You're right. I had pictured you in her place, but I couldn't have asked for a better replacement. Well, not a replacement."

"I know what you mean, and I think the two of you are a wonderful team. And also the reason why I want to get married before I leave."

"I think I know what you're saying, but lay it out for us," the older man said.

"I want to know that in case anything happens to me Sophia will be part of the family and," Nico turned to his mother, "if she is pregnant the baby will be taken care of and be part of our household."

When had his son so matured? Dimitri thought.

His parents looked at each other. They didn't want to think of the worst thing that could happen. They were impressed that Nico was thinking or his responsibilities towards them, the business and his own future family. The older couple nodded to each other. "We have five days, Nico," Dimitri said.

The young man smiled. His parents had taken it well. "I was thinking maybe we could fly up to Las Vegas."

"To get married?" Irini asked.

"Yeah, in one of those in and out kind of chapels."

Irini stood up and starting walking towards the door.

"Where are you going?" Dimitri asked, wondering if he had misread his wife, or if she was upset.

Irini turned and faced the men she adored. She smiled at them and said: "I have four days to plan a wedding. I'm starting with a few phone calls. I'll keep you informed. Now, I'm off."

Nico jumped up and hugged his mother. "I love you, *Manoula*, little Mom."

"I love you too, Nicolaki. Now, let me get to work."

Irini jumped into her car and called the local Greek Orthodox church. Yes, of course they could accommodate them. The Katsopoulos' were pillars of the community, and had been present whenever anyone needed help. They had always been very generous and it was the least they could to, especially when they heard that Nico was being deployed to Afghanistan. They would be happy to perform the ceremony on Sunday. Irini then called a shop that had lovely wedding dresses. Her third call was to Sophia.

"Sophia?"

"Yes, Irini."

"Can you meet me at Heather's?"

"The wedding gown store?"

"Yes. We have to hurry. It's this Sunday."

"What's this Sunday?"

"Your wedding."

"My wedd... What do you mean?"

"Didn't Nico talk to you?"

"Yes, but I didn't think it would happen this fast. And we thought maybe something in Las Vegas."

"Are you alright with this?"

"Of course, whatever you and Nico say."

"Okay, I'll meet you there in twenty minutes."

"I'll be there."

"Oh, what about a *koumbara* and bridesmaids?"

"Uh," Sophia thought quickly, "three. One maid of honor and two bridesmaids. I'll call them to confirm."

"Good. Tell them to come to the store as well, if they can. See you soon."

Oh, Sophia loved her mother-in-law.

Irini's next call was to a lovely flower shop she had frequented for years. Of course they could do all the flowers for the church, and anywhere else she needed them for. As for the bride's bouquet they would see both Irini and Sophia later that afternoon for details.

Irini called her son. "Nico?"

"Yes, Mom?"

"*Koumbaros?* Grooms?" Irini didn't mince words. She didn't have time, and she was on a mission. She had organized everything in her mind, which at the moment was working better than a computer.

"Uh, I haven't thought about it."

"Well, think about it and then call them. Make sure they have tuxedos." She knew Nico's was in his closet. Irini always made sure his wardrobe included at least one of everything he might need, like a tuxedo, suit, sports jacket and so on. "Oh, and tell them to be at the church on time. It's all set."

"What? Oh, Mom, you're wonder woman! Does Sophia know?"

"She does. I'm on my way to meet her."

"Wow," was the only thing Nico could say.

"Oh, and start writing down names of people you want to invite. Once you have it ready call them up."

"There won't be too many."

"That's fine. It's your wedding. Invite anybody you want.

Just do it today. Remember we only have a few days."

"Okay, I'm on it."

Irini told him the time everyone needed to be 'in place'. After hanging up with Nico she called a store that could provide the crowns, the *stefana*, and the favors that would contain the white egg shaped (sign of purity and fertility) candied almonds, the *koufeta*. Anything fancy was out of the question, there wasn't time. No matter, the importance was in the meaning. Yes, they could have the favors ready for Sunday. They would place five of the white almonds in a tulle and wrap them with a ribbon. The number five was significant as it represented health, happiness, wealth, children and a long life. Irini especially prayed for the last. And odd numbers were considered lucky as they were not divisible, which is what everyone wished for the couple.

Irini's phone rang. It was Nico. "Talk to me."

"Three total. Sean Sandoval will be my best man, and Frank and Kevin from high school will be my grooms. I told them where to go and what to do."

"Excellent. That's done," Irini said, checking it off her mental list. "Oh, Nico, can you take care of picking up Sophia on Sunday?"

"Sure, Mom, I'll pick her up."

Irini screamed. "No, no, no! *Ftou, ftou, ftou*," she mockingly spit, warding off any evil spirits looming around. "That's bad luck. You never see the bride before the wedding ceremony."

"Okay, I'll have someone else pick her up."

"Nico, why don't you just order a limo?"

Nico smiled. Of course, why hadn't he thought of that? "Mom, can I be just like you when I grow up?"

"Yes, yes, now just make sure they pick her up on time."

The next number Irini dialed was a photographer. He couldn't do it, he was booked this weekend, but after hearing he would be paid double he would 'find a way' to be there.

Irini's last call was to her husband. "Dimitri?"

"Yes, *agapimou*, how's it going?"

"Very good, actually. The church is set, I'm on my way to meet Sophia and the bridesmaids for the dresses. The photographers will be there. The flowers, the *stephana* and the *koufeta* are ordered. Nico has his best guys and is calling a limo service to pick up Sophia and her girls."

"Wow, it's sounds like you have everything under control."

"I'm trying. Now, the reason I'm calling. I need you to do a couple of things, and then I think we'll be all done."

"Really? I thought weddings took months of planning."

"They usually do, but we don't have that luxury, besides its easy when you already have an idea of what you need. Now, my first question to you is about your tuxedo."

"My tux? What about it?"

"Is it ready?"

"It is."

"Does it fit?"

"Of course it does."

"Good, but do me a favor and try it on."

"I'm telling you its fine."

Ah, men, Irini thought. Why can't they just say yes. "Humor me. I don't want you to scream at the last minute that some button is missing. And check the accessories, and don't forget the shoes."

"Okay, okay, what else."

"I can't get a hold of Manolis. Can you ask him to call me when he has a minute. I need him to cater the food."

"No problem. The restaurant staff and the chef will jump at the occasion. What else?"

"Make a list of people you want to invite, and when I get back later we'll start making calls. No written wedding invitations, definitely no time for that. A phone call, a yes or no if they're coming, and that's it."

"Easy enough. What else?" Dimitri asked again.

"I love you."

Dimitri smiled. "I love you too, and thank you."

"For what?"

"For being the most wonderful wife and mother a man could ask for, and most of all for giving me a beautiful son."

"Goes both ways. Got to go. Bye."

The wedding went off smoothly. All the last minute preparations fell into place. Sophia and her bridesmaids were lovely in their gowns, Nico and his boys were dashing in their tuxedos, the guests and parents celebrated the couple's union in the church decorated with fragrant flowers for the occasion. The Katsopoulos restaurant catered their delicious specialties and everyone in attendance ate, drank and danced to the sounds of the Greek band and their bouzoukis until late into the night.

For a such an impromptu wedding it had been perfect in every way, and the photographer didn't miss any of the special moments.

CHAPTER 31

Sean, Nico and the PJ team flew to Afghanistan. The Boeing C-17 military transport, powered by four turbofan engines, flew for hours across the Atlantic, the European continent and on into the Middle East. They would arrive at their final destination in the middle of the night, after having made a couple of stops to load or unload equipment and personnel. They all sat next to each other, a mélange of military branches and units heading into certain danger, with hearts full of pride and venture. They were huddled together in seats of rows five across in the middle of the aircraft, similar to a commercial 747, or on benches with their backs against the fuselage. No frills, good looking flight attendants or drinks, but they did have their MREs. Each packet of Meals Ready to Eat contained about 1200 calories and were good for about three years. Every person that had ever eaten the food out of pouches wondered how they could survive temperatures from minus fifty to over one hundred degrees Fahrenheit, could withstand parachute drops and still be eatable.

Some, like Sean and Nico, were on their first tour of duty, others on their fourth or fifth. The latter were the ones with ear plugs and mini music players, either listening to their favorite tunes or sound asleep. They stayed that way most of the flight over.

"Hey Kats, do you realize this is the real thing? That we're going to war?"

"Yeah, Sandoval, kind of sucks, but that's what we signed up for. I just hope I can do some good and save some lives, get a daddy or a mommy back to their kids."

"Yeah, I was thinking the same. I was also wondering why these damn politicians act like mean bullies and have to have the most toys, and in doing so create misery and death."

"Synonymous with power hungry assholes."

"Exactly. This land, which is part of the Silk Road, has been under some sort of occupation since Genghis Khan. History tells us what happened to this part of the world time and time again, and it seems people just don't get it."

"What do you mean?" Nico asked, curious.

"That Afghanistan is a really fucked up place to fight a war. The topography of the land and the climate are just vicious. They've got the Hindu Kush mountains, which are nearly a thousand miles long and a couple of hundred miles wide, and runs from northern Pakistan into Iran, complete with dozens of peaks that are almost as high as the Himalayas. And in between it's decorated by deep valleys and bottomless gorges. But it doesn't end there, oh no, then for a nice change you've got this huge plateau of desert, and they aren't too far apart from each other, all of that in a country no more than twice the size of New Mexico. And to make things even sweeter there are millions of land mines strewn across the countryside, a reminder that they've been at it since the late seventies."

"Sounds lovely," Nico said sarcastically.

"Yeah. And to top it off the Afghans are incredible warriors. I just hope the better ones are on our side."

"Since they've been under fire for so long they were probably born fighting."

"Exactly, and they're a very proud people. They won't back down. What once started as a gallant fight against a powerful enemy has now come apart. The smart thing would have been to stay together as one. But they're also a stubborn people, and because of that they divided into tribes and now have groups the likes of the Taliban. They've gotten it from all sides over many centuries—the Mongols from the

East, the Brits from the West, and the Russians from the North."

"Maybe someday everybody will get sick and tired of fighting and death."

"Hopefully," Sean repeated and did wish that, but he also knew that people preferred an eye for an eye rather than communication and forgiveness. And of course being a martyr for Allah was at the top of every Jihadist's list.

The team arrived at Bagram Airfield in the Parwan Province in the middle of the night. They landed smoothly on one of the dual runways capable of handling even the largest aircraft, such as the Antonov 225 and the C-5 Galaxy. As soon as the wheels were chocked the ground crew started offloading the palettes of supplies from inside the belly of the colossal steel bird. When the passengers deplaned they noticed snow all around them and the bitter cold cut right into their bones.

"Fuck, its cold," Nico said as they carried several bags of gear off the aircraft.

"Sure the hell is," Sean muttered.

"I'm almost more worried at this point about the weather than about who's trying to shoot us."

The newcomers presented themselves to their superiors and got a quick tour of the barracks and the Tactical Operations Center. They settled into their cots and promptly fell asleep. They knew that a good night's rest might be a luxury in the upcoming weeks and they needed to keep up their energy. In the morning they got their bearings around the base, checked their gear and were ready to go. They didn't have to wait long. That afternoon they heard their first "SCRAMBLE, SCRAMBLE, SCRAMBLE!" from the TOC. It was the alarm. There were wounded that needed to be rescued, and hopefully saved. The PJs rushed to the two HH-60G PAVE Hawk helicopters. One was the trail helo with the medical team, the other the lead which accompanied them and was there for protection. Sean and Nico sat next to each other.

"Seems we're picking up a downed fighter pilot," Nico said.

Sean nodded. "Looks clear. They don't foresee any problem with insurgents trying to use us for target practice."

"Hope their intel is good."

"Hope so too."

They flew through the majestic sunset into the Hindu Kush, its peaks tall and defiant yet void of any kind of life—human, animal or any semblance of vegetation. As the two helicopters approached their destination they slowed down and flew over the area until the debris of the fighter plane strewn on the snow on one the mountain's slopes reflected the macabre outcome of the once sleek fighter plane. A couple of miles further away they found the downed pilot. The Pararescue team was ready. The rugged terrain would not permit them to land so the helo hovered above the wounded man. The PJs quickly rappelled out of the helicopter. Sean and Nico were among the six unit crew who ran toward the downed flyer and formed a circle with their backs toward him. Sean and Nico turned and slid onto their knees next to the wounded man. They started assessing the injuries—hypothermia, possible frostbite, and definitely leg injuries.

"Lieutenant? Lieutenant? Can you hear me?" Sean asked.

The pilot's eyes fluttered. "Yes," he whispered.

The hair at the back of Sean's neck stood on end. There were eyes watching him, of that he had no doubt, but the question was how close were they? The stone forming in his stomach was confirming they weren't very far at all. He looked at the pilot. He was alive, but barely. But was he really the pilot, and was he even American? The military had implemented a protocol to make sure it wasn't an enemy combatant that had donned the injured's uniform. Sean looked him over and would have sworn he was as American as apple pie, but he had to follow the regs. He asked the pilot the required password, but the man only gave him incoherent grunts. Could he even remember it? In his condition Sean doubted it, so he tried something different.

"Hey, Lieutenant, what do M&M's do?" If the guy was really an American he would know.

The pilot stared at the PJ's eyes. Sean saw the glow, as if they were smiling back at him. "They melt... in your mouth... not your hands," the wounded man managed to squeeze out.

Sean grinned. The pilot had given him the answer he wanted. "Yes, Sir, that they do."

"That was brilliant, Sandoval, I'll have to remember that for some other time," Nico said.

"Let's get him patched up and out of here."

"You feel it too?" Nico asked.

"Yeah, they're out there and much too close for comfort."

A few more seconds was all Sean and Nico needed. They reached into their med kits and pulled out the necessary items to quickly splint the pilot's legs. They each did one of the man's limbs.

The flyer had been shot out of the sky by a SAM. Just a few inches and milliseconds before the surface to air missile penetrated the fuselage and lit up the chilling blackness of the midnight sky, the pilot managed to eject. As he rocketed up and out of his cockpit he thought he lost a couple of inches of height as he was sure his vertebrae had compressed. After his initial shocks—compression and still being alive—the rush of a million needles of icy cold penetrate his bones. His chute opened and once again he was jerked back up. Finally he floated toward the ominous, dark mountain peaks below him. He could just make out their shadows, but he was descending blindly. By the time he realized where he was the ground suddenly rushed up to greet him, but it wasn't a pleasant welcome, rather it was a landing so forceful and awkward that his legs became entangled between the craggy boulders. Both limbs instantly snapped as if they were mere toothpicks, and the pain that shot through his body made him pass out. The GPS he wore automatically sent out signals to units that monitored for just such incidents. Rescue units were immediately dispatched to his location.

Suddenly their earpieces crackles: "Get your asses out of there!" Sean heard the lead helicopter say over the radio, "or you'll have company in a just a few minutes." They had spotted a group coming toward them with their NVGs, their night vision goggles.

"Roger that, on our way up." Sean responded. Their instincts had been right. There were enemy eyes watching them. *This guy's ours, you're not going to get him! We're taking him home, he belongs to us!* Sean silently shouted.

In less than a minute they hoisted the downed pilot and were back in the helicopter and retreating into the sky. Sean and Nico quickly worked on the flyer. They inserted I.V.s, pumped him with lifesaving fluids and cleaned his cuts. He was dehydrated and half frozen, but happy as hell the PJs had rescued him. As the Lieutenant lay there letting the Pedros patch him up he remembered the SAM, the ejection, the explosion and the horrific pain when he smashed into the treacherous rocks. He had also believed he was going to be captured, become a prisoner, tortured or worse. "Thanks for saving my ass, guys," he said to the men working on him.

"You're going to have to get a pair of green feet," Sean said to the pilot.

He stared blankly. "Green feet?"

"On your ass, Sir," Nico added.

"What?"

"A tattoo, of green feet. Means you were rescued by PJs. It's a tradition."

The flyer grinned. "I might just do that."

As the helicopters flew back toward the base the crew looked at the Hindu Kush mountains surrounding them. They saw a campfire at an incredible 10,000 feet and wondered if the people around it were friendlies, or were the ones that shot down the pilot's plane.

CHAPTER 32

Hamzed Wazir was one of the men warming up around that campfire. He sat on the dirt cross-legged, encircled by the mountains of his beloved Afghanistan. He was wearing the local *perahon tunban*, a knee length shirt and baggy trousers. He also wore a vest and a *pakol*, a flat wool cap. His hair and beard were neatly trimmed, reminiscent of an English cut, and his nose, cheekbones and dark brown eyes were more ethnic to the region. His head was lowered toward his chest as he pondered on his life. His eyes and heart became darker by the minute.

Hamzed was born not far from where he sat, in a village high in the mountains. As a boy he grew up surrounded by war, with AK47s, grenades and mines, from conflicting tribes to fanatics like the Taliban. His country had never known peace. Foreigners had invaded his land for millennia, and internal conflict kept them in danger at all times as well. The Afghanis grew up as fighters from a very young age. They were noble warriors good at defending themselves, and they knew every inch of their land. If they could internally bond together their resistance and defense would have been one of the strongest and most impressive in the world. Unfortunately politics were their defeat, and they would never agree to unity. Instead it made them a broken people, marred by stubbornness and traditions that instead of complimenting them kept them back from progress and prosperity.

Hamzed's father had been a good man, the leader of their tribe and the chief of the surrounding land, until a bomb from an American drone exploded during a wedding celebration. Forty people were killed, including his parents, his two brothers, one of which was the groom, and all of his friends. Even the love of his life, his wife, and their little son, had perished. For some reason he survived, and as he dug himself out from under the mutilated bodies and the rubble, a piece of him died as well. And then the rage set in. The more death he saw the more he wanted revenge. He was the only one of the once revered family who survived, and the one that would have to lead and take over where his father left off. But his path was not the same as the older man's had been, of trying to better his tribe and enable them to have a more comfortable and prosperous life. His father had sent him to England to study and Hamzed became an engineer. He had excelled and proven himself worthy of the sacrifice his family had made for him to accomplish his schooling. He studied hard and learned not only the academics from the West, but also how they lived and thought, their quirks and downfalls. He was a smart man, and well respected by his peers and mentors. He graduated at the top of his class and was looking forward to going back to his homeland and helping his people. He had been honored by the privilege of being chosen, as he was meant to take the reins from his father at some point in his life. But it was to be later, not this soon, and definitely not in such a devastating way. Now, as he reflected into the past he pictured the future the Americans had deprived him of. He, in turn, would offer the infidels a future as well, one that would be just as dark and painful as his own heart was.

The Afghan leader lifted his head and started talking to his men. They listened attentively. They respected him, but they also feared him. He had an explosive temper that would flare up unexpectedly, and they didn't want to be victims of his wrath.

"Allah's wish, Peace be upon Him, is also our mission." Wazir looked at each one of his men, deep into their eyes, and slowly said: "And that is to exterminate the Americans like cockroaches. Our goal is to annihilate the infidels from the face of this earth."

"Yes! Yes!" They answered back excitedly.

"Our mission is immediate and continuous, and we must do whatever it takes to accomplish this task."

"*Baleh! Baleh!* Yes! Yes!"

"We must all sacrifice." Wazir's eyes grew darker. "Most of us here already have." The men nodded. They knew what he meant. They had lost people in the drone attack too. "We will fight the enemy!"

"*Baleh!*"

"Until all the infidels are dead!" Wazir's voice kept rising.

"*Baleh!*"

"Until the last drop of blood is drained from their bodies!"

"*Baleh!*"

"Until the last American head has been chopped off!"

"*Baleh!*"

The men picked up their AK47s, stood up, waved their rifles in the air and danced around the fire.

"We will be victorious!"

"*Baleh! Baleh!* We will be victorious!" They chanted.

Wazir had them exactly where he wanted them. They were practically in a frenzy. "What will we be?" He shouted to his men.

"Victorious!" They shouted back.

Wazir was standing among them, their arms around each other's shoulders. They danced in a circle around the fire. "What will we do to the infidels?" He asked.

"Kill them!"

"What will we do?"

"Chop their heads off!"

"Will we accomplish Allah's wish?"

"*Baleh!*"

"Will we accomplish our mission?"

"*Baleh!*"

The men continued to dance. Wazir looked around and then signaled to one of them who immediately went to his leader.

"Kamal."

"Yes, Hamzed."

"Come, I need to talk to you."

The two men walked off.

"Praise Allah, we will accomplish our mission," Kamal said.

"Peace be upon Him, we most certainly will, and this is why I wanted to talk you. I have an important assignment I want you to undertake."

"Of course, anything you wish. I will accomplish everything you ask of me."

"You are good man, Kamal. May Allah bless you."

"*Tashakor,* thank you."

"How is your son?" Wazir asked, the pain in his heart for his own dead child overwhelming.

"*Khob, tashakor*, fine, thank you."

"Good. Now let me explain your mission."

CHAPTER 33

"SCRAMBLE, SCRAMBLE, SCRAMBLE!" And they did. The Pararescuers ran toward the two waiting helicopters and jumped in.

"What do we have?" Nico asked.

"Young boy stepped on a mine. Legs are in shreds, one is severed below the knee."

"Aw, fuck." Nico said.

All casualties were painful for the crews, but none were as heart wrenching as when they were women and children, especially the children. They were supposed to be playing with a ball, not getting their limbs blown off.

They flew to the landing zone. As soon as they were wheels down the crew jumped out. The American soldiers on the ground rushed the local Afghan father who was carrying the wounded boy in his arm up to them. The child was bleeding profusely from what was left of his little limbs. The PJs quickly climbed back into the helicopter after taking the boy from Kamal. It was mandatory that the father go along as a child was involved. He of course knew this. Before following his son into the helicopter he was frisked by one of the soldiers. He was cleared and the Afghan boarded.

The blades of the steel machine chopped away making a cloud of dust. After a few moments they were wheels up. In the meantime Sean was trying to insert an I.V. into the boy's arm, but couldn't get it in. He couldn't find a vein that would hold. He pulled out an I.O., an intraosseous device. He looked at the boy's face. It was caked with dust and tears and distorted from the pain.

"Hey, little man, I'm going to put this needle directly into your humerus just above your elbow. It's going to be fucking painful," Sean said, pretty sure the child didn't understand a word he was saying. Man and boy looked at each other, a definite connection, and both hoping for the best.

Sean lifted the sleeve of the boy's shirt, felt for the bone in his upper arm and swiftly inserted the I.O. into the bone. Sean felt the boy's scream pierce all the way to his heart. "I'm really sorry, little man, but that was the worst of it, I promise." Nico was holding the bag of lifesaving fluids above the two of them. He hung them on the cables hanging below the ceiling of the helicopter and knelt down next to Sean. The two men worked on the boy, cleaning, removing debris and when they finished with all they could do they bandaged him up. That would be the extent of their capabilities. The next step would be at the hospital, the medical specialists alerted and waiting. The Pararescuers looked at the boy. He was sleeping, thanks to the medication they had pumped into him. Once at the hospital he would have a good chance of survival as they were still in the 'golden hour', the critical period after the inflicted wound. They just needed to get there as fast as they could.

Nico kissed the boy on his forehead. There was nothing glorious about war, no matter what people thought. Maybe if those politicians saw their handiwork, like with this innocent boy, albeit indirectly, maybe they would think twice about starting something so vile and destructive.

Kamal watched the care these two men were giving his son. It made his stomach churn, especially when the man kissed the child. He now focused even more on his mission. He had no doubt he would accomplish it, and knew Wazir would be proud of him.

Nico and Sean went to sit on the side of the chopper with the door open to the air. They didn't say anything, they were both lost in their thoughts. Their legs dangled over the side as they watched the scenery.

"Hey, Sandoval, look down there."

"What?" He shouted over the noise of the rotor.

"Snow."

The chopper was flying very close to the mountains, just above the white carpet.

Sean nodded. It reminded him of New Mexico—mountains and desert. He missed home. He missed his family, but he missed Angela most of all.

Inside the cabin the father looked at his son with tears in his eyes. He was sorry he made the boy step on a mine, and for the pain it was now causing him, but he knew it wouldn't last too long as they were on their way to meet Allah. It would be a better life for both of them, and they would take some of the infidels with them. He looked at the Americans with hatred in his black eyes. It was time. *Khuda hafez, goodbye, my son. We shall meet in Heaven.*

Kamal inconspicuously reached under his long shirt into his groin area. He had been searched by the men in uniform, but they had not found the concealed V-40 mini grenade. A string at the top of his penis held the attached ring. The orb below it, which was a little smaller than a golf ball, rested between the membrane and his testicles. The man carefully removed the pin from the grenade and mentally counted—*one*, he stood up, *two,* he crouched next to the cockpit, *three,* he shouted: *"Allahu Akbar!* God is Great!" Sean heard him and whipped around. Out of the corner of his eye he realized what the man was doing, but it was too late. *Four,* the grenade detonated behind the pilots. At the same instant Sean grabbed Nico's shirt and pulled hard. Both men flew out of the side of the helo. A flash of fire spread throughout the cabin and burgeoned out the door where the two men had been sitting.

"What the f..." Nico screamed, as he and his best friend plummeted fast toward certain death, their arms and legs wind-milling to break their fall. A split-second later a second explosion devastated the rest of the helicopter. As the two men plunged to earth they saw chunks of the steel bird boomeranging out and then down toward the mountain and crash on the snow and trees. The rest of the crew and the once pristine medical helicopter became thousands of dark and grotesquely twisted pieces. One of those fragments impelled itself into Nico's leg in mid-air, right before the two men smashed into the white covering of snow on the side of the mountain they had been looking at. They hit hard. As Sean tumbled down the slope like a broken toy he pictured himself as a doll that had been thrown in anger. Bodies rolled and legs and arms cartwheeled as the two men tried to survive the brutal ordeal. Helmets and parts of the equipment they carried were flung away and lost to the elements. Sean and Nico kept rolling down the slope, unable to stop their descent. They hit and bounced off of boulders seemingly strategically placed to provide even more pain. It propelled the men off the snow and they would land time and time again even harder, they were sure, than the previous impact. As they were being shaken and slapped by an invisible giant hand they wondered if they would actually survive the ordeal. And if they did how badly injured would they be. After what seemed an eternity and a couple of miles the bodies finally stopped at the edge of a forest. Sean and Nico lay completely immobile.

The lead helo circled back and searched the area. The crew found the site and the result of the explosion. Their throats tightened at the macabre sight. Different size pieces of what once was a helicopter lay grotesquely deformed and scattered across the snow. They circled to make sure there wasn't anything they could do, but they knew that nothing could have survived the double eruption. Their peers and compatriots, noble military personnel who were doing their duty by trying to save lives, lost theirs in the process. They were sure the malefactors were people on Jihad dedicated to eradicating not only Americans, but Muslims who didn't believe in exactly what they did. As far as the crew was concerned they were just murderers. They radioed the base and brought them up-to-date. The flight back would be a somber one.

CHAPTER 34

Sean moaned as his body told him how much pain it was in. He lay in the snow, not daring to move. Everything hurt, and he was sure every inch of his battered body was bruised—inside and out. Even his breathing seemed to be a torture device every time his lungs expanded. His eyes fluttered open. It was probably the only part of his anatomy that wasn't screaming in pain. He slowly tried moving, assessing the extent of possible injuries. Sean was sure his body had turned to brittle. Would it crack? Would he break? Was it already broken? And how badly? Slowly and carefully he tried moving each limb, each finger. To his amazement they responded, painfully, but with no signs of breakage. He was grateful he didn't have any serious injuries and thought about his buddy. Sean remembered pulling him out the door. Had he survived the fall? Was he still alive? Where was Nico? He looked around and found the man a few yards away, lying face down in the snow. Sean hurried over to where he lay, falling and crawling until he reached him. He turned him over gently and brushed the snow off of his face and the rest of his body. Nico was out, from either a hit on the head or his injuries. Sean quickly checked his pulse—it was weak, but still there. He was alive! He dragged Nico from the snow and into the edge of the forest that lined the side of the slope. He didn't know if enemy fighters had seen them, and would maybe come around to check if there was anything left from the helicopter. They would especially be interested in crew members and possible survivors.

"Kats! Can you hear me?" Sean asked, slowly shaking him. No answer. He shook him again. "Kats!"

"Mm, yeah," Nico answered groggily.

"Kats, listen to me. Do you remember what happened?"

Nico's eyes fluttered open as his mind tried to focus. "Oh, fuck! Yeah. You pushed me out and then the helo exploded." He groaned and his eyes became slits. "Shit, everything fucking hurts!"

"Yeah, I know what you mean. Keep your voice down, I don't what's happening around us yet."

"Got it."

"Let me check the rest of you out. Don't try moving until I finish."

Nico nodded. "Did you get hurt, man?"

"Not too bad, but I'll probably look like a black and blue checkerboard by tomorrow," Sean answered, thinking that his entire body was probably bruised. Even his lungs hurt. He figured his chest had hit one of the boulders and they were bruised too. But he was grateful it was no worse than that.

As Sean checked Nico for other wounds he never thought that he would be working on his best friend. He quickly assessed that no vital organs had been harmed, and the tough PJ didn't have any broken bones. There was, however, one large piece of shrapnel that had pierced Nico's upper left leg. It seemed deep. The area surrounding it was covered in blood. That one did worry Sean, but he didn't think the femoral artery had been cut. He automatically went to reach for his medical supplies, but realized that the impact and their tumbling down the slope had been so forceful that both their vests and helmets had been ripped off and were now long gone. They didn't have any of their medical gear, radios or weapons. All Sean had was his knife. Nico had even less. The leg continued to bleed. Sean quickly took off his belt and made a tourniquet out of it. Nico moaned in pain, trying vehemently not to scream.

"Kats, listen, I'm going to see if I can find any supplies.

Seems the fall and the slope claimed all of it. I'll be back as soon as I can."

"Okay," Nico said weakly. "I'll be a good boy and wait for you."

"Very kind of you. I'm going to pull you farther into the woods."

"Okay."

Sean dragged him into the forest and covered him with some leaves. Nico wanted to scream, badly, but used all the willpower he possessed not to.

"I'll be back as soon as possible."

Nico nodded. "Watch your six," he whispered.

"Always."

The sun was rapidly disappearing and Sean scrambled as quickly as he could back up the snow-covered slope toward the chopper's scattered debris. He ached all over but he pushed on. He thought of their SERE training, how they had to walk back up the slopes they had skied down and how Johnson would be cursing the entire walk back up. But it now came in handy and didn't seem to be such a colossal endeavor. He climbed fairly fast, even with all the aches and pains screaming from his body. He had to reach the wreckage, there had to be some things that he could use to help them survive. The snow was packed pretty solidly and Sean used his hands and feet to climb up the slope. He slipped a few times but persevered. He tried to keep his mind away from the agony pulsing through his body and thought about his family and Angela, and about Nico and Sophia who had just gotten married. The wedding had been lovely, but it wouldn't be right if the new bride suddenly became a widow. He swore he would get Nico back to his wife, or die trying. He also thought about his own family and Jack and Ryan, their avalanche in the Alps and how long they had been laid up. They too had been in excruciating pain and had suffered, but they never gave up. Sean swore he wouldn't either. He pushed himself in the difficult ascension and started seeing pieces of debris.

Sean searched the scattered objects for anything that

could be useful. As he combed the area he found some dog tags. He gently brushed them off. They were the pilot's. He would make sure they would get back to his family. He put them in one of his pockets. His eyes took in the evidence and the fate of the rest of the people that had been on board. He clenched his jaw and cursed the father that had blown them up. How could he have done that to his little boy? Why would he do that to the Americans, when all they were doing was helping the people and the wounded? He put the thoughts aside and concentrated on finding supplies. He spied a piece of rappelling rope which had been singed and was now only about ten feet long. He picked it up. Everything could come in handy. He didn't know how long they would be on their own, or even if someone would come out to search for them.

Sean looked around some more and spotted a bag against the side of a rock. He quickly went over and grabbed it. The medical kit had been a victim of the blast, but some of its original contents were still intact. He took account of his inventory: two large bandages, two space blankets, a tube of lip balm, several fentanyl pops, a rectal thermometer, three plastic zippered bags each of a different size, a penlight, and a Penrose drain. Sean would have to work with what he now had. He shoved everything in the pockets of his pants and jacket. He really needed his suturing material, but it was gone. He would find another way to help Nico. He also found one of the weapons but it was bent, twisted and totally useless. As Sean started back down the slope he noticed a large piece of metal protruding out of the snow. He pulled it out. He thought maybe it was a piece from under the helo's nose. It was about three feet long and two feet wide, one of its sides turned up. He put it on the snow, the curled up side toward the front and knelt down onto it. Sean put his hands on top of the curl. The piece of metal slid easily and very quickly gained momentum. They sped down the slope and Sean wanted to shout like a kid as they barreled along. He silently thanked Jack and Ryan who had taught him how to ski and snowboard. Sean laughed out loud as the wind hit his face and the adrenaline pumped through his body. Even though Sean was very aware of the circumstances he now found himself in, he took a moment to enjoy the rush. He thought his uncles would be proud of him, and maybe James Bond would be too. As he got closer to where he left Nico he tightened his grip on the upturned metal and lifted it up. The back dug into the snow like a ski brake and he started slowing down. Sean leaned over and fell off, still hanging on to the piece of metal. He went into the forest and found Nico where he had left him. His eyes were closed.

"Kats! Kats! Wake up.

"Mm, yeah," he answered as groggily as he had before.

"Listen, Kats, it's your leg."

"How bad?" He asked through clenched teeth.

"Well, it's not that bad," Sean lied, "but we have to get you to a doctor."

"You're just as good, you can patch me up."

"That's all I can do, but even that won't be very good, I don't have any equipment, just a couple of bandages and some pops."

"Oh, that sounds good."

"I'm going to give you one now, take some of the pain away."

Nico nodded. "Glad that was one of the survivors." His eyes grew darker. "Anybody else make it?" He asked grimly.

"I'm afraid not." Sean handed him the medical lollipop. It was a dissolvable lozenge with some sugar at the end of a stick, the fentanyl more potent than morphine.

"Okay," was all Nico replied. He was trying very hard not to scream from the pain as he waited for the lozenge to take effect.

"I need to take a look at your leg."

Nico nodded. "Okay."

Sean inspected the damage with the penlight. His hand cupped the light, being careful not to give away their whereabouts. He looked into the wound. Thankfully, as he had hoped, the femoral artery had not been severed but it needed attention. "I'm going into the woods to find some supplies I need."

Nico gave him a weak thumb's up.

Sean went deeper into the forest. He took his knife and started cutting bark off of a tree, as well as a couple of branches. He went back to Nico.

"Hey, Sandoval, what are you up to?" he asked, the pain having greatly subsided.

"It's getting cold but I'm not going to start a fire, I don't know who's out there."

"I understand," Nico said bravely as he trembled with cold.

"I found the space blankets."

"That'll help," he said weakly. Nico was slipping away, falling asleep.

Sean wrapped his buddy with the strong Mylar insulation material. It would help the wounded man retain ninety percent of his body heat and it was waterproof. That would have to do for the night. He sat next to him with the bark from the tree. He started chewing and made it into a paste. He then spit it into the smallest of the plastic bags. When he had about a handful he stopped. It was a long process. It had taken about an hour and his jaw hurt, but it also kept him alert.

"Kats? Are you awake?"

Nico woke up. "What is it?"

"I need to take a look at your leg."

"Again?"

"Yeah, I've got something for it."

"Okay," Nico said. He knew Sean would try his best to help him.

"Here's a branch."

"Oh, shit."

"You can do this Kats."

"Why?"

"You've got a piece of fucking shrapnel sticking out of your leg. I've got to take it out."

"You do?" Nico knew he did.

"Uh huh. Are you ready?"

Nico put the branch in his mouth. "Ready," he mumbled as his teeth clenched down on the wood.

"Alright, don't move." Nico nodded. Sean carefully, yet

swiftly, pulled the shrapnel out of the man's leg. Nico wailed as quietly as he could and bit down harder on the branch. Sean looked inside the wound. Muscle, tendons and ligaments had been sliced so there was no way the leg would function. Sean knew that he would have to sew it up so that it wouldn't get any worse. And that would only be temporary.

"Kats?"

"Uh huh."

"Hang tight, man."

"Uh huh," he mumbled again.

Sean started by cleaning the leg up as best and as quickly as he could as it was still bleeding. He took the paste from the baggie and spread it carefully on the man's thigh.

"Holy shit!" Nico whimpered, holding back tears and screams. The slightest touch sent searing arrows to every nerve ending of his body. He bit down harder on the stick.

"Keep quiet, Kats."

"I'm trying," Nico grumbled through the branch.

Sean continued with the poultice until the wound was covered. Between the tourniquet and the paste the bleeding stopped. He prayed this would not only work in the healing process, but would keep away any infection. Sean quickly wrapped up the leg as gently as possible. "Okay, Kats, done for the moment."

"Thank God! Fuck that hurt."

"I'm sorry."

"No, not you, you were great."

"Listen, the bandage will hold for a little while but it's cut up pretty bad and I'm going to have to sew it up."

"I thought we didn't have any supplies."

"We don't. I'll be back as soon as I can. Maybe find some food too."

"Try to catch something besides a rat, or God forbid any of those cockroach looking things," he said, remembering the SERE training.

"Weavels?"

"Yeah, those sons of bitches."

"I'll do my best to bring some back for you."

Sean left Nico and went back into the forest. They needed food. They would need the energy. Who knew how long they would be out in the wilderness, and how long they could survive. Nico's injury was bad. At least it wasn't infected *yet,* and Sean knew he had to fix it up. There was only about a half an hour of daylight left. He would have to hunt his prey quickly. Sean looked at the earth. After a few minutes of searching he found was he was looking for— animal tracks. He followed the freshest ones until he was close. He could smell the little creature. He quickly made a snare from a piece of vine. He laid it between two small branches he stuck in the ground, covered it with some leaves and crouched behind a tree. He pulled out his knife and slowed his breathing. He stayed perfectly still, his senses heightened, and patiently waited. After about half an hour he saw it. Any small creature would have been fine, but a rabbit was a bonus. The animal, curious, ventured close to the snare and put his head through the loop. Sean pulled. Before it could escape he swiftly killed it with his knife as his father had taught him so long ago. He remembered the rabbit 'puzzle' he had pieced together, and thought lovingly of his parents and the day they had ridden their horses on the land. He quickly brought his thoughts to the present, thanked the little being for its sacrifice and went back to Nico who was sleeping. Sean accomplished what he had come to do. He thought of the expression 'killing two birds with one stone' and he had done just that—found the food and supplies he needed, but did it with one rabbit.

Sean filled the medium plastic bag with snow, zipped it shut and put it between his jacket and shirt. It would slowly melt into drinking water. He then skinned the rabbit, sliced up the meat and organs into chunks and put them in the largest of the bags which he left in the snow. He ate a couple of pieces before closing it up.

Sean used all of the rabbit, including the intestines which he washed off with some snow as best he could and meticulously cut them into strips. He managed to make them as thin as angel hair pasta. As they dried they became glutinous and he spun the threads together. Sean took one of the rabbit's ribs which was slightly circular and carved it until it was no thicker than a needle. At one end he shaped it into a sharp point. On the other end he made a small hole. He also cut out four round shapes from the pelt. He poked some holes close to the sides and threaded the Penrose drain through the small perforations. He went to Nico, being careful not to wake him with two of the four mittens he had just fashioned. He covered Nico's hands, the furry side on Nico's skin, tied the drain together with a knot and closed them. He kept the other two for himself. If their hands weren't cold they would expend less energy to stay warm.

Sean organized his supplies before waking his friend. When he was ready he put his hand over Nico's mouth. He didn't want the man to make any noise and knew that he automatically would, as the pain would surprise him. And he was right. When Nico woke him up he cried out in pain, well, he tried, but Sean's hand stifled the noise.

"Sh, Kats, don't scream. I haven't seen any signs of life, but that doesn't mean they aren't out there." Nico nodded and almost screamed again as he saw the 'animals' on his hands. He looked at Sean frantically. "Relax, man, I made you some bunny mittens so you could stay warm," he chuckled. He removed his hand from Nico's mouth.

The man picked up his arms and looked at the white fur. "You found a rabbit?" He asked incredulously.

"I did."

"Wow, good job, and yeah, they're nice and warm. You're such a crazy Indian," he slurred.

"You know it. I'm glad you like your mittens."

"I do."

"Listen, Kats, I've got to sew up your leg, man. Are you up for it?"

"Uh, do I have a choice?"

Sean chuckled. "Nope."

"S'what I thought." He knew it would be painful as hell, but he had full confidence in his fellow PJ.

"Stick?"

"Uh huh."

Sean put one in Nico's mouth. "You can do this, Kats."

"Make it pretty," Nico mumbled through the teeth holding the branch.

"I'll try." Sean threaded the gut through the hole in the rib-needle. He held the wound together, inserted the point into the skin and pulled the improvised thread across both sides. A muffled growl came from Nico's throat. Sean continued, being as gentle as possible, although he knew how much pain his friend would have to endure. He continued suturing. Nico bit down harder and harder on his stick every time the needle went in and came out the other side. By the time Sean had sewn three quarters of the wound Nico bit through the branch and passed out.

Sean sat next to his friend through the night. He checked on him periodically, made sure he didn't have a fever and kept watch. He didn't know who or what lurked around them, and he was happy when the first rays of sun crept up over the mountain.

CHAPTER 35

Nico woke up shivering in the early morning. This time, although he was in pain, he didn't make a sound.

Sean was watching him. "Hey, Kats, how you feelin'?"

"Hey, Sandoval. You mean besides the pain? Not too bad."

"Listen, I went scouting. I found a way to get off this mountain. I can't believe how high up we are."

"I don't know if I can walk."

"You can't. I'll carry you."

"Don't be crazy. You go on by yourself and come back with the troops. It'll be a hell of a lot easier, and definitely faster."

"Can't do that."

"Why not?"

"Not leaving you."

"Listen, Sandoval, go get some help and come back."

"I said I'm not leaving you, and that's final."

Nico knew Sean meant it, and would never be able to change his mind. "Crazy Indian."

"You know it."

"Are you sure about this?" Nico tried one more time.

"Absolutely. Let's get going."

"What, no coffee?"

"Suck on one of these," Sean said handing him a lollipop.

"Okay." Nico put the stick in his mouth.

"And drink some water before we go." Sean gave him the bag. Nico took it and swallowed a few gulps. "Ready?"

"As I'll ever be."

"Right. Let's go."

Sean helped Nico up, who then stood on his good leg. He lifted him up into a fireman's carry, the wounded limb dangling in front.

"Is this okay?"

"Very comfy," Nico lied and gritted his teeth.

Sean started walking down the mountain. It was treacherous and he went slowly and carefully. He didn't want to drop his load. He also kept close to the edge of the forest. They would be a little more inconspicuous that way.

"How you doin', Sandoval?"

"I'm good. How about you? How's the pain?"

"Uh huh."

"Does that mean you need another lollipop?"

"No, I'll save it for when it gets really bad."

"Okay."

"We lost all our equipment, huh?"

"Yeah, unfortunately, but we'll be okay."

"By the way what did you use for sutures?"

"Bunny gut," Sean chuckled.

"You didn't!"

"I did."

"Oh, Sergeant Smith would be proud of you."

"And my Dad too. I'm really glad I learned a few tricks from him growing up."

Nico was thinking about the gut. "I've become rabbit stew," he exclaimed theatrically.

"Speaking of stew, are you hungry?"

"What do you mean?" Nico knew that Sean hadn't lit any fires, and even if he had he wouldn't have cooked a stew."

Sean handed him the plastic bag. "Help yourself."

Nico did. He ate a couple of the raw chunks. He knew he needed all the protein and fat the little animal provided.

After a couple of hours Sean took a break and gently put Nico down. "You okay?"

"I think it's time for that lollipop."

Sean fished into one of his pockets and handed him the pain killer. "We'll take a few minutes break and then we'll move on some more. We need to get as far as possible down the mountain before the sun goes down. It's going to be bitterly cold tonight."

"Is that your Navajo or your pilot skills telling you that?"

"All of that and Pararescue training."

"Whatever you say," Nico said weakly. The trek had exhausted him. The pain had been excruciating even though he knew Sean had done his best to make him as comfortable as possible. He waited patiently for the medicine to kick in.

After a little while Sean lifted Nico back on his shoulders and started back down the mountain. When the sun went down the icy cold took over and burrowed into their bones. Soon Sean could barely see and he didn't want to take a chance on stumbling and dropping his load. So far he had been really careful and hadn't fallen once. He went deeper into the forest. He found a spot that was dense with foliage, where he was fairly sure they would not be spotted unless the insurgents were practically on top of them. Sean leaned Nico against a tree. He could tell his buddy was exhausted, in pain and getting weaker.

Sean decided to build a fire. He dug a hole in the earth with his knife and gathered twigs and small branches. He cut bark off a tree, scraped some of it into tinder and quickly built a fire which he surrounded one side with flat stones. He cut another larger piece of bark and shaped it into a cup, put the shavings into the vessel, added some snow and rested it on stones around the fire. Soon the water was bubbling.

Nico watched Sean from where he was leaning against his tree. He wanted to help the man who had carried him for hours, but found that he could hardly lift his arms.

"Hey, Kats, hot tea?"

"Oh, yeah." Nico took a sip. "Kinda bitter."

"Just a bit, but it's hot."

"That it is."

"You know what I miss, Kats?"

"What's that?"

"Brisket taco plate, smothered with salsa, guacamole and pico de gallo!"

"Oh, sounds good, and I'll have a souvlaki with tzatziki on a pita bread, and lemon roasted potatoes."

"And a nice cold local beer!" They said at the same time and laughed.

"When we get back, Kats. We'll call our families and put our orders in."

Sean gave Nico some of the rabbit chunks and both men only ate a couple of pieces each. They knew they had to conserve what they could.

"Sean?" Ever since their first meeting at Lackland back in Texas, Nico had never called him by his first name.

"Yeah, man?"

"I want you to know something."

"What's that?"

"You mean more to me than even a brother."

Sean knew where this was going and also knew that Nico had to stay with it, psychologically and emotionally. "Are you trying to tell me that you're batting for the other team?"

"No, hell no, asshole. Just listen."

"If it's something stupid I don't want to hear it."

"Thanks for everything you've done, man. If I don't make it back I want you to tell my family how much I loved them."

"Kats, shut the fuck up."

"Please."

"You're not leaving us. Your parents and Sophia will see you again. That's a promise." But Sean didn't know if it would be dead or alive. Either way he swore he would bring his brother back.

"Sean, seriously."

"Yes, I promise, and I love you too, man."

Sean looked at his best buddy. He had fallen asleep. It took two years to become a Pararescueman and less than a second for them to get blown up while trying to save a life. No, he swore again, he would get him back and very much alive. Sean was lost in his thoughts. He contemplated on his life. It had been good, and he missed it. He wanted to be back with his family and with Angela, especially his Ajei. He took the letter she had written him out of his pocket and read it for the hundredth time. He also had her picture. He looked at it long and hard and kissed it before putting it back.

Sean cut the chunks of rabbit into thin strips and let them cook on the hot stones around the fire to preserve them. After a little while he let them dry out. They would have rabbit jerky for a few days. Sean fed the fire every couple of hours. He didn't want to make it big to warn anybody, but he wanted Nico to be warm.

As Sean had predicted the weather worsened. The temperature dropped and the snow came down forcefully. Sean was glad they were in the forest, protected pretty well from the elements, but it was bitterly cold. He huddled next to Nico and managed to cover both of them with the waterproof space blankets. He cradled his best friend. Their body heat just enough to keep them fairly warm and dry.

Just before dawn Sean woke Nico up, gave him another cup of hot brew and a piece of jerky.

"Breakfast of champions," Nico chortled.

"Drink up, man."

Nico did. When he finished Sean picked him up in the fireman's hold and they continued their trek. Even though they were next to the woods the walking was difficult and Sean almost fell several times. He was warm enough as he was exercising, but Nico was trembling.

"Hey, Sandoval."

"What's up?"

"I have to take a piss."

"Go right ahead."

"Seriously, man."

"I know. Best thing you can do. It'll keep you warm."

"You're right." And Nico did. The warm liquid spread down his legs. It was one of the tricks they had learned in survival training.

By the third night Sean's body was aching. His bruises and pain were better, but his muscles were throbbing and cramping. He brushed it off, but he knew he had to do something different with Nico. They were much farther down than where they started and almost out of the mountains.

Sean cut down two small trees and broke off all the branches.

Nico stared at him. "What are you up to, man?"

"Making a travois for you."

"A what?"

"A litter, Navajo style."

"For me?"

"Uh huh."

Nico watched as Sean put the contraption together. He took the two small trunks, laid them on the ground parallel to each other, the top opening a little closer together. He then crossed them with branches. He cut the rope into pieces and tied everything together. He also cut the bottom of the logs and made them flat so they could slide better. Sean thought of the piece of metal he had used to slide down the snowy slope, but had left it there as it wouldn't have been any help.

"Kats, give me your rigger." Nico complied and gave him his belt. Sean took his off as well and attached each one to the top of the travois. He looked over the litter one more time, double checked the rope and looped the belts around each of his shoulders similar to a parachute harness. He took a few steps and the litter glided behind him.

Nico appreciated Sean's creativity. "Wow, it really works!"

"Did you have doubts?"

"Absolutely not."

"Good, because that's your bed from now on. We'll start off early in the morning."

"And where are we going?"

"Bagram."

"You know where the base is?"

"I have some idea," Sean answered, and hoped to God he was right.

Early the next morning Sean woke up. He had fallen asleep sometime during the night cradling Nico. Both men were still in the same position. They were so exhausted neither one of them had moved. Sean carefully woke Nico up. "Hey, sleeping beauty, I need to get you on the travois. You can go back to sleep when you're on it."

"Okay, you crazy Indian," Nico said groggily.

"I have a couple of pops left, you want one?"

"Yeah, I do." Nico was in excruciating pain and wanted to scream, but for Sean's sake he didn't. He appreciated all the hard work the man was putting in for him, and he wanted to at least try to make things as easy as possible.

Sean gave him the painkiller, lifted him up and gently put him on the litter. He crouched down in the front and put the harness around his shoulders. He pulled slightly until it was taut and slowly stood up. The top of the travois lifted off the ground. "How is it, Kats?"

"Just like my mattress back home."

"Asshole," Sean said and smiled.

"Truth be told it's really good, Sandoval." And Nico meant it. Traveling on top of Sean's shoulders for hours had been excruciatingly painful.

CHAPTER 36

Sean continued pulling Nico toward their destination. He was happy with the litter, it was working out well. He must have done a decent job as Nico had quickly fallen back asleep. He was sure he was more comfortable lying down than being wrapped around Sean's shoulders. Since he didn't have to carry his buddy anymore different sets of muscles were now being used. The ones that had been carrying the wounded man were getting a break. By sunset they had traveled several kilometers and Sean stopped. He looked around. They were in another forest and he could hear water. Was it a river? A waterfall maybe? And then he heard something else, his worse fear—militia, and they were coming straight for them. He quickly lowered the litter to the ground, put a finger to his lips to warn Nico not to make any noise and hurriedly covered him with leaves. He crouched behind a tree away from his friend. Two men were walking toward them, their AK47s by their side. Nico was well hidden, but he could see everything that was going on. The men stopped. One of them was Hamzed Wazir.

"The infidels are here," he said to the other man who was wearing a brown scarf around his neck.

"How do you know?"

"I can smell them. Westerners have a certain odor."

They looked around.

"There!" Brown Scarf said, "behind that tree."

The men ran to where their enemy was. Sean took off running, wanted to get them away from Nico, but they caught up with him. One was behind, one in front. All Sean had was his knife who threw it at Brown Scarf. He never saw it leave the American's hand. It landed in his throat. He immediately went down gurgling blood. It only took him a few seconds to die. At the same time Sean lunged into Wazir like a professional linebacker and knocked him to the ground before he had a chance to lift his rifle. It fell and the two men rolled together in a deadly embrace.

Sean and Wazir fell apart and jumped to their feet.

"You will die, infidel!" He screamed in English.

"Why do you want to kill me so badly?" Sean asked, trying to steer him away from the knife that was sticking out of the dead man's throat.

"Because you must!"

"That's a great explanation," Sean said sarcastically. He was impressed by the way the man spoke his language. He must have lived in England for a few years. "Your English is excellent. Spent some time over there?"

Wazir lunged for the knife at the same time Sean did. They collided and the Afghan man lost his footing and started swinging his arms like a propeller. The American immediately understood what was happening and grabbed Wazir's arm as he was going over the edge of a cliff. Sean fell on his stomach holding the man who was dangling above the gorge. "Hold on!" Sean screamed. "I'll pull you up!" They were holding on to each other's forearms, but they were both slipping. "Grab my other hand!"

Wazir looked at him, hatred in his black eyes. "I curse you, your land and the people you love," Wazir said and violently let go. As he did he noticed the name on Sean's sleeve. Although he only had moments left to live it would be one of the last things he would remember.

"No!" Sean screamed, as he watched the man fall into the river and to his death. He followed him with his eyes as he splashed into the water. Wazir floated face down and drifted away as the current claimed his motionless body.

"Asshole!" Sean swore at the Afghan, "you would rather

die than let an 'infidel' help you. That's the problem with all of you idiots. Your way or no way. Don't you realize that we all live on the same planet, and that there's enough room for all of us to coexist?" Sean was angry, cursing the man that wouldn't take his help and talking to him as he were still standing on the edge of the cliff. He couldn't understand the misguided pride of a man who seemed educated and worldly and would prefer to die. What a wasted life. Sean lay on his stomach watching until Wazir disappeared, anger and disappointment etched on his face. When the body was no longer in sight Sean stood up and went to his wounded pal.

Nico had watched the struggle from his hiding place and seemed to read Sean's thoughts. "You did everything you could, man. Don't let it get to you."

But it did. Sean was in the business of saving lives, not losing them, at least not in such a stupid way.

Four days later Sean was still walking, still dragging the travois with Nico on it. The topography was gentler as they had gone beyond the mountains, but he knew the base was still a long way ahead of them. He calculated it would take them another week, and that was without any interference from people like the fanatical Taliban or Mujahedeen. He hoped Nico would last that long. He was now really weak and his mind was playing tricks on him. He would talk to Sophia, or to his parents, and usually in Greek. Of course Sean couldn't understand what he was saying, but every once in a while he would pick up some words, like *moussaká* and *beera*. They decided to travel at night since they were now in the high desert, and finding a good place to hide was becoming difficult. It provided better cover for them and it was less of a toil on their bodies. It was better to move around in the cold night than in the heat of the day.

The good news was that Nico's leg wasn't getting any worse, but Sean knew the man wouldn't last much longer. He had lost a lot of weight and his body couldn't keep up with its demands. He was dehydrated and hallucinating, and his organs would soon be shutting down. Sean had done all he could, but he was getting very weak as well. Suddenly, and for the first time, he lost his footing and crumpled to the ground. The litter crashed with Nico on it. The man hardly even moaned.

Sean lay on his back for a few minutes trying to recuperate as he took a short break. He stared at the black canvas above him, peppered with white stars. They were winking at him and the exhausted PJ wondered if they were making fun of his failure to save his friend's life. Out of the blackness he heard the scream of an eagle and firmly believed he was hallucinating like Nico. Eagles didn't come out at night. Or did they? He couldn't remember. He looked up. Of course there wasn't anything there, and definitely no eagle. And then he heard a helicopter, or did he? Was his mind playing tricks on him too? He listened carefully. He could still hear it. Yes! It really was a helo, but it was pretty high up. They would never be able to see the two men, especially in the dark. Sean quickly took the penlight from his pocket. He moved it back and forth and flashed a message in Morse code: 'PJs Sandoval and Kats, pick us up.' He repeated it several times. He waited for some sort of confirmation and then jumped in the air and pumped his fist several times when he saw the helo circle back. It was really there, right? When Sean heard the motor coming closer he smiled triumphantly as he realized it wasn't a dream and that they would survive.

"He shook Nico. Wake up, Kats, we're going home!"

"What?"

"Helo's on its way."

With all the energy Nico had left, which was practically nonexistent, he managed to open his eyelids and look up. For the first time he really believed he wasn't going to die, although he had come to terms with his imminent death. At times he wished Sean hadn't pulled him out of the exploding helicopter. But Sean had done more than that. He had saved his life, several times, risking his own many times over. God, how he loved the man.

Sean helped him out of the litter and held him up on his good leg as the helicopter was almost on the ground. "Close your eyes!" He hollered as the rotor churned the earth and engulfed them in a cloud of dust. The personnel jumped out even before the wheels touched down. They immediately carried Nico and helped Sean into the steel bird. One of them was Ted Johnson.

"Good to have you back, you crazy New Mexicans," Ted said grinning from ear to ear. He was delighted his buddies hadn't perished in the explosion.

"Good to see you too, Florida boy," Sean said as he crumpled in the big man's arms. Johnson gently laid him down on the floor of the helicopter. They took off into the black sky and the crew immediately worked on both men, inserted I.V.s and checked Nico's leg. They smiled when they saw Sean's handiwork.

"Hey Sandoval, what the fuck did you use to sew up Kats's leg?" Johnson hollered over the noise of the engines.

From his spot on the floor Sean looked up at his fellow PJs and answered: "It's called a bunny stitch."

Johnson wondered if there was such a thing.

As they flew toward the hospital Sean realized that he had used all the items he had recuperated, except for the rectal thermometer. He figured Nico would be happy about that. The exhausted man fell asleep with a smile on his face.

The doctors and nurses at the hospital at Bagram took care of Nico and thankfully he wouldn't lose his leg. Sean's chewed up bark poultice had saved the man's limb. He would be going on to Landstuhl in Germany to the military hospital. After a few days there they would send him home to New Mexico. It would take a several months to get his full mobility back, and he would get a medical discharge.

"I'll see you Stateside, my friend," Sean said as they carried Nico onto the giant Hercules waiting to medevac several wounded service members.

"That you will. And Sean…"

"Yeah?"

"Thanks for everything, man."

"It was a pleasure."

"Asshole."

"Love you too, man."

Both men still chuckled as Sean turned away from the plane. He would miss his buddy. It wouldn't be the same without him, but he still had a job to do.

Sean would be the awarded the Air Force Cross for his travails. He was also given a couple of weeks leave. He flew back to the States.

CHAPTER 37

When the Hercules C17 troop carrier landed at Kirtland Air Force base Sean felt his loins grow hard. He always had this reaction at take-offs and landings, on any plane, helicopter, hot air balloon, and anything that connected him with air. As soon as the wheels were chocked the service members came out and breathed the aroma of the land, of the mesa and the sun. It was the smell of home. He inquired about Nico and was thrilled that he would be flying in from Germany and to New Mexico in just a few days. He would be able to see him before going back to Afghanistan.

Sean's parents were waiting. They were anxious to see him. It had been almost a year since he had deployed to Afghanistan.

Fiona was the first to see him. She rushed up and fell into his arms.

"Mam!"

"Oh, Sean, it's so good to have you home!"

"I think so too!"

"Let me see you," she said, looking him over. "You look good, healthy and happy. A little thin perhaps." Fiona of course immediately understood that her boy had lost too much weight and wondered why. She knew that at some point Sean would probably tell her.

"I feel great Mam, really great."

Fiona looked at him. Something was up.

"Nílchi Deesdoi!" Tibah exclaimed seeing his son.

"Dad!" The two men embraced.

"You look great! You've lost quite a bit of weight. Ah, no worries, nothing your mother and the local cuisine can't fix."

"So what's up, *a stor*?" Fiona asked.

Sean looked at his mother with that 'how-did-you-know-look?' "Are your Celtic buddies kicking in and telling you things?" He chuckled.

"Ah, lad, you'll always be my little boy. Every mother is a bit psychic when it comes to their children. So, come on, out with it."

"I met a girl," Sean announced proudly.

Fiona was aware that her son had great success with the ladies, but this was the first time he was talking 'girls' with his mother. She tried to be as nonchalant as possible. "Oh?"

"Uh huh."

"Now that sounds serious."

"It is," Sean confirmed.

"Really?"

"Yes."

"Tell us about her." She looked at her husband. "You saw that smile too, Tibah, didn't you?" Fiona asked him.

"I did."

"Man, I can't get anything past you guys!"

"No," both Fiona and Tibah said at the same time.

Sean roared with laughter, and then repeated: "I met a girl. No, I met *the* girl."

"Ooh, so this *is* serious," Fiona said.

"Yeah, Mam."

"When you wake up is she the first thing your mind sees?" Tibah asked.

Sean grinned as only a man in love could. "Yes, Dad."

Both Fiona and Tibah went to their son and hugged him. "It's time we met your angel," Tibah said.

"How did you know her nam… never mind," Sean said, "forget I asked."

"Come, Nílchi Deesdoi, your mother made a feast. Let's eat. We need to fatten you back up."

"Home cooked food! I'm right behind you, Dad. I do have

one question, though."

"What is that?" Tibah asked.

"There's always something that clinches the falling in the love thing. What was it for you?"

"He called me a beautiful horse," Fiona said.

"What?"

Tibah chuckled as he remembered the first time he laid eyes on his beautiful flame-haired wife.

CHAPTER 38

"Tibah watched his pensive son who was sitting on the couch. He had a glassy stare that looked straight ahead, but it wasn't his eyes that were seeing, it was his mind.

"Nílchi Deesdoi, I believe it is time for the lodge."

Sean looked up from his reverie. "I believe you're right."

Fiona walked into the living room. She looked at the men conversing. Tibah saw her and got up. He hugged her. "It is time," he simply said.

"Is he alright?" She asked apprehensively.

"He is pretty good, but there is some healing that needs to be done to the warrior's heart. We will be gone for a day or two."

"I understand. I will pray for you."

"That is good, thank you, my dove."

Tibah and Sean rode out to the lodge, tied up the horses and built a fire. They waited for the embers and the stones to turn hot.

"Spirits of the North, Spirits of the South, Spirits of the East, Spirits of the West," Tibah said each time he turned in the direction of the cardinal points. He invoked and prayed to the Spirits as the two men held hands above their fire. He prayed for protection, for peace, for healing, for wisdom, for purification, for release of all negativity. Tibah picked up the mother of pearl shell that contained burning sage. They smelled its sweet aroma and Tibah brought the container above Sean's head. With an eagle feather he fanned the smoke all around his son. Sean did the same for his father. When they were done they started drumming and chanting. The sounds from the skins and from their voices were putting them in a trance, and they danced around the fire to the rhythm of the music and their hearts.

The ceremony was similar to the one they had done before Sean's departure for the other side of the world, but this time the younger man had new burdens weighing him down. Tibah was fairly certain that his son had witnessed or been part of some traumatic experiences in Afghanistan. He was also pretty sure that a certain number of people he had worked on, or had come in contact with, did not survive. It was an unfortunate fact of war, and probably the main reason the younger man needed to spend some time in the lodge. And of course Tibah had been told about the explosion in the helicopter and the fight for survival he and Nico had been through. The older man knew Sean had to release these mental and emotional demons, had to lighten his load and continue to walk the path of his life.

They sat in the lodge. After a little while Sean was seeing the Afghan man, their hands holding on to each other, his body dangling over the gorge. He knew how hard he tried to hold him, but he also saw the incredulous stupidity of the stubbornness as Wazir pulled away from Sean. The image of the hatred on his face would stay with him forever. His eyes followed him down into the water at the bottom of the canyon. Sean saw himself watching from above, his body morphing into an eagle and hovering over the floating body. He had no doubt he was the enormous raptor as he saw the piercing green eyes.

"Am I *chindi*, bewitched, by this man, Dad?" Was his father following his dreams? Was he able to see what Sean was seeing? He could somehow sense that he was.

"No, my son, he is not that powerful. He will not be a problem. You must let him go."

Sean kept seeing Wazir deep in a cave in Afghanistan.

The dead man's body was not solid, rather it was made of waves of gray smoke that undulated in front of his eyes. Every time the ghost-like Wazir approached Sean he would try to provoke him into a fight. Sean couldn't understand how the man could want such a thing. One of them was alive and made of skin and bones, the other was in a different world whose body was made of haze. Wazir kept trying to lure him into a lagoon of murky water in the center of the enormous cave. Sean looked at the mini lake and knew that it was evil. Suddenly a hundred replicas of Wazir's open hand, the one that Sean had tried to hold on to, kept rising and falling in and out of the water. There was no doubt in Sean's mind that they wanted to pull him in and hold him under the water under he drowned. Wazir wanted him dead and he used any means he could to achieve this from the other world.

Sean drifted in and out, as did Wazir and his demonic hands. Tibah was by his son's side the entire time invoking the Spirits, chanting, drumming, carefully watching his son and his visions. The Sandoval men stayed in the sweat lodge for twenty-four hours, detoxing and releasing the demons and negativity that were haunting Sean.

Tibah knew his son needed the session in the sweat lodge. He needed to alleviate his burdens and pains, both physical and emotional. He needed guidance and wisdom from the spiritual entities.

Tibah followed the news about veterans returning from war zones and wished they would all spend time in sweat lodges, especially the ones afflicted with PTSD. Some of the V.A. hospitals understood the benefits and built sweat lodges for the veterans. They found the results more powerful than conventional medicine. They understood that these places were refuges where the minds and bodies of the wounded warriors could heal.

CHAPTER 39

Not too far from where the Sandovals lived stood one of the largest casinos in New Mexico, the *Yeibichai*, the *Night Chant*. It was on Navajo land and it was close to the Sandia Casino, and although they were both hotels and gambling institutions they were not in competition with each other. Their design reflected the New Mexican and indigenous architectural tradition, but they were still different and unique. People enjoyed themselves when they went to the casinos and delighted in the facilities. There was plenty to go around, and the claim to fame of the *Yeibichai* was that it was a venue that celebrities loved performing at. Sean looked at the impressive structure and appreciated what the gambling facility had done for the Reservation. It provided jobs and incomes for many of the inhabitants, and one of them was his father who supplied them with his produce. It made Tibah financially very comfortable. He was even prouder of Joe, his best friend from high school who worked at the Yeibichai. The day Sean landed at Kirtland he had immediately called Joe and they agreed to see each other right away. As Sean now entered the establishment he was eager to see the changes he had been hearing about his friend.

After the fire Joe walked around the trailer he and his mother called home, barely more than a dilapidated box with four walls that was falling apart. Water seeped through the roof when it rained and thankfully that wasn't too often. The home was as hot as a sauna as soon the sun came up, and the freezing night temperatures of the high desert forced them to sleep under several blankets. Both Joe and his mother were overweight, from a diet that consisted of Ramen noodles, Spam and fry bread, or bologna covered with chips and buried between two pieces of white bread.

Joe kept walking around the trailer, as if in a permanent daze. The fire had really scared him, made him feel more vulnerable than he had ever been, and made him take a good look at his life. Would he always be called Fat Joe? Would his mother, who was at the moment in her forties, always look twenty years older? Why did his father, who had been overweight, have to die of a heart attack, leaving them to fend for themselves? Why did the Navajo, the *proud* Navajo, become third world citizens? Yes, of course the white man had stripped them of their land and dignity, and of hope and expectations. Because of these circumstances they turned to despair, to being lazy and indifferent, and to a solace in the shape of a bottle or drugs. His people had the highest rate of alcoholism, diabetes and heart disease in the country, and it had been killing them for years. This also contributed to the Diné having one of the lowest economies in the nation. Granted it started with the white man, but the continuing decline was by their own hand. They had to turn things around.

Teenage drug use and drinking were rampant and destructive, and Joe did not want to be included in those statistics. Hadn't all these problems contributed to the fire being set because someone was drunk? He knew this to be true. He was tired of all of it, fed up with being so damn poor, always scraping for change to get the bare necessities they needed to survive. And especially tired of being made fun of, whether it was about his weight or his lack of will power.

Joe decided he wasn't going to waste his life and follow in that detrimental path. It was time, time to turn his life around. He also wanted that for his people. He knew he wouldn't be able to solve all the problems, but he firmly believed he could make a difference. He sat on the earth against a fence and watched his mother fry her bread in the outdoor oven. Yes, he would make a difference, he insisted. He would get his mother a better home with all the comforts. He no longer wanted to see her get water from the well, he wanted her to be warm when it was cold, and cool when the scorching sun burned down. He wanted to be a son she could be proud of, wanted to buy her anything she could wish for or needed. He wanted her to eat the healthiest, freshest food. Joe wanted the same for himself. He would become thin and healthy, and somehow, some way, he would help his people as well. Joe was proud to be a member of the Navajo Nation, and wanted to preserve the culture, ceremonies, traditions, spirituality and language. He didn't want any of it to die out. His generation had to keep it going, just as previous ones did, but even that was an uphill battle. But Joe made a pact, with himself, to try to make a better world for the people he cared for, for his tribe, for the noble Navajos. He didn't want this once proud people to disappear.

Joe, Sean and Charlie had grown up together. They were fairly good students and Sean and Charlie knew what they wanted to do with their lives. Sean was going into the military and Charlie, who had always been an amazing athlete and who rode since he was small, was already on the rodeo circuit. As soon as he graduated he would tour the country. Sean and Charlie had made their plans, but what direction would he take? Joe wondered.

While he watched his mother making fry bread his mind was putting a plan together. He knew he could enroll for free in a college and he did. He also found a job helping Sean's father with his produce when his buddy left for his military training. It was a match made in heaven. Tibah not only paid the boy he also insisted he eat his meals with them, and take some of the fruit and produce home to his mother. Fiona always made extra for Joe and his mom and carefully prepared the meals that would help them lose weight. They were grateful and the young man found a new zeal he never knew he possessed. The Sandovals' house was not too far from his own and he would walk to it early in the mornings.

He would help Tibah, caring for the produce and then loading the pickup. They would drive together to the casino and deliver it to the restaurant. Joe was smart and quick and picked up details of the trade. One day one of the managers saw him watching.

"Hey, Joe, I could use an extra hand, do you need more work?"

Joe's heart skipped a beat. Of course he needed more work, but more importantly he wanted to learn the business of the restaurant.

Tibah saw the shine in the young man's eyes. He was proud of him. Joe had been with him for almost a year and had been a great help. He was also trim as he kept his word to Tibah and ate only the food Fiona caringly prepared for him. In addition he worked hard in the field and lost all the extra weight he had been carrying around for years. He also kept himself busy with his homework. He stayed home at night and didn't go out drinking with the rest of his age group. Joe studied hard, his objective a degree in business. He even took extra classes so he could get it faster.

Joe looked at Tibah, a little embarrassed. "I'm already working for Mr. Sandoval," he answered.

"I know, I just need you for a few days, two of my guys got in an accident and will be laid up for a couple of weeks. I sure could use the help. Let me know when I see you tomorrow."

Joe desperately wanted to see how the restaurant was run, but he was also loyal to the Sandovals.

"Alright Joe, let's get going," Tibah said.

"Right behind you."

They climbed into the pickup and drove out.

"Listen, Joe, I want you to know that you've been a great help to me this whole time."

"It's been my pleasure, sir, and I want to thank you for what you've done for me. I'm very grateful. You gave me a job and you've given me hope, and even got me thin and healthy. I don't know how to repay you and Mrs. Sandoval, and I certainly won't take the job at the restaurant and let you down."

"I'm proud of you, Joe. You turned out to be a fine and loyal young man, and Fiona will be thrilled that you like her cooking."

"Oh, yes, very much."

"I also know that you've set your sights beyond my fields, and that's how it should be. You must follow your heart and find your path in life. I have a feeling that you might know what direction that is, and I'm behind you one hundred percent."

Joe loved this family and he regarded Tibah Sandoval as the father he never really had. "I appreciate that more than you could ever know," Joe said.

"Listen, Joe, everyone needs a helping hand once in a while, or maybe a second chance. But I'll tell you a secret: the one giving the help feels just as good, if not better. There's a sense of accomplishment and pride when there is success. I see this success in your life, Joe."

Tibah had witnessed the hunger in the younger man's eyes and knew he would go far. If he could help him along the way he was glad to do it.

"Thank you, Mr. Sandoval."

"I mean it, Joe. So, let's talk about the restaurant. I think it would be a good idea, and a wonderful job opportunity for you."

Joe started the very next day and Tibah watched the boy mature into a young man full of ambition. He began by washing dishes and graduated through the positions of cook, waiter, host and eventually manager. It had taken him just over a year. For extra money he cleaned the rooms in the hotel, became friends with the cleaning staff and the employees at the front desk. He learned as much as he could from them about the mechanics of reservations and the running of the hotel. At the same time he finished his degree in business. He also learned the gambling end of the enterprise, all the games offered at casinos and became a croupier. Joe could tell that his plans were coming together.

Joe worked hard for everything he accomplished. He had climbed the proverbial ladder and was proud to have moved on from an assuredly wasteful life. He had learned and worked at probably every position in the casino. His preference was the entertainment side of it, especially the shows and more specifically the singers. He watched every detail, from the construction of the sets to the costumes to the quirks and habits of the some of the biggest stars in the world.

The casino's manager followed Joe's career from the first day he washed dishes in the restaurant. Nothing escaped him, and when his assistant suddenly died of a heart attack he summoned young Joe.

When Joe entered the manager's office he thought he was there to get fired, although he couldn't think of anything he had done wrong. He hadn't even taken a complimentary bottle of shampoo. He was an honest man and didn't want to risk losing his job for any reason whatsoever.

"Come in, Joe, have a seat," the manager said.

"Yes, Mr. Rivera."

"Do you know why I've called you in?"

"No, sir. Uh, have I done anything wrong?"

"No, Joe, on the contrary, you've done everything right."

Joe stared at him. What did he mean? "Sir?"

"I've been watching you. As a matter of fact I've been following your progress here at the casino since your first job as a dishwasher."

"Yes, sir."

"I know all the positions you've held and I must say I'm impressed. You've done this in a very short time. Usually people are happy with one thing or the other and they stick with that job for years, but you seem to know and worked about all of them."

"I found them all very interesting, sir."

"Tell me, is there one particular job you like best?"

"I'm not sure. Is there a position that has to do with all of them?" Joe asked honestly.

The manager roared with laughter. "I like you, Joe, and your answer is perfect! And it also confirms that I made a good choice."

"Sir?"

"I'm offering you a job."

"A job, sir?"

"Yes. As I'm sure you know I just lost my assistant and I need someone to be my right hand, I want you to take over the duties of the assistant manager."

Joe held his breath. In a blink of an eye he saw his life flash before him—the difficult childhood, the loss of his father, the struggling with his mother, the fire, the despair and the hopelessness. And then the turn of the tide with the help of the Sandovals and his very own accomplishments at the different casino jobs and his business degree. He had arrived, had accomplished his goal after so many years of despair and then of hard work. Joe wasn't bitter about anything, on the contrary, he was proud of his achievement. His plans had come together and manifested. "It would be an honor, sir."

"Good. You start tomorrow."

As in his previous jobs Joe excelled. In less than a year the manager was grooming him to take over as head of the entire casino enterprise as he wanted to retire. Joe achieved that dream as well. He was the youngest to ever occupy a managerial position in any casino around the country. He was damn proud to be the manager of the Yeibichai casino.

Now Joe waited for Sean, the man that risked his own life to make sure he still had his, to walk through his door. When he heard the knock he immediately jumped out of his chair and went to greet his old friend. The two men embraced.

"Hey, Sean, how are you? How is our local hero, the great Pararescue superman?"

"I'm great, Joe, or should I call you 'skinny Joe'? Wow, you look like you're in great shape, man. I haven't seen you since we graduated from high school. My parents told me you lost weight. You really look terrific, Joe."

"Your parents had a lot to do with it, and I never want to go back to 'Fat Joe'. The fire put my life in perspective, and if it hadn't been for you…"

"I'm just glad I was there."

"Have a seat."

"Thanks." Sean looked around, taking in the office filled with Navajo art and crafts. It was beautifully decorated. "Office looks great, Joe."

"Yeah, I like it."

Sean laughed. "You should, it's gorgeous."

"Thanks."

"I'm proud of you, man. I know you worked hard."

"I did."

"Are you happy?"

"Very. I can finally give my mother everything she needs."

"Yeah, I saw the house. I'm really happy for you both, you deserve it."

"It's not too big and it's cozy. We're happy with it. As far as work this is my dream job. I put in a lot of sweat to get here, but I was also lucky. Your parents started me off. Without them I know I would never have gotten this far."

"I know how proud they are of you."

Drink?"

"No, I'm good."

"What can I do for you? Name it, you got it."

"You're the best Joe, and yes I came not only to see you, but to ask you for a favor."

"I owe you, Sean, you know that. Now, tell me."

"I met a girl."

"Oh, this sounds serious, but I like it. Tell me more, Nílchi Deesdoi."

"She's beautiful, smart…"

"Of that I have no doubt."

"…And sings like an angel."

"Really?" Sean had just peaked Joe's interest.

"Really."

"And?"

"And I'm asking you to give her an audition. If you think she's good hire her to sing here at the casino."

"Interesting," Joe mused.

"Well? Could you do that? What do you think?"

"I think you're in love."

"You think right."

"I'm impressed. I've never seen this side of you."

"I hadn't either. It's new, but it's the best thing in the world."

"I see she makes you happy, Nílchi Deesdoi."

"Like nothing else in this universe."

"Is she local?"

Sean shook his head. "No, she's not from here. I met her when I was in training."

"And this angel lives where?"

"North Carolina."

Joe whistled. "I see."

"She's really good, Joe. If she wasn't I would never ask you for such a favor, or put you in an awkward position. I think you could give her a chance to make a career for herself, and more selfishly, I'd like to have her close by."

"This really is serious."

"Joe."

"Yes?"

"You're killing me. Will you help out?"

"Yes, of course, Sean. I'll set it up. And by the way, you had me at 'I met a girl'."

"You're the best, man. Thank you!"

"It's the least I can do. Besides, if she's everything you say she is, which I believe, this will be a good for all of us."

"Oh, one more thing."

"Oh, oh."

"She can't know that I set this up."

Joe raised an eyebrow, then nodded. "Understood."

"Thank you, Joe."

"Don't mention it. So, what are you up to these days?"

"Just a few days off and then back to Afghanistan."

"You watch your ass over there!"

"I try to. Okay Joe, I'm going to see my parents and a buddy who was wounded who's from here, see how he's doing."

"Okay, give them my best, and thank your buddy for me."

"I will. Thanks again for everything, Joe." Sean gave the man Angela's phone number.

"Her name is Angela?" Joe asked.

"That's right."

"Of course it is, why am I not surprised?" Joe sighed.

The two men embraced and Sean left.

Joe looked at the back of the door and smiled. He loved Sean. He was a good man. Without him he wouldn't be alive today. He reached for the phone. "Stella? This is what I need…" he said to his assistant.

CHAPTER 40

Angela's phone rang. She picked it up. "Hello?"

"Ms. Angela Moreno?"

"Speaking."

"Ms. Moreno, my name is Stella, I'm calling from Albuquerque, New Mexico."

Angela looked at her phone. Did they have the wrong number? Or was this one of those calls asking for something. And then she gasped—had anything happened to Sean?

"Yes?" She asked apprehensively.

By the time Angela hung up with the woman she was in a daze. Could this be a turning point in her life? *The* turning point?

In less than forty-eight hours Angela was on a plane to Albuquerque. She was excited. The Yeibichai casino was well known. It was one of the largest in the Southwest and she knew how much entertainers from around the world loved playing that venue. The stars were some of the biggest names in the business. And now they had called her. Yes, *me,* Angela Moreno, her mind screamed. How had they heard of her, this young woman from Sammy's in North Carolina? Did Sean have anything to do with it? She thought back to the phone call. Stella had been so nice. She told her the general manager wanted her to audition for him, and that her ticket and all expenses, including the nights she would miss at the bar, would be covered. And she of course would stay in a suite at the casino. Her reply had taken about two seconds, enough time to figure that even if she didn't get the job she would have a paid vacation to a place, from what she had read and was told from Sean, was a beautiful part of the United States. As Angela looked out of the window of the aircraft she studied the landscape passing by below her. As she flew over Texas she thought the topography was an extension of Mexico which made her examine her life so far.

When Angela was three years old the great earthquake of Mexico City shook the buildings so violently that most of the city center was devastated. Her parents were both doctors working in one of the hospitals, two of the more than nine hundred patients, physicians, nurses and medical personnel that lost their lives during the brutal quake that left the building in rubble. The series of quakes and aftershocks killed a minimum of 10,000 people. Estimates climbed to 40,000.

Angela had been at home with her nanny when the house came crumbling down. She was found later that night by a stray dog who was barking at the crying baby. They also found the nanny on top of her who had saved the little girl's life by giving hers. They took her to an orphanage where she stayed until her Aunt found her six months later after frantically searching for her. The two women were the only survivors of the Moreno family. The older woman took her niece to the United States where she had been living and working as a nurse in a hospital in Fayetteville, in North Carolina. She raised the little girl as her own until she died of cancer when Angela was in her senior year of high school. The aunt had some savings and in her will she left everything to her only family member. Angela didn't know what she wanted to study, but she enrolled in a local community college. The one thing she adored was her music. She loved singing and playing the guitar, and knowing that the savings her aunt left her would not last long, decided to find a job. And she did, at Sammy's, a bar near a military base. By day she would go to school and study, in the evenings she would sing. It wasn't bad. She didn't mind working there as the pay was decent and the tips were good. She was fluent in both Spanish and English and her repertoire included songs in both languages. She was well liked and kept the bar full with the customers coming back. The men all tried to take her out, but she wasn't interested until one made her heart sing. Where was Sean now? Was he in danger's way? She missed her man. She was going to his town. It was a pity he wasn't around.

When she landed in Albuquerque she marveled at the airport. It wasn't enormous like so many others, rather it was a convenient size and easy to get around. As she walked toward the exit she saw lovely shops and a magnificent statue of a glorious Native American. She immediately thought of Sean. Sunport was constructed to look like an adobe, a typical New Mexican architectural design. As she descended the escalator to exit the airport she gasped as a hot air balloon, in all its glory, was proudly displayed for all to see, *inside* the building. She had never seen one close up and something about it made her want to sing. It just made her unbelievably happy and made her think of Sean the night they met at Sammy's. She loved the way he had flirted with her, using music and hot air balloons. She so longed to see him, to hold him, to make love with him. She wished he were here, and not on the other side of the world.

Once outside a chauffeur waited for her with a limousine. He took her luggage and they drove to the casino. It wasn't very far and on the way she appreciated the city, the views of the Sandia Mountains and the mesa. Even the casino looked like a lovely huge adobe. Angela Moreno now understood why Sean was so attached and proud of his homeland.

CHAPTER 41

Hamzed Wazir heard bees around him. Where am I? Is this paradise? With insects? He listened more carefully and heard his native language of Dari. Am I still alive? Hamzed opened his eyes. He took in the room and recognized the walls of a village dwelling as well as several people talking behind the wall of where he was. That is why he thought he was hearing bees. He then remembered the river, falling from the top of the gorge, Sandoval's hand... Sandoval... and then it all flooded back, including the dark anger in his soul.

"Praise Allah, he is back!" A woman hollered.

Wazir looked up at the woman who discovered that he was no longer sleeping. "Who is in charge here?" He yelled.

Between the woman's enthusiastic hollering and Wazir yelling, a middle-aged man came running in. "Praise Allah! Hamzed, calm yourself. You are safe and healing nicely. You are lucky to be alive!"

I'm going to find Sandoval and *he* won't be so lucky to be alive. I will make him pay for every Afghani he and his country have killed. "How long have I been out?" He asked the man.

"Almost four months."

"That long?"

"It's a miracle you are alive and woke up. Your injuries have healed nicely. You should have your full strength back in a few days."

Wazir had been in a coma for four months. Sandoval had stolen even more from his life. "You took care of me?"

"Yes, my family and I."

"I owe you."

"Please, it is our pleasure and our tradition. We thank you for the opportunity."

"Again, that's very kind of you. *Tashakor*, thank you."

"Don't mention it." The man saw the woman bringing a tray with *tchai* and fruit. "Please, drink and eat, you will feel better."

Hamzed took the glass of tea from the tray and drank it slowly. He stared at the brew and began devising his revenge. He had a valid passport from his studies abroad. His first step would be a flight to London where he still had contacts, and then he would continue on to the United States where Sandoval lived. He didn't know where that was, but he would most definitely find out.

CHAPTER 42

Sean called Angela's cell phone.

"Hello?"

"Hi Ajei."

"Sean! What a fantastic surprise! I didn't recognize the number, other than it has a New Mexico code. Oh, I have so much to tell you, but first how are you?" Angela said all in one breath.

"I'm fine. Nico got wounded but he's doing good."

"Oh, my God!"

"He'll be fine, I promise."

"Thank God!"

"So, what about you?"

"I'm actually really great!"

"Really?" Sean of course knew where this was going.

"Yes! I got a job, a great job!" She said excitedly.

"Singing?"

"Oh, yes! And guess where?"

"I give up."

"At the Yeibichai casino!"

"In Albuquerque?"

"Yes! I arrived yesterday and did an audition. They liked me, really liked me!"

"That is great!"

"Yes, and I'll be moving here. They gave me a lovely little apartment right in the casino and I'll be singing here permanently. And the salary, divine. I couldn't have asked for more."

"That's amazing!" Sean exclaimed. He was delighted. Joe had come through as promised, and he knew that with Angela's voice he wouldn't have felt compelled to hire her because Sean had saved his life. "So, are you there now?"

"Yes, I'm at the casino."

"Does that mean I can come see you?"

There was silence on the phone for a few seconds and Sean heard her gasp. "Are you here, in Albuquerque?" She whispered.

"I am," he whispered back.

She screamed and Sean had to hold the phone away from his ear. "Sean Sandoval, get yourself over here right now!" She commanded.

"Yes Ma'am, give me about an hour."

Sean called his longtime friend.

"Hello?"

"Joe, its Sean."

"Hey, Superman, how's it going?"

"It's going great. I wanted to thank you. I just talked to Angela, she told me everything. Thanks, man, you're the best!"

"Actually, I should thank you, she truly is a gem. What a voice, and yeah, she's a beautiful girl. Well done, Nílchi Deesdoi."

"Thanks Joe, for everything."

"You're welcome."

Sean arrived exactly one hour later. He found Angela's apartment and knocked on the door. As soon as it opened she jumped on him. He held on to her tightly, they both did. Sean closed the door behind him and as their bodies slightly parted they looked into each other's face and hungrily kissed. All the anxiety, emotion and anticipation dissipated with that one kiss. They were together, and that's all they wanted at this moment in time. They made love, talked about their last year, made love again and ordered room service.

"I'm going to take a shower," Sean announced after they finished their meal.

"Want company?"

"Of course."

"Uh, how is little Sean?"

"Dying to make his beautiful lady happy."

"Doesn't he ever get tired?"

"Not when it comes to his Ajei."

"I really like that little guy."

Sean grinned and picked her up on their way to the shower.

CHAPTER 43

Sean and Angela held hands as they walked onto the enormous field. It was October, his favorite time of year in Albuquerque. The weather was perfect and it was the beginning of the Balloon Fiesta. The timing of Sean's leave had been coincidently perfect, and he was thrilled that he would be showing Angela the first of what he was sure would be many of these festivities. The park was over seventy yards long and hundreds of hot air balloons lay on their sides waiting to be inflated. As they walked on the sidewalk where the food vendors were selling their goodies they heard an announcer on the loudspeaker stating the national anthem would be sung. Everyone present stood silent as they listened to a choir singing and watched the first balloon lift off. Below the basket it sported the American flag. Sean looked at the woman he loved. Her eyes glowed as bright as the fires from the burners, and he wondered if it was because of the momentous event, or because they were together. He decided it was both.

When the ceremony was over the balloonists started inflating. Everyone present, no matter what age, became a child. All were mesmerized by the colors, by the enormity of the event, by the joy it brought to their hearts, by the uniqueness of hundreds of balloons inflating at the same time. Angela was no exception as she too became a youngster.

"Sean, look at that one!" She exclaimed as one of the special shaped balloons started ascending.

"Yes, Ajei, out of all the balloons there are at least a hundred special shapes."

"This is magnificent, Sean. Thank you for bringing me here."

"It's my pleasure, and believe me it never gets old, no matter what age you are."

"I believe it."

They watched the balloons take flight one by one. He watched the French balloon, it was sporting that country's flag. He smiled when he saw *Annonay* inscribed on the lower portion of the envelope. He remembered his boyhood dreams with the Montgolfier brothers, and that they were from Annonay in the Ardèche, in the southeastern region of France.

"We'll have to do this every year."

"Oh, yes, let's!"

"Do you think you'd like to ride in one?"

"Oh, yes! Can we?"

"Absolutely. I'll set it up. Of course we have to book this in advance."

"I understand. Hundreds of people probably want to ride."

"I have a surprise for you, Ajei," Sean said to the love of his life.

"You do?"

"He does," a voice behind her said.

Angela whirled around and saw Nico. He looked good, a little thin and leaned on crutches, but good. "Nico! Oh, it is so wonderful to see you. You're alright?" She hugged him, truly happy to see the man, and so very glad he was alive.

"I'm great. And you look happy and wonderful too. I heard that you're going to be a resident of our great state."

"I am!" She said proudly

Nico pulled Sophia forward. "Angela, this is Sophia, my wife."

The women hugged, an immediate connection.

"So good to meet you."

"Yes," Sophia agreed, "and we have some really special guys."

"Absolutely!" Angela said.

"Hey, let's get some burritos, they're the best around," Sean said.

"Let's go."

Once they had eaten, and of course Sean and Nico had two large breakfast specials each, they went back to the field and watched more of the balloons inflate and ascend.

Sean was standing behind Angela, his arms wrapped around her waist, his chin on her shoulder against her hair. "I have a question for you, Ajei. A serious one."

"Do you?"

"Yes." Sean paused and watched one of the balloons gently lift off the ground. The gathered crowd clapped in delight.

"Well, what is it?"

"How would you like to get married in a hot air balloon, in the middle of the sky?"

Angela who had been watching a special shape take off suddenly turned and stared at the man she loved. He was holding a ring in his hand. She gasped as the sun hit the diamond perfectly and made it sparkle. "Oh, *mi Amor*, are you asking me to marry you?" Sean nodded. "And do the ceremony in a balloon?" He nodded again.

Sean stared at her and knew he would always remember the glow on Angela's face. This was what a woman looked like at her happiest. Sean thought his heart would burst through his chest.

"Oh, yes, my love, yes!"

Sean placed the ring on her finger, lifted her off the ground and kissed her. Nico and Sophia, and the spectators who had gathered around them, and who had been holding their breath, finally let out a cry and clapped profusely.

Nico lovingly smacked his best friend's back. "Well done, Sandoval."

"Thanks, Kats."

"Pretty amazing, isn't it?"

"Like nothing else."

This was indeed a special day at the balloon fiesta. It was also time for Sean to take Angela to meet his parents. He could hardly wait.

CHAPTER 44

Sean's two weeks of vacation came to an end. He was leaving for Afghanistan the next day and the lovers spent their last night together at Angela's apartment.

"I hate that you have to leave, Sean."

"I know, Ajei, so do I, but this is what I do."

"I understand. Just please be careful."

"I will, I promise."

They spent the rest of the night talking and making love. They didn't sleep. Angela didn't have to sing until the next evening and Sean could sleep on his long flight to Afghanistan. And still they thought the hours passed by too quickly.

Nico picked Sean up and drove him to the air base. It was easier for Angela. She was having a hard time, and knowing how long they would be apart depressed her. But her greatest fear was that he possibly could be hurt... or worse. She tried putting the negative thoughts out of her mind, and prayed for his safe return.

"It won't be the same, Kats. It doesn't feel right. Last time we flew it together."

"I know. It doesn't feel right to me either. You'll be there, and I'll be here."

"Yeah, I'm not as excited, and I'm leaving a lot more behind."

"I know," Nico repeated, "you just watch your six. Don't let anything happen to you!"

"I'll do my best."

"You do better than that, Sandoval!"

"You got it."

"At least you won't have to carry me around."

Sean laughed. "As I said, it won't be the same."

Once they arrived the men got out of the car and hugged.

"Take care of yourself, man."

"Yeah, you too, and check on Angela and my parents every once in a while."

"I definitely will, and Sophia will too."

"Thanks, Kats."

Sean turned, walked away and waved. Both men had a lump in their throat and a stone grinding in their stomach. Their instincts were warning them. There was danger ahead.

CHAPTER 45

Hamzed Wazir fully recuperated from his fall into the river and now his only focus was on revenge. He was obsessed, and failure was not an option. He thanked the family that had nursed him back to health and went to the mountains, to one of the deep caves. He brought some food, water and a prayer rug. Wazir was all alone. He told the men who were loyal to him that he would be leaving and finishing his mission in the United States. They would know of his success from the news—it would make big, worldwide news, like the towers in New York and the marathon in Boston. He stayed two days in the cave, praying and devising his plan.

Wazir boarded a flight from Kabul to Istanbul. As the plane took off and climbed he looked down at his beloved Afghanistan. He burned the image, in his mind and in his heart, of the land he would never see again. He once thought that he wanted to be buried with his noble ancestors, but knew that would no longer be possible as he would die in the land of the infidels. Once the plane leveled off at its cruising altitude Wazir put his head on the headrest and closed his eyes. For the rest of the five hour flight Wazir's mind was filled with ways to kill Sandoval. That's all he could think about. He held his anger back as he had to pay attention connecting at Istanbul's Atatürk airport. He went through and boarded his fight to London. Another four hours and he would be in the country where he had studied for his engineering degree. He would now use his expertise to destroy instead of build.

As Wazir landed at London's Heathrow airport he showed his passport to customs and immigration. He had no problems entering the country, and walked out into the terminal. He found a public phone and made a call.

"It's Wazir," he said into the earpiece.

"I'll meet you at Wembley."

"At the stadium?"

"Anything wrong with that?" The cold voice said.

"No, not at all."

"I'll leave a ticket for you at the box office."

Even though Wazir was completely focused on his mission he had to smile. Like most of the world he loved football. "Who's playing?"

"Arsenal, Liverpool."

Wazir whistled. "That should be a good game."

"I'll see you there," the voice said, and hung up.

Wazir stepped out of the terminal and looked at the sky. It would be cold and rainy. The weather in England never changed. He would get soaked at the game. He took a taxi to Wembley. When he arrived he was a bit disoriented as he realized that the stadium had been rebuilt since he had been there. As an engineer he was duly impressed. It was a beautiful construction and to his joy he noticed a retractable roof that would cover most of the thousands of expected spectators.

"Lovely, isn't it?" The driver said.

"Yes, very nice indeed," Wazir agreed. He paid the cabby and walked toward the building. He passed the statue of Bobby Moore, the captain of the 1966 English world cup winning team, and went to find his ticket.

As Wazir entered the stadium he first noticed the manicured green grass and the seats that were all red. The crimson spread throughout the stadium. He immediately pictured Sandoval completely red as well—from his own spilled blood—and Wazir would be a witness to it since he would do the honors.

The sports arena was almost filled to capacity and Wazir was just one of the spectators. He found his seat and sat down. A few minutes later another man sat next to him. They looked at each other.

"Maloof," he said and held out his hand.

Wazir shook it. "Thank you for the ticket."

"It should be a good game," he smiled.

Wazir understood that 'business' would not be conducted in the stadium so he decided he might as well enjoy a game of football. He had to admit the Brits were good players, although the Afghan teams were doing pretty well. How wonderful would it be to see his national team in a world cup.

The two Afghan men watched as the teams walked into the stadium. Liverpool, all in black, and Arsenal from London, in red shirts and white shorts. The red triggered Sandoval again and Wazir forced himself to concentrate on the game, and not his enemy.

Liverpool lost to Arsenal with a score of 2-1. As in every stadium and in every country around the world the fans were fanatical. The winners were screaming in delight, and the losers had long faces and cursing their no good wanker players.

As Maloof and Wazir left Wembley Stadium they walked for about fifteen minutes in London's borough of Brent. That was the reason Maloof told Wazir to meet him at the stadium. It was close to the house they would be staying at. Wazir noticed that the borough was very ethnically diverse. He saw people from Africa, the Caribbean, India and South Asia. He also recognized a diversity of Muslims including Afghans. Wazir followed Maloof into an old Victorian house. They entered into a dark foyer and went to the kitchen.

"Hungry?" Maloof asked.

"I am actually. I only had a snack on the flight over."

"Right. Have a seat. I'll heat up some food." Wazir did as he was asked and Maloof brought out some containers from the refrigerator and heated them up in a microwave. When the food was ready Maloof slammed his foot twice on the floorboards. In moments two men entered the kitchen from a door which led to the basement. They went to the counter where Maloof had laid out the food and served themselves.

"Wazir, grab a plate and help yourself."

Wazir did and was amazed that the food was Afghan. He took some lamb kebabs, salad and pilaf. "Does someone cook this?" He asked.

"Don't ask too many questions," Maloof said.

"I'm sorry."

"The food comes from a local take-out restaurant."

"Understood."

"Now eat. This is Ghazwan," Maloof said, "he's our resident computer expert. He can find anything you want. And this is Mohammad. He's an expert in other things."

Wazir didn't ask. They all shook their hands.

"And this is Wazir. He has a mission. We are going to help him."

The men nodded and ate their food.

Wazir would stay at the Victorian house where he would have a bed and food. It had been set up as a network to help individuals in their missions.

"So, Wazir, tell us about your thoughts."

"I need you to find a man by the name of Sandoval. I saw his name on a patch on the sleeve of his uniform. I didn't get a chance to see his first name. That's all I have," Wazir said to Ghazwan, the computer expert.

"In the name of Allah the Merciful, do you know how many Sandovals there are? Millions. You said he was in the military, still too many Sandovals. Do you have anything else for me to go on?"

"He is a Pararescueman. I saw the patch on his uniform."

"Impressive."

Wazir's temper flared, but he kept it in check.

"Alright, we'll start with that right after we eat," Maloof said. "While Ghazwan is trying to find this Sandoval why don't you get some sleep."

"But I..."

"We'll wake you as soon as we have something."

"Alright, a couple of hours will do me some good."

Wazir went to the room he had been given. It was small and dark with wallpaper that showed off distorted flower designs which probably dated back to the seventies. The room had a bed, a night table and a lamp. That was it. That's all he needed. And some information. Then he would be on his way. As he lay on the bed he wondered how many others had used this room, and what their missions had been.

A few hours later Ghazwan called Wazir to the basement. Hamzed rushed downstairs. "Any news?"

"I have the information," Ghazwan said with a pleased look on his face.

"You found him?"

"I did."

Maloof and Mohammad were present as well.

"Tell me."

"He's from New Mexico, lives on a Reservation near the city of Albuquerque..."

"Reservation?" Wazir interrupted. "He's an Indian?"

"Half Navajo, half Irish. He's also a pilot."

"A pilot?"

"Yes," Ghazwan continued.

"So why is he a Pararescueman?"

"He's not a military pilot, he's a hot air balloon pilot."

"A balloon?" Wazir laughed raucously. "He likes to play with toys."

"Not exactly."

"Fine. What else do you have for me?"

"He's in Afghanistan."

And I'm *here*, Wazir thought, when I should be *there* with my people, his anger intensifying every time he thought of that bastard Sandoval.

"So, you are set on killing this man, perhaps some of his family members?" Maloof asked.

"That's correct. The more the merrier, praise Allah."

"Praise be to Allah. We can assist you in this matter, however I have a bigger picture for you."

Wazir looked at the man, wondering what the head of this organization had in mind. "I'm listening."

We can provide you with a contact in the United States who in turn will provide you with all the material you need."

"Material?"

"Explosive material."

Wazir looked at the man, not understanding. "What did you have in mind?"

"Have you ever heard of the Albuquerque International Balloon Fiesta?"

"No." Wazir thought about it for a moment. "Sandoval is a pilot there?"

"It's more than that. Let me tell you my thoughts."

The men at the network trained him in the explosive materials, and Wazir was attentive and learned well. They formed a meticulous plan, down to the last detail. They covered everything, went over it day after day until all they could see and dream were the intricate details of the mission. Wazir learned that the Fiesta was at the beginning of October, which meant that he had several months to prepare.

Half a year later Wazir landed in Denver, rented a car and drove to Albuquerque. He had to admit the scenery in Colorado was stunning. When he crossed the state line into New Mexico he flinched, as the landscape reminded him of home, of Afghanistan, of a place he would never see again. Sean Sandoval was going to pay dearly for that.

CHAPTER 46

Sean had been in Afghanistan several months. He was relaxing on his cot when suddenly the men heard the familiar SCRAMBLE! SCRAMBLE! SCRAMBLE! And as so many times before, they did. They ran to the waiting helicopters and jumped in. As soon as they took off they headed for the LZ and the wounded.

"What do we have?" Sean asked his fellow PJ, Ted Johnson, who was still in country and hadn't left.

"Fucking IED in a convoy. Lots of wounded and fucking firefight still raging. It's a bad one."

Sean groaned. Johnson was right. It was going to be bad. Sean just didn't know how bad the outcome would be.

The helicopter landed in the cloud of dust the rotor was churning up, and rushed out to the wounded men. The PJs did their magic, a well-trained team retrieving injured warriors. They seemed to be performing a beautifully choreographed dance, each step precise, each movement defined for a specific purpose. They carried the wounded fighters to the waiting chopper, their eyes assessing as much as they could of the injuries while they rushed them to their helo. The other helicopter kept watch, scrutinizing the area for enemy combatants. Every once in a while they fired when they saw insurgents aiming their rifles.

The PJs were ready to leave. They had retrieved their wounded and were inside the steel bird. Sean was bringing up the rear and would be the last one in the helicopter. As he was about to jump in he heard a high-pitched scream. He turned and straightened up to see where it was coming from.

The ear-piercing screech sounded as if it came from an eagle, like the ones back in New Mexico. It was so loud Sean wondered if the raptor was right next to him. At that instant one of the well hidden insurgents, a sniper, had his sights on the American leaving. He fired. The bullet hit his mark—under Sean's arm and into the left side of his chest. A grotesque red rose exploded out of the side of his body. If Sean hadn't turned around and straightened out to see what the scream was about the bullet would have pierced the back of his neck. As he crumpled to the ground his young life flashed before his eyes in a nanosecond: the Montgolfier brothers, Jack and Ryan, his parents, Nico and his Ajei. As he lay on the earth the light faded from his being, but not before he saw the faces of the people he loved in a heavenly blue sky, intermingled with hot air balloons and an immense screeching eagle who Sean would have sworn was smiling at him.

Ted Johnson was among the team. The big man quickly jumped back out of the helo and picked up Sean with one arm as he fired his weapon at what he was sure was the insurgent who had shot his buddy. A stream of automatic fire answered back and stitched a pattern in the dirt just in front of his boots. Ted kept firing as others from the pararescue team pulled Sean off of the big man's arm and into the helicopter. As the steel bird started its lift Ted jumped in. The PJs worked fervently to keep Sean alive until they arrived at the hospital. Johnson stared at his wounded brother, praying for him and remembering the good times they spent together in the snow and training in the Washington wilderness.

"Don't you fucking die on us, Sandoval. Hang in there, man, you can do it." And Sean did, with the help of the amazing team that worked on him in the helicopter and the subsequent doctors who performed a pneumonectomy on his left lung and saved his life, a life that would, in all probability, be physically normal. However, his life as a PJ out in the field was over.

CHAPTER 47

Nico and Sophia watched Angela's performance at the casino. They marveled at her talent and kept thinking how they were going to tell her about Sean. After the show they went to see her in her dressing room.

Nico knocked on her door. "Angela, its Sophia and Nico, may we come in?"

The door opened and they saw the thrilled expression on her face. "Absolutely! What a lovely surprise." Nico knew she wouldn't think so in just a few minutes. "Come in." They hugged and kissed and then sat down.

"You're amazing, Angela, and your voice is just magnificent.

"Thank you, Sophia."

"Uh, Angela, we've come to tell you something," Nico started.

"What's up?"

"It's about Sean."

Angela's mind flew to the worse possible scenario and she turned paler than she ever had in her life. "Is he…" She couldn't get the words out. Her heart skipped a few beats and when the rhythm came back it pounded out of her chest.

"He's alive," Nico said quickly.

"What happened?" Angela asked.

"A sniper shot him."

"Oh, my God," she whimpered, "how bad is it?"

"He was shot in the chest. The bullet just missed his heart, but damaged his left lung. They had to remove it."

"Oh, my God, oh my God," she kept repeating. She covered her mouth, afraid that her emotions would come out and she wouldn't have any power to stop the screams.

"Angela, the main thing is that he's alive and he'll recover. He probably won't ever climb Mount Everest, but then again, knowing Sean he might just prove everybody wrong," Nico chuckled, trying to comfort her.

"Many people live a full life with only one kidney or one lung. He's going to be fine. He just needs a little time to get better and heal," Sophia added.

"He's really going to be okay?" Angela asked, hope coursing through her being as a little color came back to her face.

"Really," Nico said. "On the good news side he's at Walter Reed in Washington, and as soon as possible they'll fly him home. They'll be giving him a medical discharge."

"That is some good news." And that also means I won't have to worry about him getting hurt, and he'll be able to stay with me, she thought to herself. "Do his parents know?"

"Yes, they were told. They're flying to Washington."

"I'm glad," she said graciously, and wished she were with them.

"We thought you might want to go as well."

Angela looked up at them and then her eyes lowered to the floor. "I would love to, but it's not that simple. I can't just leave and I need to get a ticket."

"Actually it is that simple."

Angela looked up. "What do you mean?"

"We spoke to Joe," Nico said. He and Sean go back a long way, and Sean even saved his life when they were teens. It's not a problem. He wants you to take all the time you need. He said to not worry about anything and to come back whenever you're ready."

Sophia opened her purse and handed Angela an airline envelope. "And here's your ticket. You leave on the first flight tomorrow morning. We'll take you to the airport."

"I don't know what to say other than I really love you both

very much." Angela stood up and hugged them. "As you know I have no family and you are the closest people to my heart."

Nico and Sophia hugged her back. "We are family, Angela. You and Sean are closer than even blood relatives," Nico said.

"Sounds like my big fat Greek family," Sophia said.

It was the first time that evening they laughed. Life would once again be good, maybe even better than before.

CHAPTER 48

Sean was discharged from the hospital and recuperated in Albuquerque, spending his days and nights either at his parents' home, or with Angela in her apartment at the casino. The couple were resting in bed in each other's arms, and Sean was trying to figure out what he would do as far as work.

"I don't know what I'll be doing, Ajei. I can go back to the military, maybe train new PJ recruits, or, God forbid, a desk job. I could be an EMT, which would be easy enough since I have all the credentials. I could maybe teach at a hot air balloon pilot school. In time maybe I could pilot my own balloon and make a business out of it."

"Listen, Sean, I don't want you to worry. I make a really good salary at the casino, I can support both of us. Besides, I want you to get well, that's all. If you don't ever want to work again that's fine by me too. You don't have to work if you don't want to. Besides, it would be great fun having you all to myself."

Sean looked at the woman he loved. He knew she meant it, but he also knew that he couldn't do that. He wasn't meant to be idle. He knew he would soon figure it all out.

Sean had been back almost two months and they decided they didn't want to wait any longer. They set the date for the wedding for the beginning of December. They would get married in a hot air balloon just like they planned, and would take off from the Sandovals' land.

On the day of the wedding Sophia, Angela's maid of honor, arrived early at her apartment at the casino. She had coordinated everything with the wonderful staff. Joe had been very gracious and acted like a loving brother. He had insisted on paying for everything Angela needed, including the wedding dress. The 'gang' was all there: Sophia, the hair stylist, the manicurist for a last minute checkup (she had been there the day before), and a couple of women who worked at the casino who had become friends with Angela. The chauffeur waited with the limousine.

"There. Even the last little hair is in place," the hair stylist said with finality. "Now close your eyes because I'm going to put on so much hair spray that a bird would bounce off if he tried flying into it." She didn't want any of the hair falling out of place when Angela was saying her vows up in the sky in the hot air balloon. She didn't want to take a chance on it being windy.

"Stand up, let's take a look at you." Sophia said.

Angela did. The women didn't utter a word. "Well?" The bride asked, starting to worry.

"Oh, girl, you are gorgeous," Sophia said. "Sean is going to faint when he sees you!"

"I hope not! But really, I look okay?"

"Look in the mirror," one of the friends said.

Angela did. After a few moments she smiled. Yes, even she believed she was the most beautiful she had ever been. It was just the way she wanted it for Sean on their wedding day, and for herself as well. "Not bad, huh?"

"Not bad? I'd say more like incredibly beautiful," Sophia said.

Each one of them went to hug her and wish her the best.

"You're drop dead gorgeous," the other friend said.

"Okay, girls, time to go," Sophia announced. "Let's get this bride in the limo and to her wedding."

At the Sandoval home Sean emerged from his boyhood bedroom in his Air Force dress uniform. His short vest, bowtie, cummerbund and pants were dark blue. His shirt a crisp white. On his vest he sported small medals. Among the accolades the Air Force Cross and the Purple Heart were the most prominently displayed above more than another dozen citations. Directly above the ribbons of the medals Sean's badges were aligned: the Pararescue badge, the free fall parachutist's badge, the scuba badge and the SERE badge.

"Well? Mam, Dad, how do I look?" He asked.

Tibah looked at the merits on his vest, duly impressed. "Quite sharp, Nílchi Deesdoi. You make me a very proud father."

"Thanks, Dad."

"Oh, Sean, you look so handsome! And your uniform is beautiful." Fiona's eyes were glowing, fighting the tears that were forming under her lids.

Sean hugged his mother and whispered. "You are the beautiful one, Mam, inside and out. I am honored to be your son. Thank you for everything." Before Fiona could reply Sean said: "Now don't cry, you'll ruin your makeup." He let go of her and Fiona held her boy's face in her hands. She smiled. She knew she didn't have to say anything, Sean could read how proud she was and how much she loved him.

"It's waterproof. I came prepared."

"Aunt Sheila?" Sheila, from Dublin, and Fiona had kept in touch via monthly letters. They were still the best of friends, even with the distance between them. Sheila had done well for herself. She had enrolled in an accounting school after Fiona left for the States, and after a few months received her degree. She worked at the same firm where she started over twenty years ago, and was pleased with her life. It was quiet and comfortable, and she was blissfully independent. She had her beaus, but never wanted to marry. She was content, and when Fiona told her about the wedding she never hesitated and flew to New Mexico. There was no way that Fiona's little boy would marry without his 'Auntie' present.

"Oh, boyo, you look fierce and a fine thing, you do," she replied, as proud as a real aunt.

Sean stared at her. Fiona came to his rescue. "That means that you're a real good looking guy."

"I thank you, Aunt Sheila."

"My pleasure, Sean, and you're marryin' a bang on lass."

Fiona was ready to jump back in, but Sean put his hand up. "Got that one, Mam."

"I wish you both every blessin', lad."

Sean hugged her. The woman had a dear, big heart.

"Alright, everybody," Tibah said, "we need to go outside and get this boy married."

They followed him out of the house.

Three hot air balloons were being inflated. One of them was the *Rainboyws*. Sean had been part of the Albuquerque ballooning community since he was a child when Jack and Ryan first brought him along. He had grown up with them, and they had come to love the boy. Today they were celebrating the man marrying his bride. Jack and Ryan would provide the balloon for Sean and Angela. Accompanying them would be Nico and Sophia, the best man and maid of honor. Two more would join them: a priest (Angela and Fiona's idea) and a Shaman (Tibah's idea).

The second hot air balloon would carry Sean's parents, Nico's parents, Sheila and Joe. The third balloon would carry six Pararescuemen, Sean's closest Pedros, present to honor him on the joyous occasion. Ted Johnson was among the PJs. The balloon rides were the pilots' way of giving one of their own a wedding present, that way their family and the people they loved would be close by and witness the ceremony. Charlie and Joe's mother, and many from the Reservation who had known Sean since he was a child were among the crowd and would watch from the ground. Some came dressed in traditional attire with exquisite silver and turquoise jewelry, buckskin jackets and woven dresses. They all waited for the bride and the bridesmaid.

The hot air balloons were almost fully inflated as the pilots were in constant communication with the limousine driver. The stretched out car came around a bend in the road and arrived with the two pretty women. Tibah and Dimitri went to the vehicle and opened the doors. Dimitri escorted his daughter-in-law Sophia and started walking towards the *Rainboyws*. Sean's father gave Angela his arm and the young woman came out of the limousine and hugged the older man.

Tibah looked at his future daughter-in-law. "You are absolutely exquisite, my dear."

"Thank you, Tibah. You look very handsome yourself, and I can hardly wait to see Fiona. I'm sure she must be stunning."

Tibah pictured the love of his life. She was wearing a green dress that matched her eyes and the dove pendant he had given her the day their son was born. "Oh, yes, quite a beautiful horse."

"What?"

"I'll explain some other time," he chuckled. "Angela, I want you to know that both Fiona and I love you very much, and we want to thank you for making our boy happy."

"Thank you, Tibah, but I'm the happy one. Not only am I marrying the most wonderful man in the world, but his parents are just as special."

Tibah kissed her on the cheek and said: "I think everybody is waiting for us. Shall we?" He asked as he crooked his elbow. Angela gently put her arm on his and Tibah walked her 'down the aisle', a pathway covered in flower petals. It led to the *Rainboyws* where everyone was gathered, and where Sean and Nico were standing and waiting. As his father and future wife approached Sean was sure his heart was forgetting to beat. Everyone present clapped at the beautiful bride. Tibah handed Angela over to her future husband. Sean took her hand and kissed it.

Everyone who would be ascending was ready and inside the basket of their hot air balloon, except for Sean and Angela. The chase crews held down their respective baskets. John and Adam, who were still with Jack and Ryan, held the *Rainboyws* for the soon to be newlyweds. Sean saw them and started laughing as both men were wearing a t-shirt that looked like a shirt and bowtie from a tuxedo. Deep down John and Adam were still big kids, even though they had graduated with honors from UNM and went on to pursue their careers. However, they still chased for Jack and Ryan as much as possible. Hot air ballooning would always be in their blood. And they of course would never have missed the wedding of the boy they had met so many years ago.

Sean turned to Angela, picked her up and lifted her into the basket. He climbed in behind her. Sean nodded to Jack at the controls. The *Rainboyws* slowly lifted off, the other two hot air balloons followed. They floated higher every time the burners fed them heat. After a few minutes they were at the designated altitude.

"The view is magnificent!" Angela exclaimed. "Oh, Sean, we're floating in the sky!"

"Flying is the spirit of living, being in the air gives you complete freedom," Sean said.

"I like that, Sandoval," Nico said.

"Thanks, Kats."

"Oh, Sean, you have taken me into the winds, let me soar in the sky like a bird. Thank you, mi amor."

"There's nothing freer than being in the air."

"Oh, that one's good too," Sophia said.

Sean turned to the catholic priest who would perform the first ceremony. "This one's for you, Father, as told to me by none other than our gallant pilot: We are breathing the same air that angels do, and we are closest to heaven."

"I said that?"

"You did, Uncle Jack."

The priest, who was a young man and not afraid of heights, gave him an answer: "You're right, Sean, I like that a lot. 'Breathing the same air as angels'. Very nice indeed. So, are we ready?" He asked Jack.

"We are at the desired altitude."

The *Rainboyws* and the two other hot air balloons were suspended very close together, no more than a few feet away from each other. Everyone had a perfect view, not only of Sean and Angela, but of the infinite land below them.

Sophia took Angela's bouquet. The priest performed the ceremony. Nico nervously held the rings. He imagined dropping them and watching them fall through the cracks of the wicker, tumbling to earth and landing somewhere where no one would find them for a hundred years. It was *finally* time to hand them over, and he was relieved that they made it to Sean and Angela's hands. The priest told the newlywed couple they could kiss, and they did just that. The onlookers from the other balloons cheered, clapped and wiped away tears. In the wedding basket hugs and kisses were exchanged as well. The people watching from the ground were just as enthusiastic and hollered with joy.

The priest, who was greatly enjoying the ride and the unusual event, squeezed himself into one of the corners and watched as the Shaman took over. It was his turn.

"We usually have a basket of corn mush," the wise man announced seriously, "but since we are *in* a basket it is even better and we will do the ceremony a little differently." He took a small bundle of sage out of his bag. He looked at the gas cylinders and decided not to light it and swept it across the bodies of the bride and the groom. Then he removed a handful of corn pollen, sprinkled it above their heads from east to west, then north to south. Next he sprinkled more pollen in a circle on the floor of the basket. The final item he pulled out of the bag was a drum. Sean's eyes widened when he saw that it was the drum his father had made so many years ago for the sweat lodge ceremony. Father and son exchanged nods and smiles across the sky from one hot air balloon to another. The Shaman started drumming rhythmically and chanting. Tibah, from the other balloon, accompanied them. The Navajos on the ground joined in and performed a traditional basket dance. When they finished singing the Navajo master of ceremonies put his hands just above the newlyweds' heads. He asked all present to close their eyes and told them to pray for the couple. They all did. Sean and Angela were now married—twice—and were congratulated by the little group on board. The people in the other two balloons and the ones on the ground cheered and clapped some more. It was a unique ceremony no one present would ever forget.

Ryan signaled to the other two balloons. They knew what to do. They coordinated to land first so that they could all see

Sean and Angela arrive. Two of the PJs had been filming from their balloon and continued after they landed. The entire day would be recorded.

The *Rainboyws* slowly came down and landed softly.

"You will always be the master, Uncle Jack," Sean said.

"And you will always be our *petit Montgolfier*. Ryan and I wish you and Angela a lifetime of happiness."

"Thank you both, for everything." Sean hugged the two men who had started his love affair with the hot air balloons. "I love you guys."

"We love you too," they both said.

"There's one more thing, something for Angela," Ryan said.

"What is it Uncle Ryan?" Sean asked.

"It's the balloonist prayer, but we added a couple of words."

Jack and Ryan recited it to her:

"The winds have welcomed you with softness,
The sun has greeted you with its warm hands,
You have flown so high and so well,
That God has joined you in laughter and matrimony,
And set you back gently into
The loving arms of Mother Earth."

"Oh, that is beautiful Uncle Ryan, Uncle Jack, thank you both so very much for everything," Angela said. Sean nodded in agreement.

The Pararescuemen, also in dress uniforms, had quickly jumped out of their gondola and stood at attention, their swords in their hands, the blades almost touching the right side of their bodies and pointed upward. They formed an alley just beyond the basket and waited for the newlyweds.

Sean lifted Angela out of the gondola and put her down. The PJs lifted their swords and formed an arch. The newlyweds started walking through when the first two Pedros lowered their weapons straight out keeping them from going through. Sean turned to Angela and kissed her. The swords raised, they were allowed to continue, and they did, but the next set of swords were lowered as well and they stopped again. They kissed, but the weapons did not move. Sean kissed his bride passionately and they were able to continue. They kissed every time they went up to another pair of PJs. As they went through the last pair Angela received a gentle smack on her behind with the sword from Ted Johnson. Everyone laughed and the newlyweds went to greet their family—one big loving, caring family, who had been cheering the happy couple ever since the limousine arrived.

The chase crews quickly packed up the aerostats and the customary après balloon ride champagne started to flow. They toasted the newlyweds. The party was just beginning. It would continue at the Katsopoulos' home. They began to leave and get into their cars, as did Sean and Angela. Just before they entered the limousine they noticed the 'Just Married' in the back window. There were also dozens of stringed mini plastic hot air balloons and champagne corks that looked like mini hot air balloons as well. The limousine driver had decorated the car right after the women he drove to the ceremony had exited.

CHAPTER 49

The wedding party drove to the Katsopoulos' home. They came out of their cars and went in. Irini was in her glory. She had meticulously prepared the feast, with help from the restaurant where they cooked the food and then brought it to the house. Several of the waiters also came to help out and serve. The guests were impressed with the spread across the long, enormous table and they enjoyed the food and the hospitality. In addition a bartender was patiently waiting for orders.

Dimitri beckoned Nico and Sean to his favorite room in the house, the den. They obediently followed the older man.

"Have a seat, boys. Oh, don't worry, I won't keep you too long," he chuckled. Sean and Nico laughed. "How about a brandy, gentlemen?" He asked them, as he poured one for himself. "I need one after that ride. I think I'll keep my feet on the ground from now on, thank you very much." Dimitri did not like heights, and perspired during the entire ceremony.

"I'll take one," Nico said.

"Yes, thank you, the Greek brandy, of course."

"Of course!"

Dimitri took a seat in his beloved armchair. "So Sean, I'm sure you know Nico isn't quite into taking over the restaurant business."

"Yes, Sir." Sean listened, not sure where this was going and why was he bringing this up on his wedding day?

"Which is fine by me," Dimitri continued, "but he is still young, still adventurous."

"I understand, Mr. Kats." Sean really didn't.

"How about the two of you go into business?"

Sean stared at Dimitri. "At one of your restaurants?"

"No."

"I'm afraid I'm a little confused, Sir."

Nico was watching his father's Greek ways and could only smile. He knew what was coming. Father and son had of course discussed this at length before saying anything to Sean.

"Okay, you saved my Nico's life." The man didn't waste many words.

"It was noth…"

"Sh! Let me finish, please," he said putting up his palm.

"Yes, Sir."

"That means that to me you are a son as well."

"I'm honored, Sir."

"Are you still interested in your own business, with the hot air balloons?"

"Most definitely, that would be a dream come true. Somehow, someday."

Dimitri pulled out a photograph from his inner jacket pocket. "Sean, listen to me carefully."

"Yes, Sir, I am."

"First, you will not call me 'Sir' anymore. I prefer Dimitri or Jim."

"How about Uncle Jim?" Nico chimed in, having let his father have the fun so far.

"Yes, I like that," Dimitri said.

"I can do that, Uncle Jim," Sean said.

"Bravo! So, as you know, I have a few pennies."

"Yes, Sir… I mean Uncle Jim." Sean knew the man was incredibly wealthy.

"So, I would like to give you a gift, as a thank you for saving my boy's life, and as a wedding gift. I would also like you to take Nico with you on this venture, if you think that would be a good idea."

Was the older man giving them a cruise or an exotic trip

somewhere? Sean couldn't imagine what he was up to. "I don't know what it is, but I would go anywhere with Nico. He is a brother to me."

Both Katsopoulos men smiled. They knew Sean meant it, and they felt the same way about him.

"Here, take this, Sean. With all my love, my great respect and especially my gratitude," Dimitri said and handed him the photograph. "I also wish you and your lovely wife all the happiness in the world, and many beautiful babies."

"Thank you, Uncle Jim."

Sean took the picture and tried to understand what looked like a big ball in the middle of the photograph. And then he gasped. "Is this what I think it is?"

Nico now jumped up, having held himself back. "Yeah, Bro, it's your balloon, man!"

Sean looked up, still stunned. "Are you saying this hot..." Sean didn't dare say the words.

"Yeah, Dude, it's yours. You are the proud owner. Oh, and I'm your business partner, if you want me, and maybe even co-pilot. Of course you'll have to show me a few details, like how to fly the thing."

"I... I don't know what to say. I don't know if I can accept this..."

"Of course you can. Don't be so American. We Greeks love giving gifts, so just say *efharisto.* Besides, refusing would be insulting." Dimitri said, grinning. Like all Greeks he was generous and loved it. He knew that giving was even better than receiving.

"Efharisto," Sean repeated.

"Means thank you," Nico said.

"Efharisto very much," Sean said again as he hugged Dimitri.

"Parakalo, you are very welcome, my boy. I'm glad I could do this for you. Confucius said 'if you love the work you do, you never work a day in your life'. He must have been Greek."

Sean laughed. He really did like Dimitri, no, he loved him like an uncle. "You know, you've not only made me a very happy man, you've changed my life!"

"For the better?"

"For the best!"

"Good. Now you two boys go out and play," Dimitri said to the younger men as if they were still in kindergarten.

"Come on, Sandoval, let's go play!" Nico said, repeating his father.

"What?"

"The balloon, man, it's in the garage!"

"What?" Sean said again. "I'm right behind you!"

They ran out of the house as excited as school boys.

"Stop!" Nico said.

Sean did. "What?" He suddenly feared this was a dream.

They stood in front of the garage. Nico hit the remote for the large garage. The three doors slowly opened. "Wait for it... wait for it..."

Sean held his breath. Before him stood a brown van with a hitch on the back which was attached to a special hot air balloon trailer, also in the same brown color. The fire-orange lettering of *HOT AIR* was written on the doors of the van and the trailer over a hot air balloon. When Sean saw the image he almost cried. Each gore of the envelope depicted Indian feathers, in shades of oranges and browns. He finally let out his breath and shook his head. "That is the most beautiful thing I have ever seen."

"The balloon is inside the trailer of course, and it comes with the van. It's all yours, Sandoval."

"Thank you, Kats, I love you, Bro."

"Same here, Dude." The PJs hugged each other. "Oh, and here are the keys." Sean looked at him. "To the van and the trailer."

"You and your Dad are the best! Thank you."

"Pleasure. Now let's go have some fun and celebrate your wedding. Oh, maybe you would like to show the others *Hot Air*, the newest addition to the Albuquerque skyline," Nico said, knowing full well that Sean probably couldn't wait to show it off.

"We can definitely do that, partner," Sean said as both men opened the doors to the van. Sean drove it out of the garage and parked it in front of the Katsopoulos' home.

The party went on through the night. The family of course went all out, as if their own son was getting married. They ate and drank and when the enchanting staccato of a bouzouki filled the room everyone stopped and listened to the melody. The Greek band was very well versed in many types of music, including American and international favorites, wedding songs and modern Greek melodies and beloved folk tunes. The floor in front of the musicians was empty and waiting for dancers. It would not stay that way for long. A couple of notes of a famous *zeibekiko* and Nico was on his feet. The Greek dance did not have choreographed steps, rather it was an improvised dancer's prerogative where their steps flowed from their hearts and souls to their feet and bodies. The zeibekiko used to be an exclusively men's dance, as it related to warriors who would release the tension from the day's fighting. Each step, each hand movement relayed the dancer's emotions, from audacious to nostalgic, and everything in between. No two dances were ever the same. Nico went to the dance floor and offered his personal version. He swayed to the rhythms of his ancestors and his slight limp made his impromptu moves even more alluring. Several of the Greek men present were in a semi-circle crouched or kneeling, and were clapping to the beat in front of the musicians and Nico. It was part of the dance, the warriors supporting their comrade. Sean, who had been pushed to the floor by one of the men, followed suit and clapped for his fellow PJ. When the song finished Nico turned to the band and said something. The bouzouki player, who was also the leader, nodded and whispered to the other members. Nico turned to the man who had saved his life and who would always be his brother.

"This one's for you," Nico said, as soon as he heard the first notes of the popular song he had requested.

Sean looked at his best man. "How do you mean?"

"Είμαι αϊτός χωρίς φτερά, Eimai Aetos Horis Ftera, it's a well-known Greek song—I'm an eagle without wings."

"Eagle?"

"Yeah, kind of like you. Appropriate, don't you think?"

"I do. Does this mean I have to dance?"

"Uh huh."

"But I don't know how."

"Best thing about this dance, you don't have to know the steps."

"Yeah, right."

"No, man, seriously. The zeibekiko is the easiest dance in the world. It's a warrior's dance and comes from the soul."

"Like a tribal dance?"

"Exactly."

"You move however you want to. Just go inside of yourself. In your case, you know, being a crazy Indian and all you can do anything from a Navajo thing to whatever steps come from your soul."

"And it's called Eagle?"

"It starts: 'Like the eagle I had wings, and I flew, and I flew very high'. And so on."

The musicians replayed the first notes and Nico pushed his buddy toward them. "Go for it."

"Alright, I guess I'll try just about anything once," Sean said. He stood very still on the dance floor, closed his eyes, listened for a few moments. The band leader started singing and he caught the word for eagle, *aetos*, and let the music filter into his body. It only took a split-second for his mind to see the majestic raptor of his boyhood dreams. His arms slowly went up to the height of his shoulders and he gently moved them, making waves. His eyes stayed closed, his body and his feet shifted back and forth, not so much like Nico had done, but more like Native American dance steps. It was a perfect fit, especially when Sean lowered his head and his powerful shoulders seemed to gently flap his invisible wings.

The audience was mesmerized. This was more than a dance, this was more like a live dream, a trance Sean had entered into. The man's body was present, but his spirit was soaring. He moved to the rhythm, his body mirroring his emotions. He was performing from an ethereal world, describing his passions and gratitude for the gifts in his life through powerful, sensual movements and music. Sean continued throughout the long song (the band having never seen anything so mesmerizing played it twice without stopping). When it came to an end Sean knelt down, crossed his arms around his torso, let his chin rest on his chest, and folded his 'wings' into himself.

The guests clapped profusely and Nico went to his best man, helped him up and whispered: "Pretty amazing, you crazy Indian."

"Glad you enjoyed it, Kats."

"I did. So, tell me, Sandoval, who danced first? The Indians or the Greeks?" Nico asked.

"I have a feeling dance and music originated with humankind's first steps and sounds. We were all one back then anyway."

"Alright, we'll call it even."

The two best friends smacked each other's backs and went to the guests who were still clapping. Angela, who was among the spectators went up to them.

"You two looked great out there, nice dancing! And Sean, you reminded me of an eagle," she said to her new husband.

"Thank you, Ajei."

Angela turned to Nico. "Can I have a turn?" She asked.

"Of course! The zeibekiko used to be exclusively for men, but the women dance to it now as well, and let me tell you the guys could learn a few moves. They have mastered the art beautifully."

Angela giggled. "No, Nico, what I meant was I would like to sing a song."

"Oh, yeah, that would be wonderful!" Nico exclaimed.

Angela turned away from the men and headed toward the band. She spoke to them for a few moments. The leader smiled and handed her a guitar. She sat on a stool and started strumming.

"Everybody quiet!" Nico hollered. And the guests did. They watched the glowing bride caress the strings of the instrument. The happiness emanating from the woman was palpable, and they all wished the newlyweds to be just as happy every day of their lives.

Angela looked at the people in front of her. Her eyes searched for her husband. When she found him she blew him a kiss and said: "This one's for you." She had of course found the perfect song for Sean. As she accompanied herself with the guitar she sang an old international hit *Touch the Wind,* first with the English lyrics, and then in the original Spanish version of *Eres tú, you are the one.* The musicians did not accompany her. They just listened, proud of a fellow artist.

Tibah of course was the happiest father in the world. When he saw his son dancing he perhaps knew better than anyone how far he had gone in the infinite sky, and how much he had connected with his power animal. And as he watched his beautiful new daughter-in-law he was thrilled and marveled at how well she understood her son. She had managed to find the most appropriate song for him as it spoke of the wind, and the original Spanish version was just as poignant.

Sean watched, incredibly proud of his beautiful lady. He remembered the first time he heard her singing, how moved he had been and how she had touched his soul. When Angela ended the last note Sean went to his new wife.

"You are the wind that makes my heart sing, and you have touched me. Thank you, Ajei," Sean said, and kissed her lovingly. The crowd clapped and cheered for the happy couple.

The festivities continued through the evening and late into the night. Nico, Sophia and the Greeks danced continuously. Joe and his mother, as well as Charlie and some of the Sandovals' Navajo friends offered the couple their best wishes with a native dance. Tibah accompanied them with his drum. And when Fiona and Sheila did a Irish jig they were one of the night's biggest hits. Sean would have sworn the two women looked as if they were still twenty years old.

CHAPTER 50

Sean and Angela spent their wedding night in the presidential suite of the Yeibichai casino, compliments of Joe. They woke up late the next day and had breakfast in bed.

"You know, Ajei," Sean said, "in the great Navajo nation it is customary that the bride and groom stay in their home for four nights and four days."

"Smart people. Sounds good to me, and while we do that I want you to do everything you did to me that first week we were together, and everything since." Angela cooed.

"I would be happy to. If I do perhaps forget something will you help me remember Mrs. Sandoval?"

"Mrs. Sandoval would be more than happy to oblige."

Sean removed the breakfast tray and obediently complied with his wife's wishes.

Later that evening Sean and Angela headed out to the Reservation to meet up with his parents. Tibah had mentioned they needed to discuss something with them, although there was no hurry. The young couple walked into the house.

"Mam, Dad, we're home."

Fiona and Tibah embraced them.

"Yes, Sean, you most definitely are, and this is actually the reason your mother and I wanted to talk to you."

"Come in you two, have a seat, relax," Fiona said.

They sat on the couch, holding hands, curious about what the parents wanted to say to them.

"So, what's up Dad?"

"We were thinking this could be your place of business. It's perfect for a hot air balloon to take off from. Also, as you know we have quite a bit of land and we would like to build you your own home on this property. You tell us what you want and we will do it. It's of course on the land we live on, but you'll find there is enough space where we won't bother you. And if you need anything we won't be far. This is our gift to you. You have made us very happy, we hope this will make you happy as well."

"And baby-sitting services will always be free," Fiona added.

Angela looked at her husband. "Are you happy with this arrangement?"

"Ecstatic, but only if you are," he added quickly.

"I am too, but I do have one condition."

Sean and his parents held their collective breaths.

"What is it?" Fiona asked.

Angela looked at the older couple. "My condition is that you are always close by and very present in our lives, especially during holidays and celebrations. As for the babies you will have to teach them everything you know, like your native languages and your traditions, and most importantly they must have your special hearts. On that I am firm." Angela looked at her new in-laws. "Do we have a deal?"

Tibah sprang up from the chair he was sitting in and hugged her. "We have a deal!"

"Fiona?"

"I always knew my boy would pick the perfect wife. We have a deal. And *my* condition is that you of course will share your own beautiful voice and big heart with the little ones."

"Of course."

"If I were any happier I think I would explode," Sean laughed.

"I agree, Nílchi Deesdoi, I agree!" His father said.

In the last forty-eight hours Sean's greatest dreams had manifested. He married the love of his life, was the proud owner of a beautiful new hot air balloon and the base of a new business. He would help build a dream home, and was surrounded by the most amazing people in the world. Someone up in the air was working overtime for him, and he was grateful.

CHAPTER 51

On the other side of town Hamzed Wazir was in his motel room, on his knees, on a towel, praying in the direction of Mecca. Tomorrow was the day. Tomorrow he would avenge his family, his people and he would kill Sean Sandoval and many of *his* people. Tomorrow would be the last day of his life and of many Americans. Tomorrow he would meet his God, Allah the Merciful, the Benevolent.

When he finished praying he went into the bathroom, showered and shaved his beard. He put only underwear on and went to the room's large desk. It was covered by a sheet. He removed it and stared at his handiwork. Maloof and the Jihadists in London had come through splendidly. They had taught him well, everything he needed to know, down to the last detail. Their contacts in the States were perfect as well. They informed him that Sandoval was back in Albuquerque as he had been wounded in Afghanistan, but did not die. Wazir was glad he wasn't dead—he wanted to do it himself, and he wanted to see the expression on the American's face when he killed his compatriots. As far as the materials for his mission they were brought to his motel room a little at a time. Maloof's men in the area never spend more than a few minutes in his presence.

Wazir looked over every inch of his handiwork. The construction and design lay in front of him—the C4 plastic explosives, the detonators, the vest, all meticulously and strategically prepared for the most damage possible. He had worked on it for days according to the specifications provided by Maloof and his team. The contacts had brought him pieces of his instrument of death on different days, at different times. Everything was as ready as Wazir was.

The motel had served him well. It was cheap, yet clean and centrally located where he could blend in with the population and go into local inexpensive restaurants where he wouldn't be noticed. There was also a small convenience store where every once in a while he would pick up some bottled water or tea. He paid the room weekly and never mingled or made small talk with anyone. When he first arrived he told the receptionist that he was a writer and had to 'get away' in order to write in peace and quiet. He also told him that he wrote at strange hours and if the 'do not disturb' sign was hanging they should definitely not clean the room, or disturb him, as he probably would be either writing or sleeping. Wazir certainly didn't want anyone walking in on him while he was putting his explosive device together.

That night he went to one of the two beds, the one that hadn't been slept in, where his clothes waited for him. He had meticulously laid them out. He put on the jeans and a t-shirt and lay in the other bed with the clothes on. He did this so that when he woke up he would immediately know that the day had finally come. He fell asleep just after sunset as he would be up extremely early for the Balloon Fiesta.

The alarm had been set to go off, but Wazir was already awake. He sat up in his bed. This was it. Today was the day. He put socks and shoes on, went to the bathroom and looked at a picture of his family. They were all smiling for the photograph. In the background his beloved mountains in Afghanistan stood majestically. He looked at it one last time, kissed every face in the picture and lit the corner of the paper. Wazir watched it burn. At the last moment he dropped it in the toilet bowl. He would never see them again, but rejoiced that he would be united with his loved ones very soon. Today was the day. Yes, today was the day.

Wazir looked around the room and went to the desk. He

didn't check anything. He had done that the day before, besides, every detail had been thought out and perfectly executed. He put on the vest full of explosives over the t-shirt and then pulled a sweatshirt over it. The jacket was last and thankfully it would be cold outside at three o'clock in the morning in the high desert of Albuquerque. The conditions were ideal to hide the C4 under his jacket. He looked at the room that had served him well these past weeks and put on a local Lobos baseball cap.

Wazir took one of the buses the city provided that alleviated the horrific traffic that always happened during the Fiesta. There was no delay. He arrived among the other visitors, just another face with a day old beard, one of many who seemed to be wearing the same kind of clothes. It was the last day of the festivities. He remembered his visit a few days earlier when the celebration first started. He did some scouting and familiarized himself with the venue. He looked around, just as all the other people were doing, and then found what he was looking for. There he was. It was Sandoval. He had found him. Wazir could feel his blood pressure pulsing in his veins. He wanted to just walk up to his nemesis and stick a blade between his ribs and into his heart. But he held himself back. He would let him live a few more days.

Hamzed Wazir now walked onto the field and looked for the *Hot Air* balloon. Today would be Sandoval's last day. Today was the day that all the work, time and money invested would come to fruition, the day his mission would be fulfilled.

CHAPTER 52

Almost a year had gone by since Sean and Angela married. They built their dream home on the Reservation, and the business was in full swing. Nico studied hard, learned well from Sean and passed his balloonist pilot's test. The two men, who had always been good friends and warrior buddies, excelled at their new business as well. Like Sean Nico was a natural, and his parachutist's training came in handy. As far as the business, such as paperwork, neither one of them really liked it, but they had Sophia who knew the tricks and had a cunning business mind. She could always provide help or personnel whenever they needed it, and she always had brilliant ideas. This was also their busiest time of the year as they were participating in the balloon fiesta.

Sean was getting ready to leave the house to go to the fiesta field. It was very early in the morning, and as he looked out his bedroom window he saw the innumerable bright spots shining throughout the black sky. It was dark and the stars watched him and winked back. He smiled and then turned to his wife lying on their bed. He gently kissed her lips and did the same on her stomach. The happy couple were expecting their first child, which was due in just a few days. They had laughed when Tibah said that the baby would be the smallest balloon at this year's celebration.

"I'll see you later," he whispered.

"I love you," Angela whispered back, still half asleep.

"I love you too, Ajei."

"I'll see you at the park. Sophia is picking me up in a little while."

"Sounds good."

Sean left the Reservation. When he arrived at the field he drove the van with the trailer onto the field. Nico and the chase crew were already there, waiting and excited. It was the last day of the fiesta and although the week had been profitable and thrilling they were a little sad that it was coming to an end. As Sean parked the men quickly went to work. They removed the equipment from the trailer and started laying everything out. Sean looked over every piece with pride. *Hot Air* was a thing of beauty.

Sean's stomach was bothering him. It was always a sign, something was wrong. Did it have to do with the balloon? He double checked all the equipment, but knew everything was fine. Still, he couldn't shake the danger signals. He looked around the field. Others were preparing for their flights as well. It all looked normal, but Sean sensed otherwise.

Nico watched his best buddy. Something wasn't right with Sean. He had seen that look in Afghanistan when he noticed the two Jihadists coming towards them. "Hey, everything okay?" He asked.

Sean nodded back. He didn't want to worry Nico without some semblance of proof. "Time to fly," he simply said.

"Let's do it."

Wazir watched Sean and Nico and the crew preparing the hot air balloon. He was close by, just another face in a massive crowd. *Hot Air* was just about ready to lift off. As the chase crew let go of the basket Wazir quickly jumped into one of the footholds of the creel at the very last possible moment. He pulled himself over the edge and landed in the gondola. As he did he hit Nico in the back of the head with the butt of his gun. The man never saw it coming and he went down like a heavy sack. Sean watched Nico fall to the floor and looked at Wazir, who was now pointing the gun at him.

He put his hands up. "What the hell are you doing? What do you want?"

"Climb!"

Sean did as the man ordered and gave the aerostat

some fire. "You didn't answer me. What do you want? Who are you?"

"Don't you know who I am?"

Sean looked at him carefully. "You!" He suddenly exclaimed, immediately recognizing the man who he thought drowned in Afghanistan.

"Yes, Sandoval, it's me. Didn't recognize me without my beard, eh."

"What the fuck are you doing? What do you want?"

"What do you think I want?"

"I have no idea."

This seemed to infuriate Wazir even more. "You can't be that stupid!"

"You want to kill me because you fell off the cliff. If you remember I tried to hold you, but you let go."

"Yes, you will die today, Sandoval, and you will not be the only one dying!"

"What does that mean?"

The balloon wasn't moving. "Keep it climbing!" He yelled.

Sean complied and gave it some fire. "And just what are your intentions? To kill me here in the middle of the air?"

Wazir laughed raucously. "Not just you! A lot of you!"

Cold sweat ran down Sean's back. "Explain yourself."

The terrorist looked over the side. They had climbed quite a bit. The view was spectacular. They were surrounded by other hot air balloons, were above the field covered with thousands of people, and beyond the city the majestic beauty of the land was as far as the eye could see. "Not just you," he repeated, "but your people, your country, your government."

"You want revenge."

"Ah, now you get it." He opened his jacket. He carefully and slowly lifted his sweatshirt. Sean gasped as he saw several rows of C4 attached to Wazir's vest.

"You're going to blow yourself up?"

"Not just me."

"Yeah, you'll take me with you."

"And many like you."

Sean's worse fears were manifesting. The danger signals

had been right on. "You can't be serious."

Wazir looked down. "I'm very serious. Now stop the fire."

Sean did and looked down as well. The hair on the back of his neck stood on end. If the vest detonated at the right height hundreds of people would be killed or horribly maimed. "Why would you do such a thing? Not one of them ever did anything to you."

"Look at all those little people down there, and all the balloons around us. Just imagine what will happen when I detonate this vest."

Sean could picture the devastation. Dozens of balloons in their proximity filled with gas canisters would sequentially explode, and increase the deadly chaos. "You can't just kill hundreds of innocent people!"

"Of course I can, just like your American government did in Afghanistan."

"That was a war."

"They were innocent! They were my family—my parents, my brothers, my wife, my child, my village! Killed by a drone, by some finger in some office half a world away! You killed me as well that day, and destroyed my life. I was going to help rebuild Afghanistan, make a better homeland for my people." Wazir's voice was getting louder and louder as he was ranting. "Now," he continued, "I just want to destroy Americans and America! That is what you have done to me. I don't care about anything other than that. Do you understand!?" He screamed.

"I do understand, really I do, and I truly regret what happened, but that is not a solution. I know you are an intelligent man, why can't we learn to live together? We share the same planet."

"Ah, you are stupid, after all. My mistake in trying to make you understand."

"All I understand is that an eye for eye is not the solution. It is a vicious, never ending circle."

"It is not a circle, it is a solution. All we have to do is kill all of you infidels!"

"Now I know who the stupid one is," Sean retorted.

"You can think anything you want, I don't care, but now it

is time! Lower this balloon until I tell you to stop."

Sean didn't move. He had to somehow divert the terrorist's attention. "You know, I don't even know your name. I know you speak fluent English, probably had schooling in England."

"Hamzed Wazir, and yes, I received my engineering degree in England."

"So why not use your knowledge to rebuild your country, the way you originally intended, Wazir?"

"Because you infidels killed my country's dreams and all of mine when you killed my family!"

"We tried to help the Afghan people! What you're saying is wrong."

"You're the one who is wrong!"

"Listen, Wazir, let's talk about this." Sean didn't move. He had to buy time, had to figure out how to win this deadly game.

"There's nothing to talk about. You are just an American puppet, with no knowledge of foreign politics. You are so arrogant, and all of you believe you are the best country in the world."

"Doesn't everyone think that of their country?"

"Of course they do! But they don't boast about it incessantly."

"Maybe they should be prouder."

"Prouder!" Wazir yelled. "You arrogant, infidel capitalist, you are nothing but an uneducated, illiterate moron."

"You know Wazir, you are the moron! You shouldn't judge an entire nation by one action, or think of Americans as all the same. Individuals make up this country, and each person is unique. People in this land have different levels of education, just as other nations do. Of course knowledge and education is best, I'll agree with that, and if the entire world was accomplished we wouldn't have any wars, now would we!?" Sean hollered.

"What would you know about being persecuted?"

"Oh, you are such an asshole! I'm part Native American!"

"So then you should know."

"I do know, and my mother is Irish, so yes, I know about

persecution. But I also know that people can coexist, and when the damn world, especially people like you understand this, we can finally have peace."

"We will never have peace!"

"With the way you think, of course not. Which proves *you* are the uneducated moron."

"Hah! How can you say that? I have a degree, and from an English university."

"And you could have helped your people with it."

"What for? So that some trigger happy asshole on a base in Nevada can destroy it?"

"You know, Wazir, you have a beautiful country which reminded me of New Mexico, but it has become a checkerboard of land mines and mortar craters. No land deserves to be violated in such a way. No country deserves to exist without its natural beauty. And it can only be its true splendor by the people that live on it and cherish it." Sean was stalling, waiting for the balloon to slowly lower itself closer to the ground. He knew that Wazir needed to be at a certain level to inflict the most damage.

Sean continued, trying vehemently to calm the Afghan man down. He knew trying to talk some sense into him was probably futile, but he would attempt it anyway. "Afghanistan has magnificent history, it's part of the Silk Road which unites the east and the west and yes, unfortunately, has been invaded by many. But it's time, Wazir, it's time to learn to live as one world."

"Don't be ridiculous! We will never be one."

"See? That's what I mean, you won't even try."

"Stop stalling! Now lower this damn balloon faster."

"No."

"You will do as I say or I will put a bullet in him," he said, waving his gun above Nico.

"I can't do that. I can't let you kill so many innocent people."

"Of course you can," Wazir said as he pulled the trigger.

"No!" Sean screamed.

"That was a warning. The next one will not be in the floor."

The bullet hole was just a couple inches away from Nico's head.

Sean needed to come up with a solution and fast. "What is it you want me to do?"

Before Wazir could answer the radio crackled. "Calling *Hot Air*, this is *Sunglow*." It was from one of the balloons close by. "Heard a funny noise, kind of like a gunshot, did that come from you? Is everything all right?"

Sean didn't answer, which would mean there was a problem. The voice on the radio came through again and asked the same questions.

Sean didn't move. "Answer!" Wazir shouted. A few seconds went by. He pointed the gun at Nico's head.

Sean spoke into the radio. "*Sunglow*, this is *Hot Air*, everything is good here, thanks."

"Alright *Hot Air*, *Sunglow* out."

"Now lower this thing," Wazir said.

Sean reached up to pull the parachute cord. As he looked up he remembered the PJ logo: *That Others May Live*. And that's what Sean vowed to do, not only at his graduation as a Pararescueman, but today. He wasn't going to let this bastard get away with killing innocent people, even if it meant his own life. When his hand went to pull the line to open the valve he opened the burners to their maximum instead and flung himself at Wazir. The sudden movement was just enough to off balance him and took him by surprise. Sean lunged at him and both men fell down. The gun was knocked out of Wazir's hand. Sean threw a punch at the man's face, but the Afghan man stopped the blow with his forearm and managed to hit Sean in the stomach. He gasped and doubled over. It gave Wazir the opportunity to stand up. Sean grabbed the gun that had fallen, but before he could aim it the terrorist threw himself at his enemy and both men flew over the edge of the basket. The gun fell back into the gondola and instinctively both fighters grabbed the tie down rope.

The hot air balloon caught some wind and floated toward the river. The crowd, who had gotten wind of the situation, watched in horror. Many screamed, believing the men dangling from the rope would fall to their death. Sean and Wazir were holding on for their lives. They were so close they could have hugged each other.

"We could have been friends, Wazir, we just needed to agree to live on this planet together, as peaceful neighbors."

"Die, infidel!" He screamed. He punched Sean and the blow to his face almost made him lose his grip. Sean's legs wind-milled and the PJ fought hard to hold on. As he did he kicked and punched the Afghan man with his free arm. Wazir produced a knife and brought it down on his enemy. He slashed at Sean, and every time he did the American managed to bend his body out of the way. To the people watching in horror below it looked like a creative, unique yet deadly dance. Every time Wazir tried to sink his weapon he was stopped. Sean kept thwarting the knife advances with every ounce of strength, agility and acumen he possessed. The shoulder holding his body was burning, and his hand was starting to cramp up. He had to resolve this, and fast. He swung his free hand and managed to punch Wazir in the face which momentarily dazed him. Suddenly the terrorist was sure his heart completely stopped as he saw the enormous eagle, in the same spot Sean had just been. What was happening to his mind? What was going on? As the man tried to figure out the phenomenon in front of him he knew that he was going to be killed by this six foot raptor. The moment he realized it, he felt the deep incision severing his neck's jugular vein and his body ceased to respond to his mind. He tried to scream, but couldn't, deprived of that last expressive pleasure. Had it been the enormous beak, or did Sandoval have a knife? Or what it his own weapon? His eyes watched the eagle and Sean intermittently going back and forth like a badly edited film. His body was failing him, a river of blood flowed out of his neck, and the grip on the rope was becoming useless. His hand seemed frozen, the fingers non responsive. They stopped holding and loosened. Wazir slipped away, falling fast toward the land that reminded him of his own. In the last moments of his life he knew he was going to meet His God, but he wasn't going up, he was going down, and in that last split-second he understood that

Paradise was a peaceful Earth.

Sean watched the man's body fall toward the Rio Grande. It was the same area where Sean had landed on his maiden voyage with Jack, Ryan and his father when he was nine years old. Now he followed Wazir with his eyes as he plummeted toward that same area. When he hit the bank next to the river the impact forced the detonation and the C4 exploded. It sent shrapnel, smoke, fire, and pieces of the earth three thousand feet in diameter. He could see how far it reached as it mushroomed into the trees and the surrounding area. Thankfully it was an isolated area and no one was present. Sean shuddered at the thought of how many people would have been killed and injured, had it exploded at the Fiesta field where Wazir had meticulously planned the exact spot that would create the greatest devastation.

Sean searched for the Afghan's body, but the only thing he saw was his mind's eye of Wazir lying face down, floating in the gorge in Afghanistan and the images from the dreams that had been so prominent in the sweat lodge. A cold shiver ran down his back. Was he still alive? He had thought him dead once before, could he survive a second time?

Police cruisers were immediately on the scene. Sean was much too high to hear anything, but could make out the answer from the police officers' body language. Yes, Wazir was definitely dead. There wasn't anything left.

Sean dangled from the rope, bopping around like a marionette. His arms struggled to straighten his body as the pain in his shoulders screamed in agony. He also noticed that he was getting uncomfortably close to telephone lines. He knew that if the aerostat hit them he would be in grave danger and could very easily be killed. The PJ pulled himself up the rope, one hand over the other, as his feet held the cord steady between his legs and helped with the climb. He was perspiring profusely and the moisture reached his hands. Sean slipped. The crowd watching below gasped and screamed. Some covered their mouths or faces. They thought for sure that the man would fall to his death, just as the other one had. Sean slid all the way down the rope and at the last moment was able to hold on to the end of it. His body gyrated and jumped from the sudden stop. He groaned in pain. He was sure he had pulled every muscle in his body and his shoulders were straining to stay in their sockets. His hands were singed from the friction of trying to hold the rope. His nose confirmed it, as the smell of burnt chicken wafted down from his hands. Sean held on and started back up, his mind focused on getting into the gondola before they would hit the wires. He was also thinking about Nico. How badly was he hurt? He inched himself up as quickly as he could using his legs, feet and hands, now bleeding and raw. He persevered and thanked the sergeant at his first training camp who constantly screamed that 'pain is good, it keeps you sharp!' As he thought about it he wondered if he meant sharp pain. The looming lines were no more than a few feet away. Sean managed to pulled himself over the edge of the basket and fell in. His body was so sore it wasn't responding the way it normally did. He scrambled to get up and immediately fired the burners. The hot air balloon ascended just enough to whisper past the lines. He let out a sigh of relief.

Sean grabbed his radio, asked for an ambulance and told them the situation, including the detonating devices Wazir had been wearing. He saw the police stop in their tracks. They would wait for the EOD guys, the bomb experts, even though there surely wasn't anything left. Sean looked at Nico. He was still unconscious. He checked his head wound, the gash was fairly deep and matted with blood. He gave the envelope some more fire so he could concentrate on his best buddy and went into EMT mode. He took off his jacket, sweatshirt and t-shirt. He quickly put the sweatshirt back on and tore the t-shirt into strips, used some of it to clean the blood and then wrapped the rest around the man's head. Sean gently shook him until Nico started to stir.

"Good to have you back, Kats. How are you feeling?"

"Splitting fucking headache, man, and dizzy as hell."

"I can imagine. Wazir hit you pretty hard."

Nico's eyes widened. "Where is he?"

"He stepped out for some fresh air."

Nico grinned. "Roger that. Hey, I saw a really big eagle, uh, I think."

"Must have been the blow to your head."

"Mm, guess so. But, still…"

"Now you just relax as I try to get us back down."

"Problem?" Nico asked, his mind clearing.

"I think we'll be alright." Sean said. "You just stay there and don't move."

"Sounds good to me," Nico answered and leaned back against the wicker of the gondola. "Let me know if you need anything."

Sean smiled as he knew Nico was in no position to assist. He was just glad the man was alive.

Sean clicked his radio and announced that due to the circumstances, and the winds pushing him toward the field, he asked the controllers to let him land at the Fiesta park. This was a rarity as the balloons never came back down from where they took off during the Fiesta, but the air in the Albuquerque box was guiding him back to the starting point. They immediately answered that they would take care of everything and to just get back safely. Sean masterfully piloted his craft. The fliers and the organizers were a tight-knit community and Sean was well liked and respected. They knew of his prowess as a pilot and a pararescueman. He would get all the help he needed.

"Would you please tell me who that asshole was, and what the fuck he wanted?" Nico asked.

"His name was Hamzed Wazir. You remember the guy in Afghanistan, the one I tried to hold on to from falling into the gorge?"

"No! That was him?"

"Uh huh."

"And?"

"And apparently a drone wiped out his family. He wanted to do the same to us, but on a massive scale. The son of a bitch had a vest covered in C4 and wanted to do some major damage."

"To us?"

"And more."

"The balloons?"

"And the people down there too."

"Holy shit!"

The crowd watched *Hot Air* slowly descending. They were still hypnotized, never realizing in how much danger they had been. Police and volunteers were on the scene and controlling the situation.

Sean managed to steer the balloon close to where they had originally taken off. He was using all the knowledge he had accumulated over the years, and was going through the motions more on instinct and natural ability. The law enforcement personnel and coordinators outdid themselves. They were complete professionals and had everything under control, from the crowds to the ambulances to the landing zone. *Hot Air's* chase crew was ready for the landing. Sean maneuvered the basket brilliantly and gently set it down on the field, as if nothing had ever been wrong, as only a master could pull off. Everyone clapped and cheered.

The chase crew held down the basket while EMTs helped Sean and Nico out of the gondola. Ambulances, organizers, and volunteers working the Fiesta were all standing by. Angela and Sophia were there as well. They had arrived just in time to witness the danger. They ran up to their men and hugged them so tightly they were sure a rib or two might crack, but they didn't care. They were just glad they were all safe and in each other's arms.

"Hey, careful with the baby," Sean said to his wife.

"He's fine, but he wants to come out. Probably thought you could use a little more excitement for one day. So far it seemed pretty boring."

Sean laughed and then it 'clicked'. "Are you saying..."

"Yes, Sean, my water just broke." And then she double over. "Oh, that hurts," she moaned.

"Right!" Sean picked up his wife and rushed her to the ambulance just a few feet away, now completely 'with it'. "Let's go!" He screamed to the EMT standing by.

"What happened? Did the lady get hurt?" He asked.

"Not exactly, we're having a baby!"

The paramedic looked at Angela's stomach. "Now?"

"Yes! Right now! Move it, man!"

"We're off!" The EMT said. The first responders' community was fairly small, and they all of course knew their brothers, the PJ supermen.

Sean sat next to his wife who was stretched out in the back of the ambulance.

"Remember your dad saying the baby would be the smallest balloon at the fiesta?" Angela giggled.

"Yeah... how did he know?"

"Wise man."

"That he is."

Nico and Sophia saw Angela and Sean in the ambulance and rushed up to them before the EMT closed the door. Nico knew Sean's hands were torn and burned, but didn't think it warranted an ambulance ride.

"What happened?" Nico asked as he saw Angela on the stretcher. "Is she alright?" He asked.

Sean pointed to his wife's stomach. "Baby Sandoval is ready to meet the world," he said proudly.

Nico's jaw dropped. "The baby? Now?"

"Uh huh."

The men looked at each other and smiled, a smile of a camaraderie and brotherhood that started what seemed a lifetime ago, and would continue for the rest of their days. They would meet at the hospital so that Nico could get some stitches.

"You Sandovals sure know how to make an entrance."

"Like Angela said, I needed a little more excitement for one day," he laughed.

"Crazy Indian," Nico said, grinning.

"You know it, Kats."

"I most certainly do," Nico confirmed, as he pulled out an eagle feather embedded in Sean's hair and handed it to him.

Author's Note:

The Navajo Reservation near Albuquerque and the Yeibichai casino are fictitious and used solely for the purpose of the story.

All my books always include music. Some of the scenes in this book contain songs, or include some of the music featured around the characters. Please click on the link below to view, hear and connect. You will also be able to see some photographs from locations in the book. Please enjoy.

http://denisekahnbooks.com/photomusic-gallery/

I love hearing from my readers and I answer all my mail personally. Thank you for your interest and for reading! If you enjoyed the book would you be kind enough to leave a review on Amazon. I would appreciate it. Author.to/DeniseKahn

Please visit my website and blog at: DeniseKahnBooks.com
e-mail: Denise@DeniseKahnBooks.com

ABOUT THE AUTHOR

My very first memory of life was the sound of my mother's glorious voice singing to me, most likely a Brahms lullaby, and I'm convinced that is why music always has a delicious way of creeping into my writing and becomes one of the most important elements.

I spent twenty years in Europe because of my father, who was with the U.S. Diplomatic Corps, and my mother who was an opera singer. I worked mainly as a simultaneous interpreter and translator as I am a linguist and speak several languages, five of which are fluent. I also worked in the travel/airline and music industries and I have incorporated some of my adventures in TRAVEL TALES, my short travel stories series. Because of my exposure to people of different nations my writing includes many foreign settings and cultures.

I am a proud mother of a gallant Marine who served in Iraq, and among the members of our household you will find Louie the cat (aka King Louie XIX), so named because of his clawing love of Louis XV and XVI furniture, and surely thinks he must have been a king in one of his former lives.

I write about romance, suspense and thrillers in different genres: Contemporary, historical and military. I demand of myself to be accurate in my research and to produce the best work possible. I hope that my books are entertaining, perhaps enlightening and informative. I want my readers to enjoy the time we spend 'together', and that my characters are just as alive as they are to me, even when the last page is turned.
In addition to fiction I have published a photo book, 'Around the World in 80 Quotes on Photos', and 'Travel Tales', short adventure stories from different places around the globe.

Denise's books

Peace of Music

A once lost magnificent antique vase from China's 13th Century Song Dynasty reappears from the depths of the Mediterranean Sea where it comes to dwell on a piano in a doctor's home. It becomes the impetus in steering the lives of this doctor and his descendants through their heartbreaks, romances and ultimately successes. An assassination, a sabotage on a Greek island and amazing musical performances are but some of the events that strike their lives. Spanning from 13th Century China to the present, the story takes place on four continents, with talented individuals of different nationalities and backgrounds, always interrelated by music.

Obsession of the Heart

Set against an international backdrop of jet setters, music, romance, murder, terrorism and true friendship is Davina Walters, an international singer. Davina meets Jean, a young woman almost paralyzed with fear, as her sadistic ex-husband is bent on killing her. On the spur of the moment Davina decides to take her along on tour and the murderer plans his ultimate revenge in a deadly showdown.

Warrior Music

Max knew the drugs and alcohol would eventually kill him, and sooner rather than later. So he enlisted in the Marines.
His timing is unfortunate, as the events of 9/11 find him at the beginning of his military service, and he is sent to Iraq. The journey he embarks on is unlike anything he could ever imagine.
From Washington, Boston and New Orleans to the ancient sands of Iraq, Max and his entourage endure the toils of war with gallantry, patriotism, courage, heartache and passion.
Only one weapon gets them through the anguish they come face to face with... Music.

The Music Trilogy

'Peace of Music', 'Obsession of the Heart' and *'Warrior Music'* are a family saga trilogy. The three together are *the Music Trilogy.*

Split-Second Lifetime

On a business trip from the U.S. to Paris, Jebby meets Dodi on a flight. Jebby is an ethnomusicologist, and Dodi is an international photographer. They are immediately attracted to each other, but from the very first moment Dodi triggers what seems like past life memories for Jebby of a poignant and passionate time they shared together. As Jebby tries to figure out if she is "losing it" or if past lives really do exist, they embark on a path of adventure and romance where lifetimes and cultures interweave in modern day Paris, Uzbekistan, and in the old Southwest. Jebby and Dodi live their unusually diverse and rich adventure and romance, surrounded by an international cast and superb musicians. At the same time Jebby discovers where the Hopi originated from, that death is not a finality, love transcends lifetimes, and music is eternal.

Hot Air

A thriller filled with passion, romance, survival and courage.

Sean Sandoval, half Navajo, half Irish, has bravery in his blood and passion in his heart. From boyhood to one of the Air Force's elite Pararescuemen, his path in life is always connected to air.

As a hot air balloon pilot Sean communes with that air. As a Pararescuer he flies into danger to saves lives.

An enemy combatant from the mountains of Afghanistan, presumed killed, arrives in Albuquerque, New Mexico and is bent on such revenge that he puts thousands of people at the annual International Balloon Fiesta in lethal danger.

Will Sean be able to stop the extremist in time, or will the murderer accomplish his mission first?

Around the World in 80 Quotes on Photos

A photograph portrays a thousand words. A quote is but a few more powerful ones. Together they are food for the senses. They make us think, wonder, and engulf us. They represent traditions, civilizations, cultures, and offer us splendor, progress, grand vistas and minute details, all in a planet rich in majestic beauty. Embark on this journey of quotes and photographs, from ancient sands to calm seas, from sky to pebbles, from natural magnificence to man-made luxury.
Photographs were taken in several countries around the world.

TRAVEL TALES

Travel Tales is a series of short travel stories, journeys spiced with humor and interesting international characters in famous or little known places.
An American woman finds herself in an adventure in a foreign land while discovering different cultures, local folklore, food, music, and sometimes danger.

We were 12 at 12:12 on 12/12/12 (Mexico)
Entertained by the Gods (Greece)
Sai Baba's Ashram Rendezvous (India)
Gstaad Grace (Switzerland)
Thanksgiving in 24 Hours (Mexico)

All titles available as e-books

For more information please visit:

DeniseKahnBooks.com
e-mail: Denise@DeniseKahnBooks.com